Praise for Fr

"The best storyteller of the century. From the first page to the end, I fell in love with Francis Ray."
—Mary B. Morrison, *New York Times* bestselling author of *Who's Loving You*, on *And Mistress Makes Three*

"Ray . . . always writes romantic heroes that leap off the page."
—*Fresh Fiction* on *All That I Need*

"Ray pens a wonderfully sensitive story of an evil subject—spousal abuse. Though her heroine's confidence is turned on its head, she still has enough spirit to be an inspirational character full of hope and rebirth. Naomi's rocky journey to real, true romance deservedly draws the reader's full support."
—*USA Today* on *All I Ever Wanted*

"Fast and fun and full of emotional thrills and sexy chills. Everything a racing romance should be!"
—Roxanne St. Claire, *New York Times* bestselling author, on *Nobody But You*

"A wonderful read."
—*Fresh Fiction* on *Nobody But You*

"A roman⸻ ⸻ding to the next ⸻ax."
⸻ *Love Me*

Anthologies

With Just One Kiss

FRANCIS RAY

ST. MARTIN'S GRIFFIN

NEW YORK

Published in the United States by St. Martin's Griffin, an imprint of St. Martin's Publishing Group

www.stmartins.com

ISBN 978-0-312-53648-0 (mass market paperback)
ISBN 978-1-250-62407-9 (trade paperback)
ISBN 978-1-4668-0415-9 (ebook)

Our books may be purchased in bulk for promotional, educational, or business use. Please contact your local bookseller or the Macmillan Corporate and Premium Sales Department at 1-800-221-7945, extension 5442, or by email at MacmillanSpecialMarkets@macmillan.com.

First St. Martin's Griffin Edition: 2020

10 9 8 7 6 5 4 3 2 1

With Just One Kiss

Chapter 1

In less than twelve hours C. J. Callahan's life would be over, and there was nothing he could do about it.

His long-fingered hand loosely wrapped around a longneck, C. J. sat in the back booth of his bar, Callahan's, on the West Side of New York and contemplated his life . . . or what was left of it.

At 9:00 AM sharp he'd take over running Callahan Software Company. C. J. tucked his dark head, then lifted it to stare around the neighborhood bar that he'd first helped his uncle operate for five years, then owned outright after his uncle's death three years ago. The bar was as much a part of him as his hands. His uncle, Robert Callahan, the older and only brother of C. J.'s father, had felt the same attachment.

Because of C. J.'s love of Callahan's, his uncle had willed the bar to C. J. and asked him to make sure Callahan's reached the twenty-five-year mark. C. J. had accomplished that last year and looked forward to twenty-five more and beyond . . . until fate said differently.

As much as he didn't want to run the family-owned software company, he didn't have a choice.

His father's and his brother's health no longer allowed them to keep the grueling schedule and frantic pace. That left C. J., his parents' only other son.

The mournful sound of Wynton Marsalis's sax caused C. J.'s usually erect broad shoulders to sag. His unflappable sunny disposition was long gone. He felt as if every unhappy note had been written just for him. Life had done a number on him this time. It had taken him years to finally find what he wanted to do with his life, and now that he had it was going to be snatched away from him.

"It's not that bad."

C. J. twisted his dark head to see Alex Stewart, one of his two best friends, standing beside the booth. "Why aren't you still on your honeymoon?"

"Because I'm here." Alex tucked his trim six-foot frame into the booth's other side.

C. J. grunted. Alex, a lawyer and a darn good one, had an irritating way with words. He was also crazy in love with his new bride, Dianne. They'd had a big lavish wedding a little over a week ago at his parents' palatial estate in California, and were supposed to still be in Paris. When they weren't working, they were inseparable. "Where's Dianne?"

"She had a stop to make," Alex answered, bracing his arms on the wooden table. "Sin should be here any minute."

"And it won't change a thing." Sin was C. J.'s other best friend. They had always been there for each other no matter what. Sin had a way with women, thus the nickname.

C. J.'s hands closed around the bottle, then he cocked

his head as he saw Sin—tall and as physically fit as the athletes he matched with his corporate clients— making his way toward them. His bearded face was serious for once; he was casually dressed in a polo shirt and slacks, the same as Alex. C. J. preferred T-shirts and jeans. Callahan Software employees might dress casually, but his grandfather, the founder, C. J.'s father, and his brother always wore a suit to work.

"Can you get me on a private jet to parts unknown?" he asked as soon as Sin neared.

Sin was a phenomenally successful sports consultant with his own Gulfstream. Payton "Sin" Sinclair moved in some very wealthy circles, but you'd never know it. He was as laid-back and down-to-earth as they came.

"If I thought it would help, you'd already be gone," Sin answered in his straightforward way. He sat beside Alex when he slid over.

"We're here for you, man," Alex said.

C. J. knew it, but at the moment it wasn't much help. He and Sin had been best friends since they were freshmen in high school. Alex hadn't become a part of the strong bond until eight years ago, when he'd moved into the same apartment building where C. J. and Sin lived. They were as close as you could get.

"Yeah, I know, it's just—" C. J. began, but he was interrupted by a loud whistle. His head came up and around. Marsalis's sax shut off. C. J. came out of the booth to see what was happening, then he couldn't believe his eyes.

Sitting on the bar, mike in hand, was none other than Maya, a six-time Grammy-winning blues singer from New Orleans. Throwing him a kiss, she opened her mouth and moaned, low and deep, and then began to sing about love lost and never regained in her haunting voice.

For a moment he was transfixed by the sight and sound of his favorite singer in his bar in a red satin dress that showed off every generous curve to perfection. Maya had a breathy, whiskey-coated voice that grabbed a man by the throat and tugged at the emotions. She also had the homeliest face on the planet, but he loved her music. No pretense, just jaw-dropping power. Not many things were that way today.

A picture of a beautiful woman in a lavender dress tied at the shoulders flashed before C. J. Her full skirt had shown a tantalizing glimpse of black netting underneath each time she'd moved in stiletto black heels. She'd smiled up at him as he held her to him on the dance floor. He pushed the image away before he could wrap his mind around why he was thinking of *her* again.

Ever since that slow dance with her at Alex and Dianne's wedding, he'd been thinking of Cicely St. John more and more, of what would have happened if he had taken her to his room and untied that dress. There was a reason why he hadn't. At best they tolerated each other because she was Dianne's friend.

She was stuck up and had slammed his bar, not once but twice. Once to his face, the other on her irritating blog. He might have bent to be cordial for the sake of Alex and Dianne, but if he never saw her again it wouldn't bother him in the least.

"Be back in a moment," Sin said, scooting out of the booth. Alex was right behind him.

C. J. was still trying to figure out why Maya was there when he saw Dianne at the door beckoning Alex. Caught between listening to Maya and finding out what was going on, C. J. folded his arms and chose to listen to Maya. He was past due for something good.

The last time he'd seen Maya was at Mardi Gras a couple of years ago when he, Alex, and Sin had gone to New Orleans. They'd had a ball. The only time they'd had more fun was when they'd gone to Vegas for a championship boxing match. They hadn't slept for three days. Even now, the memory made him grin. What happened in Vegas definitely stayed in Vegas.

There was a commotion at the door. C. J. jerked around and frowned. Alex and Sin were coming through the door with four other men carrying a long table. Even as C. J. moved to help them and finally find out what was going on, he saw the top. Green felt. A craps table. Behind them, another man carried a roulette table, while two croupiers and three men carried slot machines.

It hit C. J. at once and made him throw back his head and laugh for the first time that day. Alex and Sin were throwing him a casino party. Seemed they remembered the vacation and Mardi Gras and were combining it into one fabulous night. Still grinning, he watched them place the craps table over the top of the pool table, push back chairs for the roulette table, and place the three slot machines on the tables pushed against the wall.

"I can't believe you did this," C. J. said, chuckling.

"Let's have some fun." Sin slapped a pair of dice into C. J.'s hand. "This time I plan to walk away the winner."

"In your dreams." C. J. turned and with an agile flick of his wrist sent the dice tumbling. Seven.

Sin folded his arms and shook his dark head. "At least the food will be better." He inclined his head toward the bar.

C. J. spun in that direction to see his cousin, Summer Radcliffe, owner of the famed five-star Radcliffe's restaurant, setting up food on the other end of the bar. Dianne, Alex's wife, was passing out tickets to the patrons. At the end of Maya's song, Dianne accepted the mike and beckoned Sin and Alex.

Alex curved his arm around Dianne's waist and took the mike. "We figured a lot of regulars would be at Callahan's on a Sunday night, so Sin and the two beautiful women beside us and I thought it would be the perfect time to throw C. J. a little good-luck party for his new job as CEO of Callahan Software."

Applause, whistles, and cheers filled the bar. Alex handed the mike to Sin.

"Summer Radcliffe, the beautiful woman in magenta, is the famed owner of Radcliffe's, so you're about to taste the best food in the state. And because we value you, the bar is closed. You can have one ticket for an alcoholic beverage and unlimited anything else. You'll also be given fifty dollars in chips to play to your heart's content." He paused and looked at C. J. "Good luck on getting a chance at the craps table. It's C. J.'s favorite."

C. J. held up the dice. "It's my party."

Everyone laughed.

"Another favorite of C. J. is Maya, who graciously came in from New Orleans for the party." Sin turned to her.

The buxom singer leaned toward him and purred, "I could use a little company on that private jet of yours back to Naw Leans."

Sin grinned, a wicked smile on his bearded face. "Sometimes a man knows when he might get in over his head." He gave her the mike. "Maya."

Taking the mike, the singer looked at C. J. "You're too handsome and too happy to feel as deeply as you do about the blues, sugar."

C. J. took her hand, brushed his lips across the top. "Blame it on that voice of yours."

Maya cocked her head to one side to look thoughtfully at C. J. and then Sin. "You two are too carefree to have had your hearts broken, but one day it will come, and when it does I want you to remember that love is worth every heartache."

Straightening, she closed her eyes and began to sing about a man giving his heart to the wrong woman, the wrenching pain, the unforgettable pleasure.

C. J. and Sin shared a self-assured grin that said no woman would ever leave them heartbroken. They were always the ones to walk away. Throwing Maya a kiss, C. J. happily headed for the craps table with Sin and Alex right behind him. If he was going to his execution in the morning, tonight he was having fun.

Cicely St. John hadn't planned to come to the party they were giving C. J. until Dianne mentioned they were having a craps table. Cicely had always been glad she didn't live in Vegas or anywhere they had legal gambling. She'd have to join Gamblers Anonymous.

There was something about the roll of the dice that pulled her. Like life, you never knew what would come up. Hers certainly hadn't gone the way she'd planned. Pushing the unhappy thought away, she entered Callahan's Bar and found the party in full swing.

People were dancing, laughing, and in general having a great time. The woman singing had a voice that made you want to move your body or cry in despair. The sight tonight was very different from the last time she'd been at Callahan's.

She'd been there with a photographer taking pictures for her fashion blog to help Dianne and Alex's new fashion line, D&A of NY, gain some much-needed publicity. As the fashion director for *Fashion Insider,* one of the top high-fashion magazines in the world, she had gained a reputation for finding the next big thing ahead of the crowd. She'd liked Dianne's designs for full-figured women and wanted to use her blog to help.

However, from the moment she and C. J. had met, they had mixed as well as oil and water. He'd been proud of the fact that his bar was a man's bar. They didn't even serve wine. He hadn't even wanted the name of the bar mentioned when she did her blog. She was happy to oblige. If he didn't want the free publicity, his loss.

Yet somehow, at Dianne and Alex's wedding they'd ending up on the dance floor together. Everyone was having a great time at the reception. The champagne had been excellent, the food scrumptious. C. J. hadn't stepped on her feet and had been a surprisingly good dancer. There had been a moment when the music ended and she'd looked up at him and had the strangest urge to press her lips against his. She'd quickly quelled the idiotic notion and left him on the floor.

Now, shaking her head, she accepted the gaming chips and drink tickets. She ordered a Pellegrino and began to circulate, the skirt of her multicolored silk dress swirling around her long legs. Bohemian fashion had been in the previous summer. She still enjoyed the free, easy look and wore what pleased her.

Searching for Dianne, Summer, and the gaming tables, in that order, she moved to the other end of the bar.

A short distance away, she saw the table and a man she'd like to forget. Never one to shy away from a challenge, she continued toward the table while sipping her water.

C. J., shaking the dice, had a hard frown on his too-handsome face. Apparently Lady Luck wasn't being kind to him. Grinning, she edged her way to the end of the table just as the dice stopped in front of her. Snake eyes.

C. J.'s gaze glanced upward. Their gazes locked. She felt a strange tingling in the pit of her stomach, and quickly attributed it to a missed lunch and a chocolate bar for dinner. With her hectic schedule, Sundays were just as much a workday for her as any other.

She'd gone over three articles for the coming issue, dropped by a fashion shoot in New Jersey, gone to a fashion show, and afterward returned home to blog until her stomach reminded her she hadn't eaten. Now she was here.

And it seemed she had arrived just in time to have a little fun.

She tipped her bottle of water. Several gold bracelets with stones the same colors as her dress jiggled on her wrist. "Hey, fellows. Looks like beginner's luck isn't with you tonight, C. J."

Alex and Sin, standing on either side of C. J., burst out laughing. Sin explained, "C. J. is an excellent player."

Cicely lifted a regal brow and took another sip. "Could have fooled me."

"I guess you could do better," C. J. challenged, his jaw tight.

Cicely didn't even think of declining. She'd had to fight all her life to fit in, fight to get where she was. Scooping up the dice with her left hand, she rounded the table and held out her bottle to C. J.

Hard black eyes drilled into her for so long that her stomach got that free-falling sensation again. She resisted the urge to rub her stomach or drop her gaze and ordered her hand not to shake. She could bluff with the best of them. She'd had to in order to survive.

Finally, blessedly, C. J. took the bottle. If he noticed the little zip when their fingers touched, he certainly didn't show it. Her unwanted reaction to him was just enough to tick her off even more and bring out the killer instinct she'd learned in the world of fashion. The weak never survived.

Facing the table, she placed half her chips on top, shook the dice in her hand, then let them fly. Seven.

Sin patted C. J. sympathically on the back. Alex whistled.

The croupier handed her the dice again along with a pile of chips. She leaned over the table. She'd show him. And she did when, in less than two minutes, she won all the chips.

A cocky grin on her face, she turned to C. J. Careful not to touch him, she took her bottle from his clenched hand, took a sip, and almost purred, "You were saying?"

C. J. looked as if he'd like to have her head.

"Cicely, why don't we get something to eat?" Summer suggested, taking her by the arm.

Dianne grabbed the other arm. "Summer, as usual, outdid herself with the food."

Well aware that they're trying to get her away from C. J. before he blew, Cicely let them lead her away. She'd made her point. She'd bested the man who probably thought the only places for women were the bedroom and the kitchen. But she couldn't resist giving C. J. one last triumphant look over her shoulder.

She laughed when she thought she heard him

growl. Sin's and Alex's gazes snapped from her to C. J. Clearly they didn't know what to expect from him, either. Remembering how hungry she was, Cicely faced forward, a smile still curving her lips.

There were several people at the bar being served, but the line moved quickly. Seeing the succulent slices of roast beef being piled on soft rolls, buttery potatoes, and asparagus, Cicely forgot about C. J.

With her plate in her hand, Cicely and the women found a relatively quiet area where she could eat. Unfortunately, she was facing the craps table.

Despite the crowd, she had no difficulty finding C. J. He, Alex, and Sin stood out, not just because of their height or gorgeous looks, but because the self-assured way they carried themselves set them apart. His gaze touched hers, and she felt that strange something again. It took all her effort to look away.

Of all the men and all the times for her sleeping libido to awaken, now was the worst. C. J. was a throwback, and even if he wasn't, she hoped to be in Paris in less than six weeks as the new editor-in-chief for her magazine's international office. She didn't have time for a man, any man.

And although she hadn't known Dianne socially until recently, Cicely knew she'd miss her, and miss Summer whom she'd gotten to know through Dianne as well. They were women who were secure in themselves. They weren't trying to use Cicely or climb over her to get what they wanted like many of the women she'd met. There wasn't a fake or pretentious bone in their slender, fashionable bodies. Cicely figured she was long overdue to meet women who could be real friends.

"Alex and I are having our first dinner party Friday night and we want the friends who helped us find happiness to be our first guests," Dianne said, her face wreathed in a happy smile. "Please say you both can come."

Cicely didn't doubt that C. J. would be invited. She could face whatever it was about him that made her body act silly or run. "I'll be there. I'll bring the wine." She wasn't afraid of C. J. or any other man. He should be afraid of her.

"I'll take care of the dessert." Summer held up her glass of wine. "To a successful dinner party."

"A successful dinner party," Cicely and Dianne echoed as their glasses touched and clinked.

Across the room, C. J. half listened to Sin while watching Cicely. Tall, elegant, she had black eyes that could tempt a man to sin from thirty feet away. Classically beautiful, she had lips meant to be kissed—often—and incredibly soft skin. His frown deepened. He hadn't missed the flash of awareness when their fingers brushed against each other. It had taken all his willpower to hide his reaction—one that, even now, puzzled and annoyed him.

How could he be attracted to the woman who slammed his bar? Just the thought annoyed him.

The bar was like an old friend, always there offering comfort and accepting no matter what. Men needed a place to come and just be, a place they didn't have to talk or try to explain the impossible or reason, just shoot the bull and have a good beer while watching a game without being asked to take out the trash or talk about their feelings.

Callahan's Bar provided that and more. Yet that didn't seem to matter to Miss Stuck-up Cicely.

When she'd blogged about Alex and Dianne's new fashion line with pictures taken at his bar, she'd said that it just proved that good fashion looked good "no matter where."

Of course he'd called Alex the instant he'd read the slanderous statement. Alex had said C. J. didn't have a case to sue Cicely for slander. Now she was here thumbing her pretty nose at him and beating him at craps.

He'd known she was trouble from the moment he'd seen her. Hopefully this would be the last time. Turning away, he put her firmly out of his mind.

Chapter 2

The next morning, wearing a gray summer suit and dark gray silk tie, C. J. parked his car in his brother's space at Callahan Software and got out. He didn't dare linger. Like bad-tasting medicine, he needed to get it over with quickly. Plus, he didn't want the employees to see him lingering in his car.

The unpretentious building was located in the Meatpacking District, which was filled with businesses, restaurants, and nightclubs. When his grandfather had purchased the property, the area wasn't as trendy. Beginning in the late 1900s, the area went through a transformation, catering to young professionals and hipsters. The land alone was worth a small fortune, but it was the company and the people that mattered most. And now both had been thrust into C. J.'s unwilling hands.

Many of the employees had been with Callahan Software since he'd worked there right out of college. They'd remember his creation of The Key in high school and later The Light and The Sword—three interactive video games that found an immediate following and became immensely popular. The sales for each had been phenomenal. With his royalties, he became a very rich man in his own right. They'd also remember he'd left a year after he started working at the company to travel the world and hadn't returned— until now.

Nodding to the employees he passed entering the building and in the hall, he saw the uncertainty in their faces. His brother, Paul, had introduced him last Friday to the employees as the new CEO to a smattering of applause. They weren't sure about his ability to run the company. He couldn't blame them. He wasn't so sure himself.

Opening the door to his brother's outer office, he saw Paul's secretary, Alice Jones, sitting at her desk, typing furiously on the computer keyboard. She'd been assigned to the man running the company since Paul's illness, but because C. J. had been dragging his feet about finding a secretary, Paul had reassigned her to him last Friday.

In her midsixties, she'd been with the company fifteen years and was extremely loyal and efficient. She wore a plain navy-blue suit. Her short black hair had traces of gray.

"Good morning, Alice."

Her hands paused over the keys. She glanced up. Her gaze was as leery as those of her co-workers. "Good morning, Mr. Callahan."

She called his brother by his first name. "C. J., please. Do you have my schedule?"

"Yes, sir. It's on your desk. Is there anything else?"

He'd felt more warmth in a blizzard. "No." C. J. continued to his brother's—correction, *his*—office.

Closing the door, he let his gaze roam around the room. The maple pedestal desk in front of two narrow windows had been his grandfather's. The black leather swivel desk chair was a later addition. One wall held accolades and awards for his grandfather, father, brother, and the company. There was also a large bookshelf filled with family mementos, pictures, and books. On the other wall were several watercolors of the sea and ships. His brother and father loved both.

Continuing to his desk, he took a seat and reached for the day calendar. He frowned on seeing only one notation—a meeting with human resources at ten regarding an opening for a programmer.

He buzzed his secretary. She picked up immediately. "Yes, sir?"

"There's only one appointment. Where's the rest? Paul must have had a full schedule."

"He did, but the department head of marketing, Elton James, is handling things to give you a chance to become acclimated," she told him.

C. J. debated if he should ask to see James and the schedule, then decided it might be best if he didn't step on any toes. James had been appointed to take charge of the company after Paul's heart attack. He had a temp secretary this morning instead of Alice. "Thank you."

"Yes, sir."

C. J. booted up the computer out of habit and for lack of anything else to do. Normally at this time he'd be at the fitness center at his apartment. By ten he'd be at the bar preparing for their noon opening. For now, his head bartender, Roy Hopkins, would stand as acting manager. C. J. had no intention of turning over the bar permanently. Somehow, someway, he'd do what he loved instead of only fulfilling a family obligation.

His iPhone rang. Pulling it from his pocket, he smiled. "Thanks again for last night, Alex."

"Glad to do it, and now I have a favor to ask of you."

"Anything," C. J. said without having to think about it.

"Dianne and I are having our first dinner party Friday night and we want our closest friends there."

The smile on C. J.'s face morphed into a frown. Cicely had been in the wedding party. Odds were she had been invited as well.

"You said anything," Alex reminded him as the silence lengthened. "You don't have to dress up or anything. The main thing is that you're there. I forgot to ask you last night."

Friends stuck together no matter what. "Wouldn't miss it. What time?"

"Eight, and thanks. Sin, Summer, and Cicely will be there. I know dinner parties aren't your thing, but this is important to Dianne."

"And you'd do anything to please her," C. J. commented.

"Without a moment's hesitation," Alex said. "One day you and Sin will fall in love and stop smirking."

C. J. chuckled. "No way. No how. I like my freedom."

"Depends on your definition of freedom. See you Friday night at eight, and don't be late. Bye."

"Bye." C. J. hung up. His time of reckoning with Cicely was coming. His day had just gone from bad to worse.

By Friday at 5:00 PM, C. J. could honestly say the past five days were the most boring and least productive he'd ever had the misfortune to endure. His was the first car out of the parking garage. He went straight to the bar to check on things. He was pleased to see business had remained good. After an update from his acting manager, C. J. left to go home to shower and dress for the dinner party that he didn't want to attend because Cicely would be there.

There was no way he would cancel at the last minute so he put his game face on and left his apartment. Since he lived in the same building, it wasn't like he had a real excuse for not showing up.

Stuffing one hand into the pocket of his well-worn jeans, he rang the doorbell, still deep in thought. Perhaps he had overestimated his sexual attraction to Cicely. Perhaps his unwanted feelings had something to do with his lack of enthusiasm in taking over the family software company. Perhaps it had been his mind's weird way of trying to focus on anything other than the company.

The door opened and it was all he could do not to gape at Cicely. She wore a short red dress that clung wickedly to every delicious curve, drying his throat and making his body ache. His hands itched to pull the dress from her tempting body.

She stared at him for a long moment, then flicked her gaze over his jeans. Irritation flashed in her dark eyes. Alex had told him it was all right to dress casual. He and Cicely seemed to piss each other off just by breathing.

"You're late."

He glanced at his watch. "One minute." And she was the cause.

She rolled her eyes. "Spoken like a man who doesn't know how difficult it is to keep food at the proper temperature for a hostess who wants everything right for her guests."

"Then what are we doing standing here?" Without waiting for a response, he stepped inside the apartment, closed the door, and took her arm all in one smooth motion. He felt her tense, felt the soft velvet skin he'd thought about so often. "Is everyone in the dining room or kitchen?"

"Kitchen," she said tightly, none too subtly freeing her arm.

"After you," he said, then realized his mistake when she started in that direction. His eyes unerringly drifted over her svelte body, stopping on the slight sway of her hips, probably exaggerated even more by red icepick heels of at least five inches. Shaking his head, he followed.

"Sorry I'm late," he greeted everyone. He was the last person there.

"Hi," they said in unison. Alex, a bottle of wine in his hand, stood beside Dianne while she stirred something on the stove. Sin, always hungry, watched Summer place parsley around a standing rib roast. "Smells good."

"Dianne is a fantastic cook," Alex said proudly, handing C. J. a glass of wine.

Dianne threw a loving smile at Alex, then dished up the asparagus in a crystal serving dish. "Thanks to your mother. Otherwise I wouldn't have had the nerve to invite Summer."

"I'm looking forward to eating food I didn't cook or have cooked in my restaurant." Summer lifted the prime rib on the sterling serving platter. "I can't wait."

"Neither can I." Sin took the dish from her, which earned him a frown. "You're moving too slow for a hungry man."

"When aren't you hungry?" Alex said, opening the refrigerator. "I'll get the salads, honey."

"I'd like to do more than answer the door," Cicely said.

"Grab the rolls in the breadbasket by the stove." Dianne shook her dark head of hair. "I invite you to dinner and make you work."

"The best dinner parties, my mother always said, were the ones where everyone was involved and enjoying themselves." C. J. grabbed a chafing dish with new potatoes. "The others were just work."

"Thank you." Dianne glanced warmly at her guests, then continued to the dining room off the terrace. Once there, she directed everyone where to place the food and where to sit.

C. J. paused briefly, noting Cicely did the same when Dianne waved him to sit opposite her. Instead of showing his annoyance, he rounded the table and politely pulled out the carved Chippendale chair. Sin was busy placing the roast on the table.

"Thank you," she murmured.

C. J. grunted and took his seat. He bet that stuck in her throat.

Alex lifted his glass. "Thanks to all of you for sharing this night with us, our first dinner with our closest friends. To lasting friendship."

C. J. lifted his glass and looked directly into Cicely's eyes. She glanced away. It was going to be a long night.

Each time C. J. looked up, Cicely was there, tempting him. He'd recall the softness of her skin, the arousing scent of her perfume that haunted his senses. He resorted to keeping his head down until dinner was finally over.

When everyone went to the living room, he made the mistake of lounging in the kitchen to try to get his libido under control. When he finally came out, Dianne motioned him to sit next to Cicely on the love seat. It would have been rude not to do so. At least this time he wouldn't have to look at her.

The second he sat down beside her, he inhaled her soft jasmine fragrance and had to stop himself from leaning over and sniffing. He tilted the glass of wine in his hand and took a big swallow.

Alex immediately refilled his glass. "Good, isn't it? Cicely says it's one of her favorites, and since you aren't driving you can have another glass."

C. J. didn't know why, but he suddenly didn't want any more. He placed the glass on the coffee table in front of him. "What are you two planning this weekend?"

Dianne blushed and Alex, his arm already around her, pulled her closer. "Spend a lazy weekend here with the phone unplugged."

"Sounds like a wonderful idea," Summer said. "I haven't had one of those in what seems like forever."

"And you wouldn't have it any other way." Sin tipped his half-full glass of wine toward her.

She smiled. "You're right. I'm living my dream."

"Glad someone is," C. J. muttered. He took a sip of wine, forgetting that he'd lost his taste for it earlier.

"Sorry," Summer said, sending him a smile. "Family responsibility can be a trial."

C. J. felt like a grouch even without the frown from Sin, who had always been overprotective of Summer, even before the accident. She'd lost her parents, his aunt and uncle, when she was eighteen, but had fulfilled their dream of owning and operating an upscale restaurant. "Your parents would be proud of you."

"Just as Uncle Robert would be proud of the way Callahan's Bar has thrived," she said. "It will continue to do so while you're running Callahan Software."

If he didn't keel over with boredom first. If it weren't for the games on the computer, he'd be a nutcase by now. He'd never felt so useless in his entire life. "Yeah. At least the company is closed on weekends and I can work at Callahan's then."

"So you're breaking family tradition," Cicely said before she thought. She shouldn't be interested in anything about him—nor did she like to think that she and C. J. had anything in common—but she'd broken family tradition as well to follow her dream.

"Depends on which family tradition you mean." He turned to her, his shoulder and thigh brushing against her. "My uncle owned the bar before he willed it to me, and my father owns the software company."

"That's our C. J.," Sin said. "A man of many talents."

But his family wouldn't disapprove of him no matter his choice, the way hers had done when she'd gone into fashion instead of academia. "At least you have a choice."

He twisted away, brushing against her again, to sip his wine. "Hardly."

Cicely felt each light brush of C. J.'s hard, muscled body, which tantalized and teased and beckoned. Her grip on the stem of the wineglass tightened. If she reacted this strongly when two layers of clothes separated them, what would happen if they were naked? Heat flooded her body. She took a hasty sip of her wine.

Alex made a motion to refill her glass. "No, thank you." She waved him back into his seat, unable to believe that C. J. made her act like a hormonal teenager. Each time she moved, she seemed to brush against him. The friction made her restless, made her want to run her hand over the tight-fitting jeans, then bite. She groaned.

"Are you all right?"

Cicely glanced up at C. J. before she thought, and was caught by the deepest, darkest black eyes she'd ever seen. They drew her, tempted her.

"Cicely?"

Cicely jerked her head around to see Dianne staring oddly at her. "Long day," she managed and placed her wineglass on the table. "Thank you for a wonderful dinner, but I should be going."

"I better leave as well. I want to be at the bar early to go over the week's receipts." C. J. stood and stared down at her. "I'll walk out with you and make sure you get a cab."

Cicely gritted a smile of thanks. After hugging Dianne and Summer, she left with C. J. a few steps behind. In the hallway, she debated whether to tell him it wasn't necessary to see her to a cab. She'd lived in New York since she was a college freshman. She decided it was best to ignore him. Thankfully the elevator opened as soon as she pressed DOWN. Silently, she stepped on and punched M.

The elevator door had barely closed before C. J. murmured from a few feet away, "We seem to have a problem."

There was such male satisfaction in his deep drawling voice that she wanted to give him a swift kick. She could evade, but that would show weakness. C. J. seemed the type of man to take full advantage of any weakness. "Nothing that can't be handled," she said with enough chill for him to check his fingers and toes for frostbite.

Being insensitive and arrogant, C. J. stepped in front of her, grinned, and tilted his head toward her face. "Let's see."

Her hand in the middle of his wide chest stopped the descent of his head. The second she felt the muscled hardness and strength, she realized her tactical mistake. Her hand wanted to curl, rip the fabric away, explore, taste. "No."

His midnight-black eyes narrowed. She'd bet her Birkin bag he'd seldom heard that word. Under different circumstances, she might have enjoyed the surprised look on his too-handsome face. "This is not going any farther."

"Wanna bet?" Determination stared back at her.

If he pushed it, she was lost. She was fighting for survival. Her chin lifted. "I know it's a foreign concept, but act like a gentleman and accept a no."

C. J. jerked upright. The hardness in his eyes became laser-sharp. He stepped back. The elevator door opened. She didn't move. In trying to protect herself, she'd unintentionally insulted him. She opened her mouth to apologize, but he stepped off, ramming his hands into the pockets of his tight jeans, his jaw tight.

She stepped off as well and stared at his stiff profile. She'd put an end to whatever it was between them, but she wished she had been able to do it in a better way. Wordlessly, he started for the front door. She had no choice but to follow him.

Outside, she said, "Good night."

He nodded once, a quick jerk of his head, his gaze fixed somewhere over her head. He didn't even want to look at her. The knowledge made her feel even worse. She might be called the Ice Queen, but she didn't like hurting people. She'd been carelessly hurt too many times to want to inflict pain on another. Men of a certain ilk ran together. Neither Sin nor

Alex impressed her as a man who took advantage of women.

Sin, gorgeous and charming, like C. J., had plenty of opportunity at Alex and Dianne's wedding. Women certainly made it no secret that they were interested. Yet after seeing Alex and Dianne off to the airport where a private jet waited to take them to Paris, she, Summer, Sin, and C. J. had said good night and gone to their rooms in Alex's parents' home.

Seconds ticked by and nothing. Silently she turned toward the patient doorman holding the door open to the cab. Tipping him, she got inside. Perhaps it was for the best, but she still couldn't resist looking back. C. J. was gone.

Chapter 3

Cicely couldn't sleep Friday night and it annoyed her. For once she had a rare free Saturday. She'd worked twelve to fourteen hours every day that week to have this time. She'd promised herself she would spend a lazy day at home, trying to salvage the wilting ivy plants she always forgot to water, read a book for pleasure, eat a leisurely meal. Maybe do some yoga, take a run to get the oxygen and ideas flowing.

Instead she was dragging herself out of bed at seven thirty-three. Tossing back the covers, she stuck her feet in her pale blue silk house shoes and headed for the bathroom. A bit grumpy, she turned on the faucets and liberally squirted in Hermès Rouge bath milk. Perhaps all she needed was a soak.

After the last two hectic weeks of putting out the monthly magazine, she'd planned to use Saturday to rejuvenate before she dove back into selecting the articles and fashion for the magazine five months away, the crazy process starting all over again.

When she walked into work Monday, she had to be at her best. Lenora Little, the vice president/

publisher, was scheduled to name the editor-in-chief of the new Paris office in mere weeks. *Fashion Insider* had several branch offices around the country, but this would be the first European office. The three top candidates were all in the New York office, and just as hungry for the position as Cicely.

Placing her clothes on the French-inspired bench in front of the vanity, she climbed into the water and sank down until the bubbles covered to her chin. It wouldn't do Charles or Eva, the other two candidates, any good to have their name on the short list; Cicely intended to get that position.

She'd worked hard and would continue to do so to show Lenora that she was the best choice. She had to keep on turning in work that stood out from the pack. She couldn't do that if she was tired and unfocused.

She picked up the bath sponge and aimlessly brushed it down her arm. She had no right to insult C. J. It was her problem that he shook her confidence. No one was allowed to do that. She'd built a reputation of being formidable—she had to in the dog-eat-dog world of the fashion magazine industry. She could handle men.

Most of them were afraid of her. A tiny number revered her. There was an even smaller number who had tried to get her into their bed, and she liked it that way. She didn't have time for a man. She switched the sponge to the other arm.

It didn't make sense that she was attracted to an opinionated man like C. J., even if he had a mouthwatering eight-pack and the looks of a fallen angel. She was better than that. She also faced her problems head-on. She didn't take shots below the belt. There was only one solution. Finishing her bath, she got dressed and went to the kitchen to cook breakfast. She'd spend the day just as she'd planned, with one exception.

Later in the day, Cicely dressed in her favorite jean jacket, a blue-and-white-striped shirt, cuffed denim jeans, and statement jewelry. She grabbed her "baby stealing bag"—as her assistant's teenage sister called the oversized supple brown leather bag, which measured twenty-four by thirty-six—shoved the wide strap over her shoulder, and left her brownstone. The sooner she got it over with, the sooner she could enjoy the rest of her weekend.

Less than thirty minutes later, she was standing outside Callahan's Bar. Instead of going in, she paused. She was a bit surprised by the steady stream of patrons going inside, but not that they were all men, comfortably dressed in casual clothes and jeans and khakis. The clientele was a far cry from some of the upscale bars she'd been to.

Customers in those bars dressed to impress and be seen. None would dare step one well-shod foot inside the "in" bar without looking their best. Clearly Callahan's was a bar people went to to drink and relax, not see and be seen or find a bedmate for the night.

The word *bed* triggered her overactive imagination where C. J. was concerned, and she squirmed, pushing away the image of them entwined in bed. Her throat dried and her heart drummed in her chest.

This was ridiculous. While she was out here getting all hot and bothered, she was probably the farthest thing from C. J.'s mind. She crossed the sidewalk and opened the door. He wasn't going to be glad to see her. He'd probably make it as difficult as he could.

It was his right. But Cicely had had enough of her apologies thrown back in her face to last a lifetime. He'd better accept her apology and be glad to have gotten one!

She glanced at her watch. It was a little past five; the bar would become even busier in the coming hours. Her best bet was to get in, apologize, and then put C. J. out of her mind.

Before losing her courage, she pushed the door open and stepped inside. It was still a man-cave, with several men hunched over at the long bar, and more sitting in the booths or around the tables. She counted exactly two women, and they were at a booth with two men. Over an old Wilson Pickett tune, she heard the cracks of pool balls hitting one another. She also noticed something else. C. J. was bartending.

He had on a white T-shirt that delineated all those hard muscles she'd thought of licking. She groaned and tucked her head. She'd never before been this hung up on a man or this horny. When she lifted her head, she stared straight into a pair of flat black eyes.

Her stomach did a fast hop, skip, and jump. Her heart decided to join in. For her own sake, she had to get this over with and leave. She moved forward with C. J.'s unblinking gaze never leaving her when all she wanted to do was run back outside, get a cab, and go home.

C. J. couldn't believe Little Miss Stuck-up had the unmitigated gall to set foot in his bar. He'd like nothing better than to toss her out the door on her curvy little behind. Instead he moved to the end of the bar when she took a seat. She was his customer, and he'd always taught his people that customer service was paramount.

"Yes?"

Up went her brow in that irritating manner of hers. He couldn't care less. "Your order. I have customers waiting."

She tossed on the bar a bag that was the size of a thirty-pound turkey—and sounded as if it was just as heavy when it landed with a *thump*. "I came to apologize, but you're not making it easy."

"Maybe because I don't hear one."

She shot him a look that bounced right off. However, when she folded her arms under her breasts, inadvertently pushing them higher in the unbuttoned neckline of her blouse, his breath hitched. He straightened away from temptation.

"I'm sorry. It was thoughtless of me to accuse you. I know you're not that type of man."

"Accepted. Bye." He moved away to safety to draw a draft beer for a regular customer. First she insulted his bar, then him. She could take her apology and—

"Beer on tap."

C. J. whirled around. He'd know that imperious voice anywhere. He couldn't believe Cicely was still there and had the nerve to order a beer. He quickly moved back to her. He wanted her gone. He didn't want her reminding him that he couldn't control his attraction to her.

"You want to inspect the glass or the tap first?"

Cicely took a ten from her wallet, slapped it on the bar, and gave him glare for glare.

He turned away before he hauled her across the bar and kissed her until she— He snatched up a glass to fill her order. Why her? Why now? Didn't he have enough to contend with?

Slamming the beer down on the bar hard enough for the foam to slosh up and over the sides, he moved away to see a couple of the regulars at the bar as well as the other bartender, who were staring at him strangely. In the bar, he was always easygoing, laughing. He might have had some rough days, but Callahan's always smoothed out the rough edges.

Until now.

It was Cicely's fault that he was snarling and annoyed. Why didn't she do both of them a favor and just leave?

Cicely stared at C. J.'s strong, unbending profile, his mouth tight, body rigid. Inwardly she berated him for being so bullheaded and worse, making her order the beer. She hated the taste of beer. But she'd drink the thing if it killed her.

Grabbing the glass, she lifted it to her lips. And grimaced. "Ugh." The taste was even worse than she remembered from college.

C. J. was back in her face in seconds, looking as if he'd like to toss her out of his bar. "Something wrong with my beer?"

She stared at him and decided he couldn't think any worse of her. "I can't stand the taste," she admitted tightly. "And before you ask why I ordered it, it was because you made me so angry. I just said the first thing that came to my mind. And regardless of what we think of each other, we have mutual friends whom we both care about. There are going to be times they are together that we'll be with them, so take the stick out of your—"

"What did I miss?" Sin asked, sliding onto the stool next to Cicely, grinning for all he was worth.

Cicely blushed with embarrassment and tucked her head. She was notorious for her ability to cut a person off at the knees without raising her voice. She'd earned the title "Ice Queen," after all. So where had all her control gone?

C. J. gave Sin a look that had his best friend reluctantly moving away and mumbling that he never had any fun. As soon as Sin left, C. J. curtly ordered Cicely, "Follow me."

Since she was sure they were going to have it out, she grabbed her handbag and followed right behind him, more than ready to stand toe-to-toe with him. She'd never backed down from anyone. She'd had to

fight all of her life. If she could stand up to her disapproving family, C. J. would be child's play.

C. J., holding open his office door for Cicely, slammed
it shut the moment she stalked in. He was pissed, but
at himself. Against his willpower, he'd let her get to
him. "I owe you an apology. I have never acted
rudely to a customer or allowed my employees to
do so. Personal problems shouldn't spill over into
work."

Slowly Cicely uncrossed her arms. She'd expected
him to blast her. She'd planned on giving it back to
him in spades. "You're right. I apologize, too. Again."
She blew out a breath and rubbed the back of her
neck, the taut muscles relaxing only marginally. "Perhaps I should have just called. I knew this wouldn't be
easy for either of us. We annoy the heck out of each
other just by breathing."

"Then why do I keep imagining kissing you?" he
asked tersely, his gaze locked on her mouth before it
jerked up to her wide eyes. His wide hands were
braced on his narrow hips.

Stunned, she couldn't think of one word to say.

"You think I'm happy about this? Your mouth is
the most tempting I've ever seen. It makes a man
weak—and then you flay him."

His statement unexpectedly made her smile. She
wasn't in this alone. What's more, he wasn't any surer
of her than she was of him. Both were on shaky
ground, but they were on shaky ground together.
She'd met few people, especially men, who were up
front with their feelings. Could she be any less?

"I've wondered about the taste of you as well." She believed in honesty up to a point. She didn't admit she'd talked herself into thinking he probably had all the finesse of a caveman, grabbing and bruising, taking without thought of giving.

Slowly, his arms lowered to his sides. His hot gaze narrowed on her lips.

Air became harder for her to draw in. She licked her lips as if searching for a taste of him, then shook her head. "No kissing. Just friends."

"No kissing. Just friends," C. J. repeated. Kissing her would probably be like kissing a statue, cold, unfeeling, with no heat or passion. "How about we have dinner to solidify the friendship?"

Cicely hesitated only for a moment. She had to be willing to do her part. She reached inside her handbag. "I'll give you my address."

"That won't be necessary." There was a smile on his lips that had probably gotten more than one woman in trouble. He folded his muscled arms across that impressive chest of his and leaned back against the front of his desk. "Dinner is here at Callahan's."

Cicely would have thought he was being obstinate if Dianne hadn't mentioned that C. J. often had dinner with his friends at the bar. "All right. I'd like my burger medium with lots of onion rings."

Straightening, he took her arm as they left his office. "I think that can be arranged. I'll show you to a table and dump the beer."

She glanced up and saw the curve of his mouth and found herself smiling. "Please. Water is fine."

"Coming up." C. J. paused beside the booth. "I'll be back in a bit."

"I understand if you're busy," she said, taking a seat and placing the handbag beside her.

"Thanks, but I have good people working for me. I'll be back."

"No need to hurry," Sin said, sliding into the booth across from her. "I'll keep her company."

"Hi, Sin," Cicely said. "It's nice to see you again."

"Same here. It's always refreshing to be around beautiful things."

C. J. scowled at Sin.

Cicely smiled and tilted her head to one side. "I see you earned the nickname."

"Beautiful and smart, an attractive combination," Sin said, bracing his arms on the table and leaning toward her.

C. J. grunted. "I'll go put your order in."

"Could you please see if mine is ready?" Sin asked. "I'm starved."

"You could always eat it at the bar," C. J. said.

"But I'd be deprived of some very nice company," Sin said, grinning at Cicely.

C. J. stared down at Cicely, whom he thought might have sense enough to see that Sin was trying to work the same charm on her that he used on all women.

"C. J., your guest is probably hungry," Sin said without taking his eyes from Cicely.

"I am a bit," she confessed.

With one last frown, C. J. walked away. Sin's laugh was like a prod to his back. All Cicely did was

spew venom and insult him, but she treated Sin as if
he were God's gift to women. He shouldn't care, but
he couldn't quite deny that he did.

Women!

Cicely turned in her seat to stare after C. J. Sin
smiled and sipped his imported beer. *Looks like
C. J. has finally met a woman he can't forget. She
appears just as interested. Very interesting.*

When C. J. returned with their food, Sin ate his
burger while carrying on an easy conversation with
Cicely. Finished, he placed more than enough money
to cover the food and a hefty tip, and lightly nudged
C. J. to let him out. Both men stood.

"It was nice seeing you again, Cicely." Sin turned
to C. J. "Catch you later. I'm flying to my Atlanta
office in the morning."

C. J. stuck out his hand and clasped Sin's. "Safe
travel."

"Safe travel, Sin," Cicely repeated.

"Thanks. Bye."

C. J. retook his seat across from Cicely as Sin
walked away. For the life of him, he couldn't think
of anything to say. Usually he was nearly as smooth
as Sin when it came to women.

Yet somehow neither the small talk nor the
charming compliments came to him. For just a moment, C. J. wished for Sin's charming mannerisms,
then just as quickly he became irritated with himself. He wasn't changing for any woman.

Besides, he reminded himself, he liked his women
uncomplicated. Cicely was anything but. So why

was he still sitting there instead of escorting her politely to the door?

Cicely couldn't help but notice that C. J. had grown even quieter after Sin left. He was as stiff as the wall next to her. Perhaps he regretted asking her to stay. He wasn't an easy man to understand. Until that moment, she hadn't realized just how much she hoped they could be friends. "I guess dinner didn't work."

C. J.'s stern expression grew even fiercer. "It might if you were half as talkative with me as you were with Sin."

Cicely watched his eyes widen, his broad shoulders snap back against the back of the booth. A muscle leaped in his clenched jaw. Cicely didn't think he'd meant to be *that* honest.

Jealous. Who would have thought it? The knot unclenched in her stomach. She picked up her handbag and scooted out of the booth. Once standing, she stepped closer to C. J., leaned over, and whispered, "You ever think it's because he doesn't make me wish for things better left unspoken?"

C. J. whipped his head around. Cicely was already walking away. Grinning, he scrambled out of the booth. He purposely waited until she was outside. Catching her arm, he pulled her to one side of the busy sidewalk. "You interest me as no woman ever has. You keep me on my toes. I'd like to get to know you for myself, not just so we won't make our friends uncomfortable around us. How about it?"

Cicely felt the heat of his body, the compulsion to

lean closer and find out about that kiss. "If I say yes, we both know it won't stay just friends."

He shrugged broad shoulders carelessly. "We could try."

She rolled her eyes at him. "And what happens if we fail? I'm not sure I'm ready for that step. I'll let you know."

"What's the matter? Scared you can't keep your hands off me?"

Since he was smiling, not acting macho, and he might be right, she didn't take offense. She pushed against his rock-hard chest and he released her. "I'll let you know."

"Can I borrow a pen and paper?"

Reaching into her bag, she pulled out a little pad and pen and handed it to him. Taking it, he shook his head. "I don't know how you find anything in there."

"It was specially made for me and has pockets for everything," she explained. "I had it when my magazine did the spread your mother and sister were in. Ariel ordered one just like it."

"I didn't think my sister was into fashion as much as our mother," C. J. said, writing on the pad. "But both were ecstatic about the article you wrote, and being on the cover sent them into fashion bliss."

"They looked fabulous," Cicely told him. "And there was a nice bump in magazine sales."

"Probably because Mother purchased so many issues," he kidded and handed the pad and pen back to Cicely. "You have my iPhone, Callahan's, my office, and my home phone numbers."

Cicely glanced at the numbers, then up at C. J. Men, in her limited experience, never gave this much information. He really wanted them to get to know each other better. She felt herself softening, then reminded herself, as she'd said, it wouldn't end there— and she planned to be in Paris in five weeks. "Good night, C. J. Thanks for dinner."

"I plan on a lot more," he said, then took her arm to hail her a taxi.

So, he was self-confident. So was she. Getting inside the taxi, she waved good-bye.

As the taxi pulled away from the curb, she looked out the back window. Unlike last night, he still stood there. Straightening, she pulled out the pad. He certainly wasn't afraid of showing he wanted to get to know her better. Despite her best effort, she wanted the same thing. So why was she running away?

"Stop. I'll get out here." Pulling a ten from her wallet, she handed it to the driver and got out.

C. J. was right. She was scared, but she was also curious. Perhaps he kissed like a slug. Laughing, she increased her pace. Half a block farther, she was surprised and pleased to see C. J. still outside the bar staring in the direction her cab had headed. Something soft and sweet unfurled inside her.

A broad grin spread across his handsome face. He'd seen her as well. Waving, he started toward her. Grinning back, she hurried down the sidewalk, sidestepping people as she went.

She expected to do the same when she saw a

scrawny kid in a jean jacket and holey jeans wrestling with the leashes of five dogs in her path. It didn't happen.

In seconds she was tangled in barking dogs, two bigger than she was, and leashes. She went down and didn't get up.

Chapter 4

"Cicely!" C. J. shouted, sprinting toward her. His heart lodged in his throat, he'd started running the moment he saw her tangled in leashes and dogs. He hadn't been able to get to her fast enough.

When he reached her, the kid and the dogs were running down the street. A small crowd gathered around her. Dropping to his knees, he heard her moan. "Cicely, don't try to move until we're sure nothing is broken."

Despite his instructions, she tried to sit up. Calling her every kind of stubborn and afraid he'd hurt her more if he tried to restrain her, he helped her.

"Where are you hurt?"

Instead of answering, she lifted her hand to the back of her head, winced and cursed. "That kid is dead meat."

C. J. wanted to hug her to him, he was so relieved. She was conscious, coherent, and pissed. All three good signs. She'd also easily pulled her legs under her and moved both arms without wincing. Then he felt a large lump, the size of an agate, on the back of her head.

"Ouch!"

"Sorry." Apparently she'd hit her head when she fell. "We need to get you checked out." He scooped her up in his arms.

"Don't—"

He immediately paused. "Does something hurt besides your head?"

"No. Shouting at you made my head hurt. I can walk."

His hold tightened as he felt her body tremble. She must really be hurting. She'd fight him harder if she weren't. "Humor me. I lost ten years of my life when I saw you go down, and since I'm not sure how many I have, you owe me."

She relaxed against him a bit more. "Never knew you were a whiner."

Her voice still sounded shaky. "One of my lesser-known qualities." Luckily a patron was going inside the bar and opened the door. "Thanks."

Inside, C. J. headed for his office, calling to one of his waitresses as he passed. "Ice pack. She hit her head."

In his office, he carefully sat Cicely in one of the leather wingback chairs in front of his desk. By the time she was settled, Mary, the waitress, was there with the ice pack.

"Anything else I can do?" the petite redhead asked.

"Not now, thanks."

Gingerly, he placed the ice pack on the back of Cicely's head. She flinched, closed her eyes. Silently he cursed. If he ever saw that careless kid again . . .

"Is there anyone I can call for you?"

Her eyes opened. "No, just call me a cab. I'll be fine."

"I'll send Mary back inside to stay with you."

"I'll be fine," she repeated.

She didn't look fine. She was still trembling and had to have a monster of a headache. If she thought he was sending her home in a cab, she was crazy. He pushed to his feet and went to the door. "Mary, could you come here, please?"

She was there in seconds. "Yes, C. J?"

"Stay with her until I get back."

"Sure thing."

With one last look at Cicely, her eyes closed, her trembling hand holding the ice pack, he grabbed the car keys off his desk and went out the back door. The Bugatti Veyron started immediately, purring like a big cat. Going down the alley and into the street, C. J. parked in front of Callahan's.

Quickly going inside, he thanked Mary, gathered Cicely in his arms, and started back outside. He knew she must be feeling worse because they had gone several feet before she asked to be put down. "I thought you were going to humor me," he said.

Standing her on her feet, he opened the door, picked her up, put her in the car, and buckled her seat belt.

Her eyes opened. "This isn't a cab."

C. J. circled the car and pulled away before answering. "Not likely. Just close your eyes and try to relax. We're going to the hospital to have your head checked out."

"C. J., just take me home."

Without thinking he reached out and clasped her hand in his. "Ask me something I can do and it's yours. You need to see a doctor."

She twisted her head to look at him. "Do you have any idea how long it takes to see a doctor in the emergency room? Moss grows faster."

He squeezed her hand, then downshifted. Humor was good. "I have a secret weapon. Just close your eyes and try to rest."

Sighing, she did just that. She didn't even protest when he covered her hand with his again.

Parking in the emergency room lot for visitors, C. J. picked Cicely up once again and headed toward the entrance. If it hadn't been so ridiculous, Cicely might admire how easily he carried and tenderly cared for her. He wasn't even breathing hard. His large hands were gentle.

But if he thought she was spending half the night waiting to be seen, he was crazy. "You better be right about your secret weapon."

"I am."

Had his cheek touched her hair or had she imagined it?

Going through the automatic doors, C. J. stopped at the receptionist. "Please page Dr. Reyes. He said to tell you I'm family."

The woman on the other side of the Plexiglas, in her midthirties, straightened and sent C. J. a warm smile. "Certainly, sir."

"Thanks." C. J. turned toward the tub chairs in the busy waiting room.

"A chair and I mean it," she said.

"If you insist," C. J. said, only half kidding. He'd enjoyed holding her. Looking around, he didn't see any seats until a name was called and two people followed the nurse back through double swinging doors. He moved in that direction. The seats were next to a young woman with a small child in her lap.

"Would you like to sit her in the chair next to you?" he asked the woman.

The woman looked startled for a moment, then shook her head. "You go ahead. Every time she moves, it hurts her arm."

C. J. noted the odd way the little girl held her arm, the dried tears on her pale face. Gingerly, he placed Cicely in the chair next to the woman.

He couldn't help but ask her, "How long have you been here?"

"Three hours since we filled out the forms." The woman bit her lower lip, visibly swallowed. "She fell off her tricycle. I'm—I'm afraid—" She blinked and sat up straighter as a nurse came out of the double doors and called another name.

"Mommy, it hurts."

The dark-haired woman blinked back tears. "Mommy knows. The doctor will make it better soon."

C. J. felt helpless and didn't like the feeling.

"Dr. Reyes called and said he'd be here shortly," the receptionist said, handing a clipboard, with forms and a pen attached, to Cicely. "When you finish this, just bring it back to me."

"How soon before the little girl is seen?" Cicely asked.

The receptionist frowned. "I'm not sure. We're really busy tonight. I better get back."

Cicely and C. J. shared a look. "Would you like me to get you or your daughter something to drink or eat?" C. J. asked.

"Thank you. I couldn't eat and she doesn't want to," the woman replied. She straightened when the double doors opened again. But this time it was a doctor in a white lab coat, a grin on his darkly handsome face. He stopped in front of C. J., who was still standing.

"You look all right, so who is it you want me to see?"

C. J. looked at Cicely, then at the little girl.

"I can wait," Cicely said. "She can't."

"Her." C. J. pointed to the little girl.

"I want all the details later," Dr. Reyes said to C. J. before squatting in front of the mother and little girl. "Hello, little one, my name is Dr. Reyes. Can I look at your arm?"

She nodded. "I fell off my tricycle and hurt it."

Dr. Reyes's gaze went to the watchful mother. "I don't need an X-ray to tell me it's broken, but we need one to see the extent of the break." He smiled at the little girl. "Let's go get some pictures of your arm and get you feeling better." Standing, he helped the woman to her feet.

With tears in her eyes, the woman turned to C. J., then Cicely. "Thank you. I . . ." She paused, swallowed.

"No thanks needed," Cicely told her.

With Dr. Reyes's assistance, they moved through the double doors.

"You aren't angry," C. J. asked, a statement more than a question.

"If it wouldn't hurt, I'd punch you," she told him, and went back to filling out the forms.

C. J. laughed, and took the seat vacated by the mother. Cicely intrigued him. She was sophisticated, but there was also a hint of vulnerability beneath her tough exterior and smart mouth.

He liked that she was unique, that he appeared to be the only one who could see the tiny crack in her composure, her toughness. He was surprised and pleased that she could be so calm and selfless. Her head had to be hurting, yet she hadn't hesitated to let a woman and child she didn't know see the doctor first.

He'd been around plenty of people who thought they were more important than the next person, thought that the world should revolve around them. Cicely wasn't snotty or pretentious, as he'd thought.

The more he thought of her, the more he had to contend with images of her hair mussed, her naked and wild in his bed.

"You're right. You'd hurt yourself, so behave," he finally answered, leaning toward her.

She looked up. Their faces were so close together, she could see her own reflection in his eyes, feel the heat, the pull. "That's what I'm afraid of," she murmured.

His brows snapped together. She turned away and

tucked her head over the forms. "I'm giving the doctor fifteen minutes, and then I'm getting a cab."

Aware she probably regretted her admission, C. J. let it slide. It looked like he still had his work cut out for him to get Cicely to trust him.

In less than ten minutes, Dr. Reyes was back. Once again he stopped in front of C. J., who stood to greet him. "Now let's try this again. And before you ask, Amy's break was clean. She'll be back riding her tricycle, this time with protective gear, in no time."

"Always knew you were the best." C. J. slapped the doctor on the back. "I'd like for you to take a look at Cicely St. John. She hit her head on the sidewalk when some irresponsible kid made the bad decision to try to walk five dogs."

"Ouch," Dr. Reyes said in sympathy.

"In spades," Cicely said, coming to her feet. "I'll be fine once I get home, but Sir Galahad thought I should see a doctor."

Dr. Reyes chuckled. "Since you're here, why don't we humor him? I like hanging out in his bar and beating him at pool occasionally."

Cicely allowed the doctor to lightly take her arm. "If he plays pool the way he does craps, it wasn't much of a challenge."

"I just had an off night," C. J. protested from behind them.

"Yeah, right," Cicely said as they continued through the double doors to an exam table in a room.

"Here we go," Dr. Reyes said, but it was C. J. who gently lifted her onto the table.

"Thanks, Galahad," Cicely quipped.

"Anytime," C. J. responded.

"Since your coordination is good, and you're pleasantly coherent, I think we can assume you only have the head injury." Dr. Reyes snapped on a pair of gloves. "I'm going to feel your head. Let me know if anything hurts."

Cicely closed her eyes and winced before the doctor touched her. "I don't think I'll be as strong as Amy about this."

"Which is a good thing," he said, gently probing her head from her forehead to the back. "I need to know if anything—"

"Ouch."

"Hurts." He turned her head to one side, parted her hair, and gingerly probed around the lump on the back of her head. "There's minor abrasion but the skin is intact." Going to a drawer, he pulled out an ophthalmoscope. "C. J., hit the light for me, please."

Darkness settled in the room. "Follow the light, Cicely. Good. Hit the light. Now follow my finger without turning your head. Good." He replaced the scope and returned. "You're a lucky woman. You have a deep bruise, but you don't have a concussion. Your neuro signs are excellent."

"You aren't going to do a CT scan to make sure?" C. J. asked, hovering over them.

"Might I ask your relationship to the patient?" Dr. Reyes asked instead of answering the question.

"He's just an acquaintance," Cicely said as she started scooting off the exam table.

Although he didn't like her answer, C. J. quickly moved to help her.

Dr. Reyes smiled easily. '"You probably guessed that C. J. and I are not related."

"I did." Cicely threw a glance at C. J. "You don't bully people."

"Ha," C. J. said. "Tell that to Mary's mother."

Dr. Reyes's handsome face grew serious. "Because she doesn't stay on her diet and do her exercise. She'd control her diabetes better if she did."

"I'd say she's lucky to have you in her corner, Dr. Reyes," Cicely said.

Unsure if Dr. Reyes was making a move on Cicely, C. J. said, "Thanks for seeing Cicely. We better let you get back to work."

"Yes, thank you again."

The doctor took her hand and just held it. "I'm glad I was here. Take it easy tonight and tomorrow, and over-the-counter medicine for the headaches. I don't think it's necessary, but have someone check your pupils in a couple of hours. I'm on duty for the rest of the week if you have concerns. For you, I'd make a house call."

"Thank you, Dr. Reyes," Cicely said, smiling up at the man.

Fighting the urge to snatch their hands apart, C. J. waited until she turned. "Thanks, Dr. Reyes," he said, taking Cicely's arm and heading for the door.

"My pleasure," Dr. Reyes murmured as they left.

"He was such a nice man," Cicely commented as

they checked out. "If I ever needed a doctor again, I'd certainly call Dr. Reyes."

C. J. just grunted, took Cicely's arm, and headed for his car.

C. J. stayed annoyed with Dr. Reyes for the next five minutes until he recalled Cicely's explanation of why it was easy for her to talk to Sin. He sat up straighter in the car seat and glanced over at Cicely. Her eyes were closed, but she was frowning.

"Do I need to stop and pick up something for the headache?" he asked.

"No," she said. "Stress headaches are an occupational hazard. I just need to lie down."

"We'll be at your place in about ten minutes," he told her. "Is there anyone you want me to call to come over?"

Her eyes opened. "This is New York, and I'm a big girl. I can take care of myself."

C. J. didn't doubt that under ordinary circumstances, but if she needed anything she wasn't going to feel like getting it. It just made sense that she not be alone. When'd he been ill, he'd certainly enjoyed having his mother there. Just knowing she was around to help if needed made him feel better.

He was concerned and a bit disturbed that there was no one for Cicely. He'd thought of calling Dianne, but she and Alex said they'd planned to spend the day at home. They probably hadn't had a stitch of clothes on all day. He couldn't leave Cicely by herself.

C. J. sensed there was no one close. The thought made his heart ache for some strange reason. He'd always had friends, family—although sometimes he'd like to forget them. He was aware of how lonely you could be even when surrounded by people. He'd stared into a lot of faces over the years, people who came into the bar not so much to drink as to not feel so alone.

Cicely was too proud to admit there was no one. That left him to take care of her. If she hadn't been coming back to see him, she'd be home safe and sound. "This is your street."

Cicely roused as he turned down the row of neat brownstones. The homes were pricey, and in demand. He was surprised she could afford the house, then a thought hit him as he pulled up in front. "You live here alone?"

Although he thought he had asked the question in a conversational tone, from the narrow-eyed look she gave him before getting out of the car, he hadn't fooled her. "Since I misspoke once, I'll give you the benefit and answer yes."

Getting out of the car, he met her on the sidewalk. "I'd like to say it wasn't any of my business, but since we were discussing kissing earlier, I needed to know."

Cicely grunted and started up the stairs. C. J. picked her up again, continued up the steps before placing her on her feet. She reached in her bag and came out with her keys. She hadn't thought of protesting. In fact, it had felt kind of nice. "You must be wearing me down."

"That will be the day."

Her smile turned into a wince as the door swung open. "You need to take something for the headache." He felt responsible and picked her up again.

"I can walk."

"Don't you ever get tired of arguing?"

"Don't you ever get tired of being macho?"

"Apparently not. Which way to your bedroom, and before you get any ideas, I'm stopping at the door."

"Never thought otherwise. First hall on the right, first door."

Taking her to the bedroom door, he gently placed her on her feet. "Take the medicine, and then take Dr. Reyes's advice and lie down."

Without answering, she entered her room, dropping her handbag on the bed as she continued to the medicine cabinet. Finding the ibuprofen, she took two, washing then down with tap water. All she wanted to do was crawl in between the sheets and close her eyes. Perhaps then, the little man with the sledgehammer in the back of her skull would take a hike.

But before she could do that, she had to get rid of Sir Galahad. She rubbed her forehead. C. J. was turning out to be more of a problem than she could have ever imagined. She'd made that crack about Sir Galahad to negate her softening toward him. No one, absolutely no one, had ever cared for her so tenderly.

Her maternal grandmother might have encouraged Cicely, but never in the presence of her disapproving daughter. But she had loved Cicely. She proved that when she left her the bulk of her estate.

Her mother hadn't spoken to her for weeks when Cicely had used the money, as her grandmother had wanted, to put a hefty down payment on the brownstone. She hadn't wanted Cicely living in an apartment.

Her mother wanted her to share the money with her brother and sister. It hadn't mattered to her that neither ever had time to visit or call Grandmother Harris in the retirement home.

Her belief in Cicely had helped her stand strong against her parents. Only her maternal grandmother had believed in her, believed in her dream. She didn't see wanting to go into the fashion industry as a waste of Cicely's time and talent. So what if she didn't want to openly go against her daughter? Cicely understood her reasons all too well. Her mother had a sharp and unforgiving tongue, which was the main reason Cicely seldom went back home anymore.

For some reason a lump lodged in her throat. She shook her head and winced at the pain. She wouldn't cry. She was stronger than this. One day her parents would look at her with love and pride the same way they did her older sister and brother. The job in Paris would do it.

Her brother might be a history professor, her sister well on her way to earning her doctorate, and while that was important to her father who was chair of the history department and her mother who was tenured and respected at the same university, none of them had an international reach. With her Paris assignment, she'd finally measure up. She certainly hadn't in all these years.

So what if Cicely had an IQ of 188? It didn't make her happy or better than anyone else. She certainly wasn't wasting her time as her family had told her over and over.

She'd proved them wrong, but it had strained their

relationship even more. To get where she was, she'd worked long hours and sacrificed friendships. There were a few people she might have called, but none would have cared for her the way C. J. had. She didn't regret that she hadn't made any true friendships in her climb to the top. At least not until now.

C. J. probably had loads of friends. So did the others at the dinner party. She had her reputation as the Ice Queen.

The little man became more animated with his sledgehammer. Opening the bathroom door, she went back to the den. C. J. came to his feet the moment she appeared in the hallway. Apparently he had been watching for her. She swallowed another lump in her throat.

"Thank you for everything," she said. "I'm going to take your and Dr. Reyes's advice and go to bed."

"Is someone coming over to do the pupil check in a couple of hours?"

Her smile slipped for a heartbeat. "You heard Dr. Reyes. It isn't necessary."

"He might be the doctor, but he didn't see you go down," C. J. said easily. "I'll tell you what. I'll check on you in a couple of hours and we'll go from there. You can't check your own pupils." He turned toward the large-screen TV on the wall. "I don't imagine you have the sports channel. Never mind, I'll make do. 'Night. See you in a couple of hours."

She opened her mouth to argue, but the little man demanded her attention. Briefly shutting her eyes, she turned toward her bedroom. He wasn't going to walk in his sleep.

For once, she let her clothes stay where they fell. Grabbing the first pair of pajamas she touched in the lingerie drawer, she plopped on the side of the bed and tried to put them on without jostling her head.

She imagined C. J., his long legs stretched out in front of him on the sofa. The corners of her mouth lifted in a smile. Wouldn't he be surprised to learn he was the first man who had gotten that close to her bed in years. Crawling beneath the soft sheets, she pushed away the unpleasant memory of when she had tried to make her parents notice her and only succeeded in making a horrible mistake.

Snapping the light off, she carefully lay on her side, closed her eyes, and willed herself to go to sleep. But she couldn't seem to shut down her mind. If she were honest with herself, and she tried to be, she was glad C. J. was there. She didn't want to be alone, but she also didn't want him to know that she had no close friends—one of the reasons she wanted to nurture her friendships with Dianne and Summer. The possibility of being friends with C. J. carried as many benefits as it did dangers.

Chapter 5

Cicely tried to sleep, but she kept rolling over on the tender spot on the back of her head. She pushed the pillows against the headboard to recline on her side, but that didn't help. She couldn't drift off. She had some PM medication to aid sleep, but she wasn't sure she should take it.

She was wide awake when a knock came on her door. She was just miserable enough not to fake being asleep. She reached over and put the crystal bedside lamp on dim. "Come in."

C. J. paused briefly in the doorway before coming into the bedroom, his dark eyes narrowed. "I hope you don't mind that I found a flashlight in the kitchen."

"No."

He stopped by the side of the bed. "You haven't been asleep."

"Every time I roll over on the sore spot, I wake up," she confessed, misery coating each word.

"Let's do this, and then I have an idea. Mind if I sit on the bed so I can see better?"

"No."

Reaching over, he turned off the lamp, then shone the flashlight into both of her eyes. Finished, he turned the lamp back on. "Like you said, Dr. Reyes is a good doctor."

"A couple of times, I didn't think you thought so," she said, very aware of his nearness and her increasing desire to crawl into his lap and be held. She attributed her mood to the head injury. Apparently she was one of those people who, when ill, liked to be pampered and babied.

"Kind of surprised me. Usually I'm not so territorial." He brushed the hair off her face.

"I must look a mess."

"You could never be anything but beautiful," he said, then looked as surprised as she was by the gallant words. He quickly recovered. "You decent under there?"

"Yes." She just wasn't sure about her emotional state. Had she been fishing for a compliment, reassurance? She'd never sought either from a man.

Standing, he snagged a lightweight blue-and-white quilt from the foot of the bed and came back to pick her up. "The movie on TV is so boring, you'll fall asleep in seconds."

"C. J., you must have something else to do."

"Yes, and I'm doing it." Leaving the bedroom, he sat on the sofa, settling her in his lap with her feet on the cushions. He spread the quilt over her. "Go to sleep."

Cicely held herself absolutely still. There was no mistaking the bulge beneath her hips. "C. J., I don't think this will work."

"Just go to sleep."

"There's something that's not asleep," she said, wondering why she was more interested than embarrassed.

"Ignore it."

"I'm not sure that's possible," she murmured, especially when she wanted to move against his arousal.

"Try. You're safe with me." He tucked the quilt more securely around her shoulders.

"I know that or I wouldn't have let you inside my home. I certainly wouldn't have gone to bed with you still here."

"Finally," he said. Cicely couldn't tell if there was teasing or censure in his voice.

"That doesn't mean this is acceptable. Why don't I just sit on the sofa beside you?" She started to rise. She didn't dare try to scoot off his lap.

"Cicely," he said, enunciating each syllable of her name very precisely as he pressed her gently back against his chest. "Please just go to sleep."

She lay quietly against him, listening to the low hum of the TV. She was sure she heard the strain in his voice. He was subjecting himself to unnecessary discomfort to help her.

A strange longing washed over her. She blinked away the moisture in her eyes, and attributed it to her head injury. She was never getting sick again. Her emotions were too chaotic.

Trying to relax, she closed her eyes and listened to the erratic beat of C. J.'s heart that slowly settled into a regular and oddly comforting beat. Without thinking, she rubbed her cheek against the soft cotton of his T-shirt as her body finally gave into the weariness seeping through her body. One hand resting on his chest, she drifted off to sleep.

What am I doing? C. J. didn't have an answer to his own question. He was a man who didn't think about the odds when it came to women because he always knew the outcome.

He glanced down at the woman sleeping so peacefully in his arms and admitted he didn't have a clue. He just knew he hadn't wanted to leave her alone. So he held her while she slept. At least his body had finally gotten the message that nothing was going to happen.

He'd held women this close before, but it was usually before, during, or after sex. He wasn't the hand-holding type. He was more the arm-around-the-shoulder, fun type. He certainly didn't carry a woman—not even to bed.

What was it about Cicely St. John that changed his game plan? The crazy thing about it was, she hadn't even tried to get his attention.

Careful not to jostle Cicely, C. J. turned off the lamp on the end table, and then the TV. The only light came from a night-light in the entryway. Closing his eyes, he prepared for another first—spending a night with a woman.

Cicely awakened slowly, her body doing a lazy stretch from her legs up to her neck, shoulders, and arms. She'd always been that way, as if savoring the final moments of sleep before she came fully awake.

Growing up, she had thought it was because she hadn't wanted to face her disapproving parents. She frowned, snuggling as she pushed away the unhappy thought.

She felt the heat and muscled hardness beneath her and came awake instantly. She sprang up in alarm. Even as she did so, she recalled her accident, felt the slight ache in the back of her head, and looked into the eyes of the man who had tenderly cared for her, held her while she slept.

"Are you all right? Your head hurt?"

She simply stared. His first words had been concern for her. How could she have misjudged him so badly? She thought she was a better judge of character.

"Cicely." His wide-palmed hand gently cupped her cheek. "You all right?"

"Yes," she finally managed, still a bit amazed that he'd stayed all night to watch over her, and that she'd let him. She'd learned to be independent. Had to when there was no one to count on.

Recalling his body's reaction to hers last night, she carefully lifted herself off his lap, taking the blanket with her, still trying to make sense of it. He'd held her while she slept—so she could sleep. A man who thought so little of women wouldn't do that, but then she'd already accepted that she'd misjudged him. Badly.

He just might be the knight, Sir Galahad, she'd joked he was. He certainly acted the part. Only she knew it wasn't an act.

Because of him, her head didn't feel as if it were

about to split and she had gotten some needed sleep. "Thank you. Again."

C. J. nodded, then came to his feet. "Do you think you could eat something?"

Her mouth quirked. "I guess I could cook your breakfast."

"You could, but I can do it while you get dressed— if you don't mind?" he said.

When she was wrong, she didn't do it by half measures. "I want to apologize."

"For what?" he asked, hands on his hips, his gorgeous face puzzled.

"I misjudged you."

His sexy mouth curved at the corners. "I'll accept your apology, if you'll accept mine."

She smiled back. "Are you sure you can cook?"

"You'll know in thirty minutes."

Cicely watched him go into her kitchen, her smile growing. C. J. was turning out to be a very interesting man.

"This is great." Cicely forked in another bite of golden-brown pancake, pan sausage, and perfectly scrambled eggs.

C. J. sipped his coffee and watched Cicely plow through another helping of pancakes. He enjoyed seeing she had a healthy appetite, plus it showed she was feeling better. He topped off her cup of coffee. She preferred it black, just as he did.

"Thanks." She picked up her Wedgwood cup. He figured she deserved something nice. His mother didn't believe in waiting for guests for the "good china."

"Where did you learn to cook like this?"

He placed his cup on the small oak kitchen table before answering. "In Europe. I like certain foods and wasn't willing to give them up." He picked up his fork. "Plus they don't have restaurants open twenty-four/seven. I got tired of going to bed hungry."

She tilted her coffee cup toward him. "It must be in the genes as well. Your mother is an excellent cook. She prepared lunch for the crew when we went out to her home for the fashion shoot and interview."

"Probably." He leaned back in his chair. "More pancakes?"

She grinned at him. "I think four is my limit. Thank you."

"I'm just glad you're feeling better."

"Because of you." She placed her cup on the table. "I'm sorry I kept you away from Callahan's. It must be difficult running it and Callahan Software. How was your first week?"

"All right." His expression closed. Standing, he picked up his plate and then hers.

Cicely knew a dismissal when she heard one. She came to her feet, taking the plates from him. "I'll get the dishes. Cooking is more than enough, especially when it's this good."

He studied her a long moment. "You're sure you're up to it?"

"The dishwasher has a pot scrubber cycle," she said, trying to reassure him. Even when he didn't want to discuss his company, he was still concerned about her. He was a good man. The only reason she could come up with that she hadn't seen it before was that she didn't want to like him, so she'd done her best to keep them at odds. Now wasn't the time to start a relationship, even a light one. Her future was in Paris.

"I better be going so you can take it easy."

"I'll walk you out." Placing the plates back on the table, she went with him down the hallway and opened the front door. "Thank you again."

Nodding, he stepped over the threshold, then turned, one corner of his mouth kicking up. "I think you were wrong."

"About what?" She frowned, unsure what he was talking about.

"After spending the night together, I think we're very close acquaintances."

Drawn and charmed by the smile, she smiled back. "I stand corrected."

"Bye."

"Bye." Cicely smiled even though she wondered why he hadn't asked her out again. His body certainly reacted as if he wanted her.

Perhaps he'd changed his mind. He hadn't even asked for her phone number. She might not want a relationship, but she could use a friend, she thought, as she watched him bound down the steps and get into a car worth a cool million. C. J. didn't act like a lot of the wealthy men she had met. He'd shown her he was down-to-earth, a good friend, caring.

To many people, running a software company

worth millions would trump running a neighborhood bar any day of the week. They'd also put that company ahead of everything else. C. J. loved his bar and seemed to barely tolerate running the software company, yet he hadn't hesitated to leave the bar last night and see that she received the medical help he felt she needed. Then he'd stayed with her to ensure she was cared for and that she slept.

C. J. pulled away without even a wave. Closing the door, Cicely went to finish cleaning up the kitchen. Perhaps it was for the best that they didn't see each other any more than necessary. It would be too easy for her to blur the lines of friendship and start thinking of something more.

Stopping at the red light on Amsterdam, C. J. activated his iPhone. He had turned it off last night before he'd gone in to check on Cicely. He'd let it stay off because he hadn't wanted to disturb her. He'd been the one disturbed by her sleeping so peacefully in his lap.

He couldn't ever recall feeling that protective about a woman he was dating. The crazy thing was, he wasn't even dating Cicely. They were circling each other. The light changed and he pulled off.

He wasn't sure anymore if he should pursue her, at least not until he figured out why he felt differently toward her. His gaze went back to the iPhone.

There were three calls—his mother, father, and brother. He wasn't surprised. In the messages each had danced around directly asking how the first week had gone, but it was undeniably the reason he was receiving calls so early on Sunday morning.

They had probably expected him to call Saturday and when he hadn't, they took the choice from him. All three calls had come before 8:00 AM. His father and brother were early risers, but his mother wasn't.

He caught another red light. When the light changed to green, he stepped on the gas. The car responded with a surge of power. He almost groaned at the analogy, because that was exactly what he had wanted to do last night, lay Cicely down and make love to her. But it had been more important that she know someone cared, that he was there for her so she could sleep.

He'd thought he'd be up all night, but he had gone to sleep as well, and awakened with her still in his arms, his body semi-aroused. He'd wanted women before, but never one so deeply.

He was restless and on edge, and it had nothing to do with the software company. The week had gone well, he guessed, but it had been boring and miserable. He liked mixing with people, not being trapped behind a desk. But his parents and brother wouldn't want to hear that.

Twenty minutes later, he passed the bar and kept going. It wouldn't open for another three hours, which left too much time on his hands to think about Cicely. She could get under his skin if he let her. It wasn't going to happen. No woman had ever gotten the best of him and none never would. Perhaps the drive to his parents' home in the Hamptons would help clear his head.

He slowed to let the inevitable jaywalker cross against the light. No matter how hard he tried, he couldn't put out of his mind how scared he'd been when he'd seen Cicely go down, how good it felt to have her awaken soft and warm this morning in his arms.

He muttered under his breath and took the ramp to the underground parking garage of his apartment building on the Upper East Side. He just needed to get away for a while and then he'd be able to put Cicely in the right perspective. And he knew exactly the place.

Less than half an hour later, after a shower and a shave, C. J. was back in his car heading for East Hampton. He wasn't looking forward to being drilled by his father and brother when he got there. He loved his parents, but not the position they'd placed him in. His father and brother felt a bit guilty, and although C. J. was aware his attitude wasn't helping, he'd never been one to fake it. His family wouldn't expect him to.

They'd always been honest—even if someone didn't like what the other person said. His mother certainly let him know she wasn't pleased by his less-than-joyous reaction to running Callahan Software. Family meant everything to her; no sacrifice was too great.

He'd never forget when he'd become ill in Florence with pneumonia and had to be hospitalized. He'd looked up the morning after he'd been admitted and there his mother was. She'd stayed until he was at home and back on his feet again. She'd fight just as hard against you as for you for the greater good of the family.

C. J. arrived at his parents' estate ninety minutes later. He'd always admired the two-story home that combined the elements of Hollywood Regency with expansive southern charm. His mother had been born in Los Angeles and loved the South for its grace and hospitality.

He had fond memories of climbing the towering oak in front. At times it had been his spaceship, others a monster he defeated to save the world. He and his brother were grateful his mother had gone against the architect's wishes to bulldoze the tree and replace it with a fountain.

His mother loved the sprawling six-bedroom house with its extensive flower gardens, tennis court, and swimming pool that backed up to the ocean. She'd made it a home with her innate sense of warmth and modesty. His father liked boating more than golf. East Hampton provided that and more.

Parking in the circular driveway behind a late-model Mercedes he didn't recognize, C. J. followed the stone path leading around the side of the house. He noted that his mother's climbing pink roses were in full bloom, reaching to the railing of the master bedroom.

She kept the gardener on his toes. When she wasn't volunteering at one of her countless club and church meetings or shopping, she was in the flower garden. She loved roses so much, she had a green-house so she could enjoy them year-round.

Opening the black wrought-iron gate, he continued on the stone path past a bubbling fountain underplanted with impatiens. As long as he could remember, whenever it could fit into everyone's schedule, his family gathered on the terrace after church just to relax. Sundays were one of the few days that his father was usually home and able to spend time with his family.

He heard the laughter and voices before he rounded a six-foot-tall trellis wrapped with pink jasmine vines to see his parents, his brother and his wife and their two young children, and his twenty-four-year-old baby sister, Ariel, at the rectangular teak table laden with food by the small reflective pool. Limestone urns planted with boxwoods squatted at each corner of the pool. Sitting beside Ariel was a man C. J. didn't recognize.

"Hi, everybody."

All heads turned. Shocked surprise registered on the faces of his adult family members. Their expressions made C. J. smile. He'd turn thirty-five three weeks from today. His mother might think it was a secret, but she was trying to give him a surprise birthday party at the house. If he was here now, that meant he wouldn't be back in three weeks. He usually came up only once a month.

Ariel's always shy face brightened with pleasure. She was up and out of her chair to hug him. With his arm around his sister's slim waist, he continued toward the gathering.

His mother, the consummate hostess, quickly recovered. "Cla—C. J.," she quickly corrected when he frowned. He detested the name Clarence. "It's wonderful to see you. This is Evan Fisher, a friend of Ariel's."

C. J. extended his hand to the slim, good-looking man in his early thirties in a tailored gray suit. The handshake was limp, the dark eyes coldly assessing.

From the way his mother was beaming at the man, it was clear she wouldn't mind him being a lot more than a friend. Not if C. J. had anything to say about it. His little sister idolized him, which counted for a lot.

Moving away from Evan, C. J. shook hands with his father and gave him a one-arm hug, then repeated the action with his brother before touching his cheek to his sister-in-law's and slapping hands with his seven- and five-year-old nephew and niece, Forrest and Michelle.

"Have a seat, C. J. I'll get you a plate," Ariel said.

He caught her hand before she could dash off. "Thanks, but I've already eaten."

"Mother made pecan cinnamon rolls," she said, a twinkle in her dark eyes.

He'd always loved them. "I guess I could eat one."

"Thought so." Smiling at him, she went inside.

His mother poured him a glass of orange juice, but when she went to stand, his father took the glass and gave it to C. J. They were a great couple. They complemented each other, and had always been in each other's corners. He'd never heard them argue. His mind jumped to Cicely and he firmly pulled it back as he accepted the tall glass of juice. "Thanks, Mom. Dad."

His father slapped him on the back. "Glad you could come up. The office can get busy."

C. J. was glad he had the glass upturned so his father couldn't see his guilty face. He sat in the office. No one came to him, as they probably had done with his father and brother. He'd tried, but they seemed to prefer it that way. "It's all right," he finally answered. With another pat on his back, his father took his seat at the head of the table.

Over the rim of the glass C. J. surreptitiously studied his family: his father at the head of the table, his mother at the foot. Next to her was his sister-in-law, Sharon, whose ambition had always been to be Paul's wife and the mother of his children. Next to his father was his brother, Paul, his cheeks robust instead of pale, his eyes bright instead of filled with fear and pain as they had been the night he'd collapsed at work and had to be rushed by ambulance to the hospital.

All of them wanted to know how things were going, but none would broach the subject until Ariel's guest was gone.

"Here you go," Ariel said, placing the pecan-encrusted pastry in front of him before taking her seat across from him and next to Evan.

"Thanks, sis." Picking up a fork, he decided to give them something to hold on to until they could speak openly. "Things went well this week."

Relief washed over his parents' and brother's faces. From his sister-in-law there was a look of profound thanks. With C. J. at the helm, she didn't have to worry about her husband having another coronary and leaving her and their two children. She and Paul had been high school sweethearts. There had never been anyone else for them.

C. J. couldn't imagine only having been with one woman—and then a picture of Cicely leaped into his mind again. He stabbed his cinnamon roll. If anything happened between them, and it was a big if, it would be fleeting, just as with all of the women before her.

"Glad to hear things are going well for you," Evan said, turning toward C. J. "As vice president of one of the most recognized banks in the world, I could see how things would go smoothly with less than thirty employees." He looked around the table before his gaze settled once again on C. J. "I oversee twice that many at our branch here in the Hamptons and things run smoothly. Our reviews are always stellar."

C. J. slowly lifted his head to stare at the braggart. He'd managed to get in his position quite nicely, and that little quip about "people under him" hadn't been just an offhanded comment. The clown probably thought most people were beneath him. He definitely hoped his sister wasn't really interested in the egotistical snob.

"Mother, you keep outdoing yourself," C. J. said, then turned to his niece and nephew. "So what have you two been up to?"

They were happy to tell their favorite and only uncle about the camping trip they'd gone on with their parents. C. J. listened to the excitement in their voices, saw it reflected in their animated faces. He glanced at his brother, who stared back at him. He'd given Paul the chance to watch his children grow up. Priceless.

"Thank you, Mrs. Callahan, for a scrumptious brunch. I had a wonderful time, but I must be going," Evan announced in the middle of Michelle's telling about catching her first fish.

A brief frown crossed his mother's face, then it was gone. "Of course, Evan. I'm delighted you were able to come."

"I am, too." Ariel came to her feet. "I'll walk out with you."

"Good-bye, everyone." Back as stiff as a poker, the smirk gone from his face, Evan left with Ariel beside him.

C. J. couldn't have cared less about his abrupt leaving, especially when his sister didn't seem to mind. "I bet your father helped you take the fish off the hook."

Michelle giggled. "Mother didn't want to touch it. Daddy threw it back in the water so his mother wouldn't miss him."

"Mine was big enough to keep," Forrest said proudly.

"I'm proud of both of you," he said.

"I wish I could say the same of your behavior," his mother said.

He might be a grown man, but she could still make him feel like an errant child. He hated to disappoint her. "He was trying to show off," C. J. defended.

"And you put him in his place," his father said, sending his wife a warm look. "He needed some of that hot air taken out of him."

"He was a guest in our home, Frederick," his mother said. She'd always been a stickler for decorum.

C.J. knew one way to get her mind off Evan. "Callahan has good folks. Everything is on track for continued success." He turned to his father and Paul. "You two hired good people."

"Good. Good," his father said, relaxing back in his chair.

His mother, beautiful and trim in a pretty pink dress, stood and began clearing the table. "I'll get these things out of the way."

"I'll help." His sister-in-law came to her feet as well. "You'll want to talk shop." She sent Paul a sweet smile. "He misses the office. I'm more grateful than you can imagine, C. J., that you're running the company."

"No thanks are necessary," he told her, feeling a bit awkward that they all were so thankful and he was just going through the motions.

His mother patted him affectionately on the shoulder. "I'll pack you a few cinnamon rolls to take with you." He was forgiven.

"What did I miss?" Ariel asked, taking her seat next to C. J.

"Ariel, leave the business to men," his mother told her. "You can take Forrest and Michelle down to the water while Sharon and I take care of this."

"But Mother, I—"

"Ariel." Her mother said her daughter's name once, quietly, distinctly.

His sister's shoulders slumped. "All right. Come on, guys." Reluctantly, Ariel took the hands of her niece and nephew and headed for the beach.

None of them had enough nerve to disobey their mother when she used that tone of voice. C. J. wished he was going with his sister and the children.

He didn't want to be responsible for other people's lives. Ariel didn't know how lucky she was not to have the responsibility. Unable to avoid it any longer, he turned to be drilled by his father and brother.

Chapter 6

Monday morning C. J. sat behind the massive, hand-carved desk that had been handed down through three generations of Callahans and felt the weight of his position as CEO more than the pride. While he deeply appreciated what his grandfather, father, and brother had accomplished, corporate just wasn't for him.

He'd always be thankful that his grandfather had been ahead of his time with computers. Ignoring the advice of close friends, he'd gotten in on the ground floor. That smart thinking had enabled him to make millions, and when he wanted to go into developing programs for those computers, he'd had the financing to do so.

The development of programs for home and business made everything run smoother, more efficiently. *Efficient* being the key word, especially for businesses. Less time spent on tasks meant more productive employees and less room for human errors, and unfortunately theft in some cases. It also cut down on overtime, thus reflecting in the bottom line.

C. J. rocked forward in his leather chair, stared at

the silent phone, and almost wished some problem to tackle would come up. In the bar, he could shoot the breeze with his employees and customers, talk to distributors, check stock, do the payroll—something.

Here, there was a product development department, marketing to sell those products, a finance department that took care of payroll and the bills, a human resources department to handle hiring and employee relations.

Meanwhile, he stayed in his office and played games on his computer. C. J. rocked back in his chair in disgust. He'd go crazy if this continued.

His father and brother often worked in development. C. J. had asked the head designer this morning if any help was needed, and was politely turned away.

He really needed to be busy. The more free time he had, the more he thought of Cicely. He was still trying without success to figure out why he couldn't think of her as just another woman.

It was so incredibly easy to imagine the feel of her soft skin, imagine it heating and yielding beneath his searching hand, the hot rush of pleasure they'd give each other. For them, it would be explosive and dangerous. He had a bad feeling that one taste would only increase his craving for more. If he were a smart man—he'd stay away.

The phone on his desk rang. He quickly snatched it up. "Yes, Alice."

"Mr. Callahan, you have a visitor who wants to surprise you. Is it all right?" his secretary asked.

Grinning, C. J. came to his feet. He didn't even

mind her refusing to call him by his first name this time. "I don't think we need to call security. Send the visitor in." Sure it was Sin joking around, C. J. hung up and started around his desk.

Alice opened the door and stepped back. The first thing C. J. saw was balloons that filled the doorway. Then, as they popped through and lifted into the air, he saw an incredible pair of legs, the hem of a short black skirt inches above knees he'd love to kiss. His heart thudded.

A split second later Cicely's beautiful face appeared. She was laughing, fighting balloons, and looking much too tempting.

He crossed to her before he had time to count the cost. "Hello. This is a nice surprise."

"I wanted to thank you," she said, grinning up at him as she held on to the balloons with one hand. "I thought about flowers, but decided you needed something more fun for your gifts."

C. J. stared down at her animated face, so full of life and so tempting, and knew he wasn't going to be smart. He reached for her, his head lowering, his mouth unerringly finding hers.

He'd been right. The jolt went straight to his midsection. He wasn't prepared for the stunning rush of passion, of need. He wanted more and saw no reason to deprive either of them since she had a fistful of his shirt dragging him closer, and was doing her best to blow the top of his head off.

Using all his willpower, he lifted his head and stared down into her stunning face, waiting for her eyes to open. He needed to see if the kiss had affected her as much as it had affected him.

"Well," she managed after several seconds when she finally opened her eyes.

"Well," he repeated, enjoying the dazed look in her beautiful eyes.

"Maybe I should thank you," she quipped

C. J. threw back his head and laughed, then drew her to him again. She made him laugh. She was also honest. Like him, she said what was on her mind. You didn't have to wonder where you stood. She was self-assured. She wouldn't need a man to tell her she looked good in an outfit. There was no subterfuge.

She'd also take a bite out of him if she thought she had cause. She was rare. She intrigued him, drew him, puzzled him as no woman ever had before.

She pushed out of his arms and he let her go—for now. Stepping around him, she wandered around his office, studying the family pictures in the bookcase, the awards, the accolades for public service, finally stopping to stare at the balloons—there had to be at least two dozen—floating to the twenty-foot ceiling.

"Sorry they got away," she finally said.

He shrugged. "I'm not. They'll remind me of you."

She tilted her head. "How so?"

"Fun, unpredictable," he replied easily.

She crossed her arms and stared him in the eye. "I'm one of three candidates for the position of editor-in-chief of our new Paris office. I've worked hard for this opportunity. In less than five weeks I plan to be on a plane to Paris."

C. J. dismissed the quick regret, the unmistakable sense of loss. "You're here now."

"And I don't do casual affairs," she replied, uncrossing her arms.

C. J. realized that was all he'd ever had—and from her narrowed gaze she'd come to the same conclusion. "Enjoy the rest of your day." She started for the door.

He had a feeling that if she left, he'd miss something; what, he wasn't sure. He stepped in front of her to block her path. "You said something about gifts. I only see the balloons."

She studied him for a few moments, then seemed to come to a conclusion. "Summer was kind enough to help me out with reservations at Radcliffe's tonight at nine thirty. Sorry it's so late, but I have another engagement earlier that I couldn't cancel."

"Might I ask doing what?" he said mildly.

"Since you put it so nicely, I'll tell you. The vice president/publisher of my magazine is having a cocktail party at her penthouse," she said. "It's important that I at least make an appearance."

"Then why don't I pick you up, take you to the party, then we can leave from there and go to Radcliffe's?" he asked.

"Nothing is going to happen between us."

"At the risk of sounding chauvinistic, I wouldn't be so sure about that."

She stepped around him and went to the door. "Good thing I like a man with confidence, but don't overdo it. Pick me up at eight." Opening the door, she was gone.

Cicely dressed with care for her date—evening— with C. J. This was part of her thank-you for taking care of her, she told herself as she applied her lipstick. The brush against her lip was a vivid reminder of C. J.'s lips that molded perfectly to hers. The moment his mouth touched hers, her body had simply acted on need. Never before had a kiss affected her that way.

Placing the brush aside, she snapped the lipstick case shut. She would be lying to herself—and she'd promised long ago that she never would—if she said she didn't want him to kiss her again. But as she'd told him, she didn't do meaningless affairs. No doubt the encounter would be fantastic, but then what? The doorbell rang.

Turning off the light, she left the bathroom and went to the front door. She could see C. J.'s broad-shouldered silhouette through the unbreakable frosted glass. She didn't like the little flutter of anticipation in her stomach, but there was nothing she could do about it.

She opened the door with a bland expression. It lasted all of two seconds. C. J. was devastating in a black tailored suit that fit his incredible body to perfection, and she wanted to rip it off. She might be in more trouble than she anticipated.

C. J. couldn't think of one word to say on seeing Cicely, so he just let his eyes drink in her breathtaking beauty. He wondered if he'd have a chance to get used to the quick stab of desire every time he saw her for the first time.

She wore a long emerald silk gown that fit her body like it had been poured on from her bust to her left hip. From there the material slanted down to her right knee, than draped and curved around the back, leaving her legs tantalizingly revealed to midthigh.

"Hi, C. J., please come in."

"Hi." He stepped inside, his gaze following her as she closed the door behind him. Ropes of pearls were around her neck and on her right wrist. "Do you know you're lethal in that dress?"

"No, but it's nice to hear. I'll have to put that on my blog tonight."

The teasing smile froze on his face. She hadn't been complimentary about his bar on her blog. "Your fashion blog?"

He looked so annoyed, she reached up and patted his cheek. "Don't worry, I'll just say my companion said it." The frown didn't clear. "What is it now?"

"Is it so hard to say date?"

"That's because we aren't dating. I'll get my bag and we can leave." She picked up the multicolored crystal minaudière in the shape of a pagoda from the coffee table and came back to him. "Might I say you look a bit dangerous yourself?"

"Progress," he said, then whisked her out the door.

Lenora Little was a fashion icon in her own right. She had the looks, the money, the style, and the power. When she spoke, thousands listened. When she did it through her magazine—with the help of the World Wide Web—that number translated into millions.

At a trim and slender sixty-five years old, she'd been married twice before deciding she liked being single better. She liked calling the shots too much to be good at anything but what she did—ruling the magazine with an iron fist cloaked in a cashmere glove.

Lenora was on the A-list as much for her wealth and fashion sense as she was for the power her magazine wielded. She could make or break a model or designer, and had been known to do so. She was known for her impromptu parties as well as her lethal tongue and biting wit. People fawned over her and ingratiated themselves because they didn't want to be subjected to either.

Cicely could have told them not to bother. Lenora made snap decisions about people. You were either in or out. Thank goodness when she'd been a junior in college looking for an internship, Lenora, for whatever reason, had accepted her and turned away the other five hopefuls who had gone with her from her university that day.

"Hi, Lenora," Cicely greeted, smiling warmly at the older woman. She wore the magenta-and-black Valentino floor-length gown as she did everything, with grace and confidence. "I'd like for you to meet a close acquaintance of mine, C. J. Callahan."

C. J. threw Cicely a grin then gently took Lenora's

extended hand, glittering with a ten-carat diamond. Diamonds circled her neck and hung from her ears. "Might I say you really know how to throw a party."

"And why is that?" she asked, mildly, sipping idly from a champagne flute.

"Two bars with prime liquor and no lines, waiters circulating with food and more drinks. A buffet table by the terrace. Nothing some people like better than guzzling the good stuff and excellent food someone else had to pay for."

She smiled. "Very astute, but then I wouldn't expect Cicely to be with anyone who wasn't."

"Believe me, I had to work for it," he said easily.

"Interesting," Lenora said, studying Cicely closely.

Cicely had seen that look before. Lenora was trying to figure out exactly what was going on. Cicely wasn't quite sure if she should take the next step with C. J., but she was well aware that Lenora believed in career first, second, and always. Anyone who didn't wasn't going to go up the ladder.

That very day Lenora had passed over a very pregnant Ginger for the position of art director, giving it to a man. That wasn't going to happen to Cicely.

She caught C. J.'s arm. "Let's get some of that food you were talking about. See you later, Lenora."

"Good-bye." He started toward the nearest waiter with a tray of hors d'oeuvres. "You skip lunch again today?"

"Occupational hazard." She picked up a napkin and a bite-sized spinach quiche. "Aren't you getting anything?"

"Nope. Once you taste the food at Radcliffe's

you'll understand why." He plucked a glass of tonic water from a passing waiter, then handed it to her as she finished.

"Thanks." She sipped the water and stared up at him. He really was gorgeous. Being attentive made him lethal.

"Hello, Cicely."

Cicely turned to Eva, one of the other candidates for the position of editor in chief of the Paris office. In her midforties, Eva looked ten years younger and prided herself on doing so. "Hi, Eva, you look great in Armani. I'd like you to meet C. J. Callahan. Eva Rutledge, managing editor of *Fashion Insider*."

C. J. extended his hand. ""Pleased to meet you."

"I'm surprised to meet you," Eva said, then smiled at Cicely. "Where have you been keeping him?"

"No poaching," a male voice commanded.

Cicely glanced around to see Fred, the other candidate. He was dressed as electric as usual in a black tux, yellow tie, and yellow Italian loafers. Fred wore the specially made shoes everywhere and had them in every color.

"I'd give him back," Eva said with a smile.

Cicely knew the other woman wasn't kidding. She dated a lot of men—on her terms. She called them disposable stress relievers. Cicely looked at C. J. to gauge his reaction. Eva looked good in the strapless purple silk crepe gown.

"No offense, but since I don't think Cicely likes leftovers, I'll pass," C. J. said with just the right amount of humor.

Fred and Eva laughed. Cicely joined them.

"Definitely a keeper." Eva took Fred's arm. "More reason to stay in New York."

"I'm getting that position," Cicely said. "Nothing has changed."

"You're both wrong." Fred said. "But don't worry, I'll invite you both over to work on the first issue."

"We'll just see about that," Eva said. "Let's get something to eat while I try to figure out if any man here is going to get lucky."

"As long as it's not me," Fred said as they moved away.

"Quite a pair," C. J. said

"Yes." She tucked her arm through his. "I need to see a few more people, then we're out of here."

"Lead on."

Cicely did just that, introducing C. J. to employees of the magazine, fashion designers, and others in the industry. He met them all with charm and self-assurance. He was just as much fun to be with as she'd thought.

Later, after bidding Lenora good-bye, they left. Cicely could feel Lenora watching her as they did.

In the hallway, C. J. circled her waist with his arm. "I don't want to see you go to Paris, but my money is on you."

"Thank you," she said, leaning against him just the tiniest bit. They'd come a long way from being two wary adversaries. It remained to be seen how much farther they'd go.

"You're sure you want to leave?" C. J. stopped in front of the elevator and stared down at Cicely. "I can promise you that Summer won't have any problems filling the time slot."

"Thank you, but you met Lenora. She's not about to base her decision on whether I stay at her party. She'll look at my body of work, my unfaltering dedication, and what I can bring to the magazine. They'll speak for themselves." Cicely punched the elevator DOWN button. "Let's go have dinner."

Cicely had heard a lot about Radcliffe's but had never been there. She wasn't surprised to see the long line outside the restaurant. "I see what you mean about Summer not having any problem filling the time slot," she said, standing on the sidewalk by the black Lincoln that C. J. had hired.

"It's like this every night." He took her arm and walked beneath the red awning to the recessed black door trimmed in red. "On some nights she serves iced tea when it's hot and coffee in the winter to those waiting. She's also been known to take their names for a monthly drawing of gift certificates to Radcliffe's."

"She certainly knows how to keep customers coming back." Walking through the door C. J. held open, Cicely was immediately charmed by the elegant European décor with wall sconces, dark wood, and paintings in graceful wooden frames.

"Welcome back, C. J., miss," the smiling hostess said. She wore a black dress with capped sleeves. "C. J., I didn't see your name on the list for tonight. Should I get Summer?"

"Hi, Toni. Try Cicely St. John, my date's name," he said.

Cicely didn't think of correcting him this time. He was having fun.

"I remember seeing her name." Toni picked up two oversized menus and handed them to the hostess standing beside her wearing a black jersey dress and fishnet stockings. "Enjoy your meal."

"Thanks. We will." With his hand on the small of Cicely's back, he followed the woman. The hostess stopped at a quiet table in front of the aquarium, C. J.'s favorite place to dine. He grabbed Cicely's chair for her then sat down and accepted the menu.

"Would you like a drink now or would you like to wait and see what you'll order?" the full-figured woman asked.

"Red wine and Pellegrino," Cicely said. "I looked at the menu online."

"Same for me." C. J. placed his menu on the table.

"I'll get that right out to you."

Cicely glanced around the busy restaurant. The hum of conversation, the occasional *clinks* of glasses were subdued. "Summer has done a fantastic job. The diners are having a great time in a relaxing atmosphere. I already want to come back."

"Let me know when and I'll make reservations." C. J. grinned across the table at her.

"Good evening, I'm Ken. I'll be your waiter tonight." He placed their drinks on the table in front of them. "Would you like to hear tonight's specialties?"

"I already know I want the rib eye, rare. Baked potato with everything, asparagus, and a Radcliffe's Greek salad." She handed Ken the menu.

"Make mine the double-cut filet mignon, baked potato all the way, broccoli, and Radcliffe's house salad. Lump crab cakes for the appetizer."

"Very good." The man took the menus and moved away.

C. J. lifted his glass. "To becoming better acquainted."

Cicely did the same. "To becoming better acquainted." She touched her glass to his, then sipped her wine. "Delicious."

"Hello, Cicely, C. J.," Summer greeted them, placing her hand on the back of C. J.'s chair.

"Hi, Summer. Thank you so much for fitting me into your schedule." Cicely smiled up at her. "I didn't realize just how much that meant until we arrived tonight."

"My pleasure," Summer said. "Just glad you're feeling well."

Cicely smiled. "Thanks. Dinner tonight is going to make me feel even better. I worked through lunch as usual."

C. J. frowned. "Summer, can you put a rush on the appetizer and her salad?"

"Already taken care of." Summer turned as a waitress stopped with a deck tray. She served them their salads and put the crab cakes between them along with fresh, hot bread. "Anything else you need?"

Cicely laughed. "With this kind of service, nothing I can think of."

"We aim to please." Summer smiled at them. "Enjoy your meal, and if I don't get back to your table, have a great night."

"We aim to." C. J. grinned.

Chapter 7

Cicely caught the look on C. J.'s face and was pretty sure how he thought the night would end. It wasn't going to happen. She tucked her head to say a blessing for their food.

Lifting her face, she stared into C. J.'s dark, mesmerizing eyes. Keeping him at arm's length might prove to be a problem.

He motioned toward the crab cakes. "Have one, eat your salad, and no more wine until you've eaten. I don't want you to get woozy or ill."

Cicely simply stared at him. He was taking care of her again. She should probably remind him of the quiche she'd eaten earlier or tell him it would take more than a couple of glasses of wine with little food to do her in.

"Eat."

Cicely speared the crab cake, placed it on her bread plate where there was already a slice of bread, and began to eat. She sort of liked having someone fuss over her. There had been no one to do so since her grandmother. "This is as delicious as you said. I'm definitely adding Radcliffe's to my list of favorite restaurants."

"It's the best." C. J. dug into his salad. "Do you often skip lunch?"

"As I said, occupational hazard." She shrugged as she finished off her crab cake. "I fully intend to eat, but I just get wrapped up in what I'm doing. It will probably be the same thing Wednesday because we're doing a fashion shoot at the Museum of Modern Art that evening. Then, too, I can't stand a messy desk or things left undone. Plus, I have sort of an open-door policy and, if anyone needs me, I want to be available. How about you?"

"The people at my bar are pretty self-sufficient. The head bartender is acting as manager." C. J. frowned before pushing away his empty salad bowl. "A cluttered desk has never bothered me. You probably don't remember the night I took you into my office."

"No, I don't." She wasn't surprised he didn't mention his office at Callahan Software.

"Your steaks." Ken set up the deck tray, then served them. "Please leave room for dessert."

Cicely stared down at her rib eye and the largest baked potato she'd ever seen. "I'm not making any guarantees," she teased.

Ken grinned back and folded the tray stand. "Understood. Anything else I can get you?"

"No, thank you," C. J. and Cicely said in unison.

Cicely bit into her rare steak, closed her eyes, and moaned. "Delicious."

C. J. twisted in his seat. This wasn't the time or place for his body to remember how much he wanted Cicely. "How long have you been an editor?"

"Fashion director." She grinned at him and put extra butter on her baked potato, already bursting with cheese, chives, chunks of real bacon, and sour cream.

"I stand corrected." C. J. cut her another slice of bread and placed it on her bread plate. He didn't believe he'd ever taken out a woman with such a hearty appetite. He couldn't help but wonder if her other, more carnal appetites were as lusty.

"Thanks. Three years. I started at the bottom as a college intern and worked my way up." She dug into her baked potato. "What's the story with you and Callahan's Bar?" She took another bite of her steak and asparagus.

"It was accidental," he said. "I was on an extended holiday in Europe when my uncle asked me to come home and help him with the place. He wanted to leave it to someone in the family and I was it. From the day I walked into Callahan's, I felt a part of it." He paused in cutting his steak. "I just knew that was where I wanted to be."

Cicely nodded her understanding. "It was the same way with me and fashion. I just knew."

"Are you following a family tradition as well?" he asked and watched the smile slide from her face. "Cicely?"

She placed her knife and fork on her plate with exaggerated care and picked up her wineglass. She hadn't drunk any since he'd asked her not to.

"I didn't mean to pry." He searched his mind for something to put a smile back on her face. "How are you going to celebrate when you get the Paris assignment?"

She placed her glass on the table. "I haven't thought that far."

"You should." He was glad to see her pick up her utensils with hands that no longer shook. "Now I know why there were all of the pictures with Parisian scenes on the walls in your kitchen, and why salt and pepper shakers in the shape of the Eiffel Tower were on your table."

"I wanted them to keep me focused. There's also a small statue of the Arc de Triomphe on my nightstand," she said.

"I missed it, but I can only hope I'll get another opportunity," he said, hoping to sound regretful and hopeful.

"That will be the day," she said, eating with gusto again.

"Night works just as well."

She put her hand over her mouth, then snatched up her glass of water and drank. Putting the glass down, she eyed him. "Summer wouldn't like it if one of her customers choked."

"I wouldn't, either, but I know mouth-to-mouth."

She groaned, not knowing if it was because he excited her or he had a one-track mind. "C. J."

"Eat up." He pointed his knife toward her plate. "What do you think we should order for dessert?"

"I can't make up my mind between the six-layer lemon coconut cake and the strawberry truffle cheese-cake."

C. J. nodded and polished off his steak. "The lemon cake is Mother's favorite, Summer's own cre-ation, and she rightly refuses to share the recipe with anyone. Since she only bakes four cakes a night and they sell out quickly, I took the liberty of calling earlier and asking her to put a slice back for you just in case."

She stared at him. "For a man with a one-track mind at times, that was very thoughtful of you."

He leaned over the table. "I want to do whatever it is that will please and pleasure you."

Heat shot through her body. Cicely snatched up the water and drained the glass. C. J. was definitely dangerous. Worse, she was beginning to like his teasing her—and thinking entirely too much of tasting him again.

Walking up the steps of her brownstone, Cicely was nervous. It had escalated since they'd left Radcliffe's. C. J. was going to kiss her. She was sure of it. It was her reaction to the kiss that had her a bit worried.

Opening the door, she didn't look up at him when she asked, "Would you like to come in?"

"Yes."

She'd known the answer. The air had been humming with sexual tension since dinner. Why deprive herself of his kiss? she thought, stepping inside and closing the door. When she turned, he pulled her to him. She went willingly. She could handle—

Her thoughts clicked off like a switch the second his mouth covered hers. There was nothing tentative. This was a man who knew how to kiss a woman, please her.

Cicely was swept away by the passion of the kiss, the raw power. She felt the sleeve of her dress slide off her arm. Sanity returned with a rush. Grabbing the front she staggered back. "Wait."

When he took a step toward her, she held up her free hand. "Wait. Just wait."

No kiss, no man had taken her under so fast. She was right. He was dangerous. Dragging shaky fingers through her hair, she tried to steady her trembling legs.

"I—" She couldn't get the words out. He scattered her thoughts and made her want, but she had no intention of giving in to the desire clamoring for him. "I'm not having an affair with you."

"Kiss me again and tell me that," he said, his breathing off kilter, desire flaring in his eyes, fire raging through his veins.

He had her there. "I don't let my body rule me," she told him, hoping she was right. "This stops here and now. Good night, C. J."

He took a step toward her, then stopped when her eyes widened. He shook his head, blew out a breath, and shoved his hands into the pockets of his slacks. "I've never had a problem with a woman saying no, but I have to admit, I'm having one now."

"Me either," she admitted, then almost smiled. "I meant saying no and meaning it. And to think, once we wouldn't have wanted to be in the same room together."

"Yeah," he said, his eyes watching her hungrily. "A lot has happened since then."

"And I'm getting that Paris assignment," she said, shoving the sleeves of her dress back up on her arms and zipping her dress. Man he worked fast. She refused to think of how he had learned to be so talented.

"And I'm betting you do, but that doesn't seem to stop me from wanting to drag that dress off you and kiss every inch of you before—"

"No," she protested, her voice trembling as much as her body. "Why are you doing this?"

"I've asked myself the same thing," he answered. "Why can't I walk away? I haven't come up with an answer, so here I am."

He was honest. She could be no less. "You make me wish I had met you long ago, but it is what it is."

"The way I see it, there's no reason not to spend time with me until you leave," he reasoned.

She shook her head. He was persistent, she'd give him that, but what successful man wasn't. "I think we both know there is."

Ignoring her statement, he said, "Alex, Sin, and I have a monthly game of pool at Callahan's on Wednesday night instead of Friday. We changed after Alex became engaged. Dianne will be there. Why don't you drop by around eight? No pressure. Just friends enjoying each other."

That was the trouble, she thought about enjoying him too much—on the bed, in the shower, the sofa. Cicely didn't have to think about her answer. He disturbed her, excited her. She couldn't trust herself around him. "C. J., don't take this the wrong way, but perhaps we shouldn't be around each other any more than necessary."

"Why?" It was one clipped, very annoyed word.

"You know why, but if you want it in clear

language, I'll give it to you." Her shoulders back, she stared him straight in the eyes. "My usual calm, decisive thinking seems to take a vacation when we kiss. I don't want to do anything I'll regret later on."

"Regret," he bit out, his broad shoulders snapping back. Cicely could put a dent in his manhood quicker, and make him hotter, than he'd ever thought possible. "Like I said, the pool game usually starts around eight. Thanks for dinner." Spinning on his heels, he left, more than a bit miffed that she thought making love with him would be a mistake, something she'd regret.

Cicely stared at the closed door. C. J. had taken it all wrong. Making love with him, she didn't doubt, would be incredible in every way, but it would also be incredibly stupid. Clicking off the entry light she had left on, she bent to pick up her purse from the floor.

When he'd kissed her, all she could think of was getting closer. But that wasn't going to happen again, no matter how either of them wished otherwise.

In her bedroom, she headed for her walk-in closet. Emptying the contents of her purse, she placed the clutch in its dust cloth, then unzipped her dress, putting it in a special bag as well. She loved and appreciated her things and took care of them. In her bra and panties, still thinking about C. J., she went to the sink to wash her face.

She'd had one lover in college, when her parents, his brother, sister, and their children went on a ski trip without her. They didn't even have the courtesy to ask if she wanted to go. She wouldn't have even known if she hadn't called her parents to wish them a happy anniversary and see if they liked the gift, a beautiful Waterford vase to go with her mother's prized collection. They'd been more excited about the ski trip. Deeply hurt, Cicely had wished them a fun time and quickly hung up.

She'd needed to be wanted. She could admit it now, accept it. The relationship had lasted a couple of months before she came to her senses and broke things off. She never wanted to be that needy, insecure woman again. If she were to make a career in the dog-eat-dog world of fashion in New York, she had to stiffen her spine and squelch her need to be needed, wanted, cared for.

She'd kept that determination in the forefront, made it her credo, and as a result had loads of acquaintances and no close friends. That was one of the main reasons she wanted to be friends with Dianne and Summer. C. J. would not make her lose sight of her goal. Paris.

Sure of herself, she shrugged on a short robe and went to her computer in her home office. Bringing up her blog, *Fashionista Diva in the House*—which, she was proud to say, now had followers approaching two million—she paused before she began to type.

Tonight was my first experience, and it won't be my last—mind out of the gutter, please—at Radcliffe's, a five-star restaurant in Manhattan. My dinner companion said I looked lethal in an emerald silk Angel Sanchez evening gown, but I was more interested in the delicious food. Women around me were in couture and off the rack, and probably had just as good a time.

The owner, Summer Radcliffe, wore Chanel with elegance and grace, but clearly it was the dining pleasure of her customers and not what they wore that was paramount on her mind. So, I repeat, whatever you select to wear, wear it with confidence. 'Night. Fashionista Diva.

C. J. turned on his computer as soon as he reached home. His blunt-tipped fingers tapped impatiently on his desk as the computer booted up. Agile fingers typed in Cicely's blog address. Previous covers of *Fashion Insider* flashed on the screen.

He leaned in closer as he followed the thread of her blog to her original comment. His eyes narrowed when he found it and read "dinner companion." What would it take for her to admit that they were more than acquaintances?

At least she had given Radcliffe's and Summer a great plug. For that, he could get over his annoyance at her. And all right, sexual frustration. She wasn't playing hard to get. She really didn't want to become involved with him, but he'd change her mind. Eventually.

Shutting down the computer, he stood and thought back to the moment he had asked her if she was following a family tradition. He almost turned the computer back on to Google her. He didn't. For some reason, he'd rather she tell him what it was about her family that brought such sadness to her face.

Turning off the light, he headed to his bedroom. *I won't hurt you, Cicely, but neither am I giving up on us. I could certainly fly over to Paris. It's not over between us.*

The next morning C. J. parked in his designated space a little before nine. The employee parking lot was almost full. It seemed the staff didn't need him to keep them on task.

Inside the building, he spoke to a couple of employees who quickly moved away. Obviously they weren't comfortable with him. He had to find a way to change that. Communication was key in their line of work.

Or in a relationship. Someone should tell Cicely.

Opening the outer office, he saw his secretary already at her desk, typing away at the computer. If he wasn't busy, it stood to reason she shouldn't be, either.

Her head came up. She momentarily tucked her lower lip between her teeth and pushed her black-framed eyeglasses back up on the bridge of her nose. She wore an unadorned dark brown suit and a beige shell. "Good morning, Mr. Callahan. Did you need something?"

In plain English, move on and let me work in peace. "No, Alice. What's on the agenda today?"

"You're free until one. You said you wanted to attend the program development department meeting."

"All right. I'll be in my office." As if he'd be anyplace else. Continuing into his office, he rounded his desk and dialed Summer's office phone. She usually made it to work by nine each morning. By now, she would have already been to the fish market.

"Good morning, C. J.," Summer greeted in her usual cheerful voice. "I hope you and Cicely enjoyed yourself last night."

"We did. Thanks for saving the lemon coconut cake. Cicely ate every bite," he told her.

"I'm glad. Do you realize you've never brought a date to the restaurant?"

Restless, C. J. fiddled with a pen on his neat desk. "According to her blog, I'm just an acquaintance."

"And that irritates you?"

C. J. reined in his annoyance. "In her blog last night, she gave Radcliffe's high marks. You should check it out. If I'm not mistaken, it should be great for business."

"I like Cicely. I'll have to call and thank her. I'm enjoying getting to know her."

"Wish I could say the same thing," he groused.

"I love you, C. J., but it's about time you had to work to get a woman," Summer told him. "They fall like ripe fruit into your lap."

He recalled Cicely in his lap and twisted uncomfortably in his chair. "You're thinking about Sin."

"He's even worse," she snorted.

C. J. knew when he was on shaky ground. "I better get back to work."

"Because I love you, I'll let you off the hook," she said with a laugh. "Thanks for the alert on the blog. Bye."

"Bye." C. J. hung up, then powered up his computer. While he had the chance, he might as well see what else Cicely had to say. Maybe he'd learn how to handle things between them better.

Cicely woke up with a headache. The pain emanated from the front of her head, not where she had fallen. Two ibuprofen hadn't helped. By the time she got out of the cab in front of her office building, the dull ache was still there. She didn't think for a second it was related to her fall. She knew exactly the reason: C. J. Callahan. He could be a problem, if she let him. If she thought of him so much now, what would happen if she allowed them to be lovers?

Her mouth thinned in annoyance as she crossed the busy lobby. He was also the reason she hadn't gotten very much sleep last night. No matter how she tried, she hadn't been able to get him out of her mind.

Merging with the crowd of people getting on the elevator, she noted that her floor number was already lit. Her hand on her attaché case tightened. She didn't have a single doubt that the office would be buzzing about her showing up at Lenora's party with C. J.

The staff would be rampant with sly looks and speculations. No one except those in upper management would dare openly confront her. She'd handle them as she always had—a cold, haughty stare she'd perfected for just such occasions.

Stepping off the elevator, head high, she went straight to her office. Her assistance, Sami Waters, was already there at her desk. Dressed in a black turtleneck and black leggings in deference to the air-conditioning, she came to her feet on seeing Cicely.

"Morning, Sami."

"Good morning, Cicely." Sami rounded the desk. "Anything I can do to help you get ready for the staff meeting this morning?"

"Thanks, I have it." Cicely continued to her office, but paused when Sami still stared after her. She turned. "Was there something else?"

"The new gossip this morning is that you're having a blazing-hot affair with a yummy hunk," Sami told her. "You were so anxious to be alone with him last night, you left Lenora's party early."

Cicely's eyes narrowed with anger. She didn't have to think who had started the rumor. "Eva."

"Right the first time. She's trying to make Lenora doubt you. She's scared—as well she should be." Sami folded her arms across her chest and wrinkled her nose in irritation. "She didn't take into consideration that Lenora knows how well you multitask. If you had a hot guy in your bed last night, you still did your blog, and you're here at work on time, looking fab as usual. I'd say that ups your capability."

Only she hadn't had the hot guy in her bed, she'd only had forbidden thoughts about him being there. "Thanks, Sami. Let's hope Lenora remembers that. Buzz me in ten minutes for the meeting."

Sami glanced at the oversized facing of her watch circled with pink crystals. "You have twenty minutes."

"I know. I want to make sure I see Eva before the meeting. I have a few things I'd like to say to her."

Grinning, Sami gave her a thumbs-up.

Fifteen minutes later, Cicely saw Eva coming

down the hall. She wore a bright yellow jacket, black-and-white pin-striped blouse, and black slacks. She looked liked the successful woman she was, but underneath the beautiful facade she could be manipulative and mean-spirited.

"Cicely." Eva raised one perfectly ached brow. "I thought you might be sleeping in this morning."

"Nice try, Eva, but spreading rumors about my supposed love affair won't work, " Cicely told her. "Lenora knows *Fashion Insider* comes first with me."

"She also knows the right man can mess up a woman's focus." Eva smiled. "There's less than five weeks before Lenora makes her decision. Yummy C. J. seemed the type of man who could change a woman's mind and make her like it."

"Not this woman." Cicely said with a conviction she hoped she could keep. "I'm getting that position."

"We'll see."

"We certainly will." Cicely brushed past the other woman, went into the conference room, and took a seat, more assured than ever that she had made the right decision about not seeing C. J. anymore except in mixed company. This was too important to chance on an affair, no matter how his kisses—

"Cicely."

Hearing Lenora call her name, Cicely's head snapped up. "Yes?" When had she and the others arrived?

"I asked you if you were ready with your report." Lenora didn't look too pleased at having to ask her twice. At least Cicely hoped it was only twice.

"Yes." Cicely opened her computer, which was

linked to everyone in the room, well aware that if she looked at Eva, the other woman would have a pleased smirk on her face.

As soon as the meeting was over, Cicely grabbed up her laptop notebook and headed for the door. She could kick herself for letting Lenora catch her not paying attention.

Opening the door, she pulled up short on seeing Sami standing there with a white bakery box in her hand, a grin on her pretty face.

"This is for you." Sami held out the box with one hand and reached for the laptop in Cicely's hand with the other.

Cicely smelled the lemon coconut. "This can't be Summer's specialty cake?"

"It is," her assistant confirmed. "Ms. Radcliffe called twice and when I told her you were in a meeting the second time, she said she was sending over a little thank-you for your wonderful post about dining at Radcliffe's last night."

"That's where you were going?" Eva asked, pique in her voice.

"Next time read my blog before you start spreading rumors." Cicely turned to Lenora. "Would you like the first slice?"

"It's impossible to get reservations there on short notice," Lenora said, sounding annoyed.

Cicely grinned, her headache finally gone. "I have connections."

"They were out of the lemon coconut cake the

night I dined there." Lenora started for her office. "I have a knife and flatware in my office."

Cicely inclined her head toward Lenora's retreating back. "Come on, Sami. You get the second slice."

"What about the rest of us?" Fred asked, his face as hopeful as the others in upper management surrounding them.

"We'll just have to see." Smiling, Cicely started after Lenora.

Chapter 8

Wednesday night, at the photo shoot in the Museum of Modern Art, Cicely wasn't a happy woman. The closer it grew to 8:00 PM, the more restless she became. She couldn't seem to stop herself from repeatedly glancing at her watch. She couldn't keep her focus. C. J. kept invading her thoughts.

"Are you all right, Cicely?" Sami asked.

"Yes, why?" She answered with a question of her own.

"You keep glancing at your watch and looking around. Is he coming?" Sami looked around the room as well.

There was no doubt which "he" she was referring to. Eva had done a good job of spreading the rumor of her and C. J.'s "blazing affair." Cicely's lapse at the meeting had only fueled the rumor. Summer's cake might have diverted her co-workers' attention, but unfortunately only for a short while. At least Eva hadn't gotten any cake.

Like most of the women at the office, Sami probably wanted to see the "yummy hunk" as Eva had described C. J. Cicely, who had never let her personal problems spill over into her work, simply stared at her assistant of a year and waited for her to bring her attention back to her. The recent college grad was quiet, attentive to detail, and didn't gossip—all very good reasons why she'd lasted so long. But those same qualities certainly posed a problem now.

"Hope he's not coming tonight. Lenora just arrived," Sami said, worry in her voice.

Cicely whipped her own head around, saw Lenora in a red evening gown by her favorite designer, and quickly moved in that direction. "Hi, Lenora. Seems you couldn't wait to take a peek at the new designs by Oscar." Cicely glanced over her shoulder at the models in day and evening wear by the designer.

"Hi, Cicely," Lenora greeted. "I was passing by and decided to stop. I'll make a better entrance at the opera if I'm late."

Cicely smiled despite the sudden knot in her stomach. Lenora, who loved fashion and the designer, didn't even glance at the models. She detested being late, and always said people who needed to make an entrance were insecure idiots. She knew Cicely would remember and, if she didn't, she'd pay heavily for the lapse.

"You look spectacular as usual," Cicely said, staying on steady ground. "Excuse me for a moment." She gratefully moved away to direct the models and photographer for the next shoot. The designs were sleek and sophisticated, and the art at the museum was a fantastic backdrop. The permit to take the photos had taken weeks. Finished, she went back to the waiting Lenora.

"I can see you're busy so I won't keep you." Lenora started for the door.

Dutifully, breathing a bit easier, Cicely fell into step beside her boss, and the woman who had the final decision on who would get the editor-in-chief position in Paris. "Enjoy the opera."

At the door, Lenora faced Cicely. "I wondered if you might have changed your mind about the editor position in Paris. We need someone who is completely focused and has the good of the magazine in the forefront."

There it was. "I want the position. I've worked my butt off to get where I am. I'm thankful to you for having enough faith in me to let me do my job and considering me for the position. *Fashion Insider* is my sole focus."

Lenora smiled for the first time. "Good. Learn from me that relationships don't last with our crazy schedule. Most men want their women home at a decent hour. That's not us."

"No, it's not," Cicely agreed. She could count on one hand the number of nights in the last six weeks she had gotten home before ten, in bed before twelve—one reason she had planned to enjoy the weekend she'd been injured.

"I better be going or I'll be late."

"You're going to make a spectacular entrance," Cicely told her boss, wishing she didn't feel just as tense now that she was leaving.

Lenora laughed, a rich, full, throaty sound that proclaimed to all who heard it that she enjoyed life to the fullest. "You think?"

"Although that isn't your goal, fashion is what we bring to women, what we are. Fashion, good fashion, is to be seen and admired and so is the woman wearing it," Cicely said, meaning every word. Lenora was a true fashion icon, and had done so much to push fashion forward.

"I've always liked you, liked that you don't blow smoke. I saw the hunger in your eyes, the determination when I took you on as an intern." Lenora, not a demonstrative person, reached out and briefly touched Cicely's shoulder. "You understand fashion. It's not what they have on but the attitude. You'll continue your climb in this business . . . if you stay focused. Good night."

"Good night," Cicely said, taking the subtle warning for what it was. She was on notice. Mess up and she wouldn't be going to Paris. C. J. was just a passing thing. He'd said it himself: All he'd ever had were brief affairs. She'd worked too hard to get this far. She wasn't tossing her career aside because a man made her body want his. Then, too, when would she have the time?

Determined, she went to oversee the fashion shoot. Paris was her future; C. J. was just a passing thing.

Cicely was positive she could stick with her decision until she saw C. J. as she started down the steps of the museum later that night with her assistant. She couldn't stop the crazy leap of her heart, the sprout of joy.

Irresistibly handsome, he drew interested looks

from the women working on the shoot, and the women passing on the street. If his face wasn't enough to garner a second look, his incredible body—with wide shoulders, muscled legs in sinfully fitting jeans—would. Arms folded across his wide chest, he casually leaned against the back passenger door of a cab. He was sin on a stick, just begging to be licked.

"Looks like your waiting is over. For once, I think Eva made an understatement," Sami said, then quickly continued down the steps.

Cicely's steps were slower. Lenora had warned her about not being focused. She should just keep walking. It shouldn't matter that C. J. watched her with an intensity that made her body tremble and want. Her life was headed in a vastly different direction. Yet she found herself stopping a few feet in front of him.

He straightened, his arms going to his sides. "The night we had dinner, you mentioned you'd be here."

But she hadn't mentioned what time. It was long past ten. An unsettling thought hit her. "How long have you been here? Did you see Lenora?"

"Not long and no, I didn't see Lenora." He shoved his hands into the pockets of his jeans.

She finally realized he was nervous. She didn't think very many things got to him. "C. J., what are you doing here?"

"I was losing," he said. "Alex was beating me, and he never wins."

"I suppose you're going to tell me it's my fault."

"The thought had occurred to me." He reached

for the large attaché case and her hand, pulling her closer. "I missed you."

"Nothing has changed," she managed, resisting the tempting pull of his mouth, the comforting warmth of his body.

"I'm not so sure about that." Releasing her hand, he opened the back door of the cab.

"I'm still going to Paris."

"He's holding the game until we get back."

She should just tell him no, but she found herself getting into the waiting cab, reasoning that whether she was with him or not, he occupied her thoughts, so she might as well have the pleasure of being with him. Looking at him, she thought of other pleasures, blushed, and looked away.

She was a weak woman where C. J. was concerned. Worse, he probably knew it.

C. J. admitted to himself as he gave the cabdriver Callahan's address that he had been half afraid Cicely would refuse to go with him. In the past, he'd never given a woman a second thought if she said no. He certainly hadn't been this persistent.

In the light spilling into the cab from the passing buildings and streetlights, C. J. caught glimpses of Cicely's profile. She was beautiful, but it wasn't just her beauty that drew him. She looked vulnerable at times, and that vulnerability drew him just as much. But it was also something else, something he couldn't define or put his finger on.

"What is it about you that changed the rules for me?"

Slowly she faced him. "I was thinking the same thing, only in reverse. Why you?"

Reaching out, he took her hand in his. "My winning personality?" he teased.

She wrinkled her nose. "I don't think that would make the list."

"Stimulating conversation?"

Up went her eyebrow. "You must be joking."

The cab pulled up to Callahan's. "Here you are, and don't forget the bonus you promised me for waiting."

"Wouldn't dream of it." C. J. placed a hundred in the palm of the man's hand, then followed Cicely out with her attaché case.

"That's a lot of money."

He shrugged and opened the door to Callahan's. "Have you eaten?"

"Long ago and forgotten," she answered, stepping ahead of him into the bar. It was as busy as she remembered, and somehow just as comfortable. There was no pretense here. You got what you saw, a place to get a cold beer, conversation if you wanted, and a quick bite to eat.

"Burger and onion rings all right?" He steered her toward the back booth.

"Perfect."

"Hail the conquering hero." Grinning, Sin slid out of the booth and crossed his arms. "Hi, Cicely."

It ran through Cicely's mind that C. J. had friends who were as gorgeous and as impressive as he was. "Hi, Sin."

"Hi, Cicely," Alex greeted, coming out of the booth on the other side with Dianne.

"Glad you made it," Dianne told her.

So was she, and finally she could admit and accept it. "Hi, Alex. Dianne."

"You're a lifesaver," Dianne said, leaning her head briefly against Alex's shoulder. "You can keep me company. Sin and C. J. say I can't watch because it makes Alex play better, and will place them at an unfair advantage."

"Take a seat. I'll put your order in and then I have a pool game to win," C. J. said.

"Dream on." Sin placed both hands on his lean hips. "You can't possibly come back from such a low score."

C. J. winked playfully at Cicely. "Never count out a man with a purpose."

Sin's eyes narrowed on Cicely as C. J. moved away to stop a passing waitress. "You're also off limits in the pool area."

Cicely was oddly pleased and held up both hands. "I won't move from this spot."

C. J. arrived back to hear her response. "Your Pellegrino is on its way. You're not going to watch?"

"She's keeping me company, remember?" Dianne said, obviously trying to keep from laughing.

C. J.'s questioning gaze narrowed on Sin. Sin looked as innocent as a baby. "I'm still going to win."

"Alex might beat both of you." Dianne kissed Alex on the cheek. "My man is smokin' tonight."

"Thanks, honey." Alex squeezed her briefly around the waist. "Come on, fellows, and take your medicine. After I dispatch C. J., I'll take down Sin."

"Your food will be here shortly, Cicely. Excuse me while I shut my two best friends down one by one," C. J. said, following him.

Sin studied Dianne, then Cicely. "I'll emerge victorious, but since they have you to console them, I'll relish my victory."

Cicely's laughter joined Dianne's as Sin moved after them. "They're something."

Dianne nodded. "They're called the renegades because they do what's right rather than what makes the most money or what others think. They care about people."

"Pellegrino." The waitress placed the bottle and glass in front of Cicely and spoke to Dianne. "You want anything?"

"No, thanks." Dianne nodded toward the back where the pool table was located. "They're having fun."

Cicely heard the good-natured teasing from the men, the crack of the billiard ball against the cue stick, the thump of the balls dropping into the side pockets. "No matter who wins, they all win."

"Exactly." Dianne sipped her soft drink. "They're friends for life. Sometimes it's difficult for men that close to accept a woman, but Sin and C. J. have never once acted as if I was an intrusion. That means a lot to Alex and me. I didn't have many friends in the fashion industry so I value friendship."

"That says a lot about the type of men they are as

well," Cicely said. She liked Dianne, but she wasn't ready to admit her own lack of friends.

"Here you go." The waitress placed in front of Cicely an inch-thick hamburger patty topped with lettuce, tomatoes, pickles, on a sesame seed bun. Beside it she set a seven-inch stack of onion rings on a platter.

Cicely's eyes rounded. "I can't eat this. I'm not sure I can get my mouth around that burger."

The waitress chuckled. "Do like my daughter, squash it and then eat from the sides. Signal if you need anything."

Cicely moved the platter of onion rings closer to Dianne. "Please help yourself. You want some of the burger as well?"

"No to the burger. I should say no to the onion rings as well, but I love them here." Dianne picked up one of the crispy fried rings. "I'll go with Alex to the gym in our building Saturday morning. Maybe this time, I'll actually get to do some exercise."

"Why the smile?" Cicely asked, cutting into her burger. "I work out, but I detest each moment."

"I was banned there as well." Dianne munched with relish.

"Disturbed things, did you?"

"After being fired for being too fat, it was nice to know that men still found me attractive," she admitted.

"But you only have eyes for Alex." Taking the waitress's advice, Dianne ate the burger from the side.

"I love him and yet that's too tame for what I feel for him. He's my passion, my life. He sees my faults and loves me anyway. No one ever had before," she said simply.

Cicely didn't say anything. She thought of her parents, who saw her faults and were quick to point them out.

"C. J. likes you a lot. He's usually easygoing and carefree. I've never seen him restless and on edge the way he was tonight. He kept watching the door, checking his phone. Finally, he said he'd be back and left."

Cicely placed her burger on the plate, and smiled when she heard C. J. shout in triumph.

"You're the cause of that," Dianne said. "I never thought about it before, but Alex's mother told me at the engagement party that loving a man was a privilege and a responsibility. He might not make it easy, but love always should be."

"Wait. Wait." Cicely said. "C. J. and I barely know each other."

"I don't think that makes any difference."

Cicely wished she could tell her she was wrong, but she couldn't. Whatever it was between her and C. J., they didn't seem to have much control over it. It was as scary as hell.

"If you could change how you feel, would you?" Dianne asked.

Cicely opened her mouth to say yes, until C. J. lifted his head and their gazes locked. She felt the pull, the desire that strained to be free. "I don't have time for this. Even my publisher is concerned. Paris has to come first."

"You're going there for an assignment?" Diane asked.

"Editor-in-chief." Cicely told her about the possible promotion.

"Congratulations, but I had Paris," Dianne replied. "I prefer having Alex. As you know, we went there on our honeymoon and it is different when you share it with someone you love. There's nothing like falling asleep and waking up in the arms of the man you love, the man who loves you."

Cicely shook her head. "You're talking about love. C. J. and I have a good case of lust."

"I'm not so sure," Dianne replied. "I've been around lustful people before. They were indiscriminate. You and C. J. seem to have eyes only for each other."

Cicely didn't know how to respond, so she didn't.

"Are you going to play or eat Cicely up with your eyes," Sin asked, both hands propped on top of the cue stick.

"She's thinking about running again," C. J. said, still watching Cicely.

"Then you'll change her mind," Alex said, standing on the other side of C. J.

"I might not be able to." C. J. blew out a breath and told them about Cicely's possible promotion. "I want her to get the position, but I don't want her to go."

"That's understandable," Alex said. "You care about her, so you want what's best for her, what makes her happy, even if it takes her away from you."

"Brother." Sin shook his head. "Marriage turned you into a philosopher."

"Not marriage," Alex corrected. "Love."

C. J. whipped his head between his two best friends. "I'm not in love. We haven't even been on a real date."

"Not necessary." Alex slapped a panicky C. J. on the back. "I always knew I loved Dianne even before I kissed her."

"C. J., don't you dare fall in love," Sin ordered sternly. "I refuse to be the odd man out and lose my two best friends."

"Whoa. Whoa." C. J. held up both hands. "I'm not in love, and I'm not getting married."

Alex rubbed his chin. "I've never seen you this way with another woman. You can't get her out of your mind when you're apart, and when you're together you can't keep your eyes off her. Usually it's out of sight, out of mind for you."

"I hate to admit it, C. J., but he's right." Sin turned to look at Cicely. "But I can't blame you. She's a looker. She has a nice— Ouch!" Sin yelped, then glared at Alex. "Why did you elbow me?"

"To save you," Alex said, nodding toward C. J. "He was in full protective mode. The way he gets when he thinks a man is crossing the line with Summer. Teeth bared. Fists clenched. Fire in the eyes."

Sin jerked his head around to stare at C. J., who now looked a bit taken aback by his own behavior. "I was going to say *laugh*."

C. J. shook his head, then laughed. "No, you weren't."

"She's that important to you?" Sin asked.

"Yes." He couldn't deny it any longer.

Sin clasped his friend on the shoulder. "Then she's important to me."

"And me." Alex clapped C. J.'s other shoulder.

"Now all I have to do is convince her."

Chapter 9

"I won."

"I knew it!" Dianne scooted out of the booth to give Alex a kiss and a hug.

Cicely stood as well and smiled in sympathy to C. J. "You'll win next time."

"Seems I'm the only one not getting any consolation." Sin frowned, then smiled. "I know what will console me. Dinner at Radcliffe's."

"This time of night she's already taken her last reservation, but that won't stop you," C. J. said. "You're brash enough to call Summer anyway."

Sin folded one arm around his waist, propped his elbow on top, and stroked his strong bearded chin thoughtfully. "Summer will feel sorry for me and let me eat in her office if she can't get me a table. It's not like I haven't eaten there before. I think I'll have a five-course meal with a pairing of wine for each course. Maybe I'll talk Summer into having a glass and sharing her chocolate soufflé with me. My jet isn't scheduled to leave until one tomorrow afternoon."

"Where are you headed this time?" Cicely asked.

"My first home. Dallas." He cocked his head to

one side. "I'd ask if you'd miss me, but I want to be able to chew my steak."

Cicely frowned, then looked at C. J., who was staring intently over her head.

"We better be going," Alex said into the lengthening silence, his arm around Dianne's waist. "I have an early court case."

"And we're working on a couple of designs for the New York fashion extravaganza in September," Dianne said with excitement in her voice. "Everything was booked for this year's events by the time D and A designs was created, but we were invited to a few exclusive events."

"We already have a spot for Fashion Week in February, and the fashion extravaganza here next year," Alex said. "Designers from around the world will be here. People will take notice of D and A."

"You're really getting into the whole fashion thing?" C. J. asked with disbelief. Alex and Sin were meticulous about their clothes and preferred tailored suits. C. J. liked to look nice, but he didn't obsess the way his mother and, occasionally, his sister did. His father and brother were the same way, obsessive about their clothes.

"Since I'm a partner, I felt it made sense to learn about the industry. That way I can help Dianne, who we all know is the real force behind D and A," Alex told them.

Dianne kissed her husband on the cheek. "I'm the luckiest woman in the world."

Alex kissed her back. "And you're all mine."

"I better get going as well. I probably should warn

Summer I'm on my way." Sin pulled out his iPhone. "Thanks for the game, although you both had unfair advantages. I might ask for a handicap next time."

"No," C. J. and Alex said in unison.

"It was just a thought. 'Night." On his iPhone, Sin headed for the front door. "Summer Radcliffe, please, Payton Sinclair calling."

"Do you think he'll get his five-course meal?" Cicely asked.

"Yes," C. J. answered.

"Without a doubt." Alex smiled. "But knowing Summer, she's not about to let him have a wine pairing with five courses this late, and well he knows it. But they'll have a good argument about it."

"Some arguments are good," Dianne snuggled against him. "I think we should be going."

Alex looked at his wife, straightened abruptly. "'Night, C. J., Cicely." He headed for the door, pulling his laughing wife after him.

"You have nice friends," Cicely said.

"They're becoming your friends as well." He brushed her hair back from her face, felt her shiver, and wanted to keep on touching her. In time. "I wish we were on our way someplace where we could be alone, too."

"I—"

"Shhhh." His hand curved downward, his thumb grazing over her quivering lip. "It's all right. Just don't run again."

Cicely glanced away and slid both hands into her pockets. "You make me feel emotions that—"

"Scare you because you can't control them," he finished.

Her wary gaze came back to his. "Yes."

"Same here, and despite my wanting you to get that job in Paris, I want to spend time with you, just us. Can you give us that?"

She bit her lip. "I'll try. I'm used to knowing where I'm going."

"And I'm not, but for you I'll do my best to be patient."

Her eyebrow lifted. "I'm going to remind you of that."

He chuckled. "I've no doubt you will. I need to go over a new vendor with the manager and then I'll take you home."

"I don't want to take you away from your work. I can get a cab."

He caught her shoulders when she started to turn away. "I want to take you home. Can you take this one step? Will you wait for me, please?"

C. J. didn't have to plead with a woman. He wasn't a patient man, yet he was being patient with her. Perhaps it was time she took a chance on the unknown and dared to see what would happen.

"I'll wait."

"Thank you." Squeezing her shoulders gently, he walked toward his office.

Cicely, what have you gotten yourself into? There was no answer as Cicely sat in the booth, her hands around the glass of Pellegrino.

There wasn't a shred of doubt that she and C. J. wanted each other sexually, but desire wasn't enough to act on. She shied away from Dianne's comment that there might be something stronger between them.

Cicely honestly didn't know which would be worse—acting solely out of lust or finally finding someone she could care deeply about only to lose him.

Shaking her head, she sipped her water. She had better decide now what her response would be once he kissed her when he took her home. His patience wouldn't extend to not kissing her, and she didn't want it to.

She twisted in her seat as desire heated her body. She'd never wanted this intently, but was it enough?

"Cicely?"

Cicely glanced up to see Ariel Callahan, C. J.'s sister. Several months ago Cicely had done a photo shoot in her magazine on mothers and daughters with their own unique fashion style. Ariel and her mother had been one of the three mothers and daughters selected. She'd liked the shy young woman immediately when they'd first met, and that hadn't changed during the arduous fashion shoot and interview.

"Hi, Ariel. It's good to see you."

"Hi." Ariel slid into the booth on the other side, placing her large handbag on the seat beside her. "What are you doing here?"

"Waiting for C. J.," Cicely said a bit cautiously. Although Cicely and her older brother had never been close, she knew little sisters could be as protective of their big brothers as the brothers were of them.

Ariel's frown deepened. "Are you seeing each other?"

"We're discussing it," Cicely answered.

"Hi, Ariel. What will you have?"

"Hi, Mary. Nothing, thank you."

The waitress nodded. "Signal me if you change your mind. You all right?" she asked Cicely.

"Fine. Thank you."

The waitress moved away, stopping at the table across from them where four men were watching dirt bike racing on a large-screen TV.

"You don't seem his type," Ariel said, placing her folded hands on the table. Cicely noticed they trembled just the tiniest bit.

"And what is his type?" Cicely asked, doing her best to keep her voice even. She wasn't about to jump to the conclusion that Ariel thought C. J. out of Cicely's league. The Callahans were extremely wealthy, and although Cicely moved in their circles, she did so as a worker.

"The couple of women I've seen with him were chesty, all teeth and hanging on his every word." Ariel leaned back in her seat. "Although I haven't seen you two together, that image doesn't go with the focused, no-nonsense woman I remember."

"No, that wouldn't be me."

"You might want to think about it a long time before you make a decision," Ariel said, biting her lower lip before rushing on. "I love my brother, but he's been known not to stick around for the long haul."

She glanced toward the front of the bar before she continued.

"Perhaps because things have always come so easily to him, when he meets resistance he moves on. He's a mathematical genius. He invented an interactive game by the time he was sixteen, then two more when he was bored one summer after graduating from college while working at Callahan's."

Astonishment touched Cicely's face. "He never mentioned it."

"I'm not surprised. The games have made him very wealthy in his own right and allowed him to live the carefree life he wanted. For six years he tramped all over the world. Like I said, he moves on when he loses interest."

Cicely's shoulders snapped back at the direct hit. "You're wrong. C. J. is not that shallow. I'm amazed you think he is. He goes after what he wants with all that he has. He'd fight anyone to keep this bar."

Ariel smiled sadly. "That's just my point. As you said, he goes after what he wants. He wants his bar so he'll do whatever it takes to keep it. He's never been that interested in Callahan Software. He isn't concerned that . . ." Her voice trailed off. Grabbing her bag, she slid out of the booth and stood. "Please don't tell C. J. I was here."

"Is there a problem with the software company?"

Fear flashed in Ariel's eyes. "I didn't say that. Please, your promise."

She'd push, but she wasn't sure she had the right to interfere in family business. "If the waitress mentions it to him or he asks I won't lie to him, but I won't bring it up."

"Thank you. Good-bye." Ariel left, stopping briefly to speak to the waitress.

Cicely slumped back in the chair. Ariel had put her in a horrible position. Although she had heard C. J. himself mention that he wasn't that interested in the software business, she instinctively knew that if he thought there was a problem, he'd work night and day to solve it.

"Why the frown?"

She glanced up to see C. J. standing by the booth. She could shake Ariel for not having more faith in her brother, and putting her in a position of keeping secrets from him. "Just thinking."

"I see I have my work cut out for me. Let's go." Taking her arm with one hand, he reached for the attaché case with the other.

She waited until they were in the back of Callahan's walking to his car to ask, "How was work at Callahan Software today?"

"Uneventful."

There had been no guile or hesitation in his response. If the company was in trouble, he was unaware of it.

Opening the passenger door for her, he went around the other side and got in. "I think the employees are trying to go easy on me for fear I'll bail and they'll be out of a job. There is no way Dad or Paul had all this free time. I'm already thinking of turning the company over to someone in a year—if I can stick it out that long—and coming back to my bar. It would be better all around."

"Why would they think you'd leave?" she asked as he backed the car out of the parking space and started down the alley.

He threw her a quick glance, checked the traffic both ways, and pulled onto the street. "Programming is long, tedious work. I wasn't meant to sit at a desk or a computer ten to twelve hours a day, working on solving a problem that can take up to six months, then doing the same thing all over again."

"So you used to work there?" Cicely asked, feeling her way.

"For a year after I graduated from college." He stopped at a traffic light. "I decided I'd rather see the world. No one objected at the time."

"But that was when your father and brother didn't have any health problems," she said thoughtfully.

"Yeah." He pulled though the light and headed toward Harlem. "A lot of people working there at the time still do. Some have kids in college now."

She heard the weight of responsibility in his voice. "And you don't want to let them down."

"I don't like being responsible for that many people." He shrugged broad shoulders as he turned onto her street. "If the bar closed tonight, none of my people would have a problem finding a job."

He cared. They were all wrong if they thought he would desert them. He took his responsibilities seriously. She could understand if his employees were unsure, but his sister should know him better. She wondered if the other family members thought the same way. "They can trust you."

He parked in front of her brownstone, then covered her hand with his. "Thanks. Does that mean you trust me as well?"

"We've already had this conversation. If I didn't trust you, I wouldn't have gone out with you and you wouldn't be taking me home," she said, opening the door and getting out. He joined her on the sidewalk.

At the entry, it took two tries of her unsteady hand to insert the key and unlock the door. Pushing it open, she walked inside, silently inviting him to follow. He moved past her, stopping a few steps inside.

Closing the door, her grip on the attaché tightened. Soft light from the night-light she'd left on bathed the foyer, casting shadows over his body. He seemed to fill the space around him.

"Can you ice-skate?"

"What?"

He grinned. "I'd like to get to know you better, and I'm hoping you feel the same way. Personally, I'm hoping you're lousy because I'd get to hold you more that way."

"You want to take me ice-skating?"

"Yes. Tomorrow evening. It will definitely be a date, so know that upfront," he said. "When you get to Paris and people ask you about New York, you'll be able to tell them. Most people in New York never see the sights people come from all over the world to see."

He was giving her time. "I can't ice-skate."

His worried gaze ran over her slim body again.

"Maybe I better rethink that. I thought you'd have at least some experience on skates."

"I'm the baby of the family. By the time I came into the picture, my parents were too busy gaining tenure at their university."

"What? Where?"

"History. University of South Carolina in Columbia." She tried to pull her hand free and couldn't. "You once asked if I was following a family tradition. I'm not. My parents, my older brother and sister think I'm wasting my time and talent working in fashion." She couldn't keep the hurt from her voice.

His hand cupped her face. "I don't, and neither does Lenora. She impressed me as an intelligent woman. She wouldn't be publisher if she wasn't. Over two million people on your blog agree with me."

Her eyes widened. She'd only recently reached that milestone. "You were on my blog again?"

"Yes. How about I pick you up at eight, and once we get there, we'll decide what to do?"

"Is nine all right?" she asked a bit tentatively. She would have sworn he'd rather have his eyelids glued together than read her blog. "There's a fashion event at Chanel I need to attend."

"If you're late I'll wait, for as long as it takes." His hands slid down her arms then curved around her waist to pull her closer. "I know you trust me in some ways, but you're unsure in others. I'm going to change that." His mouth found hers, taking her breath away, heating her body. Hands skimmed up her back, over her hips, bringing her closer to his burgeoning desire. Lifting his head, he stepped back. "See you tomorrow." Then he was gone.

She was late.

C. J. had always been impatient waiting on women, but leaning against the side of the car he'd hired waiting outside of Cicely's brownstone six minutes after nine, he found he was more anxious than annoyed. The rink closed at ten thirty. They could always do something else, but if Cicely was willing to go skating, he wanted to take her.

He shook his dark head. He'd cared about pleasing the women he'd dated, but he'd never given it this much thought. Things just sort of evolved. But then, the women had been after him as much as he was after them.

Cicely was different.

Until last night, she hadn't been so sure she wanted them to be more than acquaintances. Thankfully, she'd changed her mind. Now that she'd made that step, he planned to show her he was worth the risk. He had no intention of letting her get away from him.

He nodded to a happy passing couple who were arm in arm, and thought of Dianne and Alex. C. J. frowned as he recalled Alex's comment about love. C. J. wasn't anywhere near that big step. He wanted Cicely. She wanted him. They were single and unattached, so there was no reason not to get together.

Yet he believed there was another reason for her hesitancy. It was more than just the possibility of her going to Paris. There was also the possibility of caring for someone and being rejected, just as her parents had rejected her.

His fists clenched. How could a parent do that to a child? His parents had always supported him, even when they didn't understand. He was repaying them by taking over Callahan, he just wished he could find some satisfaction in the job. Somehow he had to break through his employees' standoffish attitude. He would. If he could get Cicely to go out with him, the employees at Callahan should be a snap.

He saw a taxi approaching and straightened, wondering if this one would keep going. It didn't.

The back door swung open as soon as the car came to a stop. Cicely stepped out, wearing a blue silk dress with a wicked split on both sides and strappy blue sandals.

He moved to help her. However, by the time he rounded the hood of the car, the cab was pulling away and Cicely was hurrying toward him.

"Hi. Sorry, I'm late. It won't take but a minute to change."

His appreciative gaze roamed over her. "I wish you didn't have to. You look incredible."

She paused on the steps and let her approving gaze run over him. "So do you."

He was in his usual after-work attire, jeans with a polo shirt. "You always outshine me," he said slowly, realizing it for the first time.

"It's my job and my pleasure to look my best and stand out. It helps that I like clothes, get unbelievable discounts, and know where to find the bargains.

You wear what you like and feel comfortable in." She smiled and continued up the steps.

"You're the epitome of what I want the readers of *Fashion Insider* and my blog to embrace: Don't dress to impress others, dress to please yourself." The door swung open and she kept going. "Please have a seat. I'll hurry."

C. J., who had never given too much thought to what he wore, stared after her as she rushed away. For a crazy moment he'd felt—he searched for a word. He discarded *uncertain,* rolled his eyes at *worried.* Cicely certainly made a man think. He wasn't sure if that was good or bad.

In her bedroom, Cicely quickly hung up her dress. Thankfully, she'd already decided what she'd wear. She changed into comfortable black cotton slacks, a long white blouse, and a pin-striped white-on-black jean vest, then checked her makeup. Retouching her lipstick, she exchanged her evening bag for a small across-the-shoulder Gucci bag. After combing her hair, she was ready.

She found C. J. still standing. "I hope I didn't take too long."

"No." He took her hand. "Besides, you're worth the wait."

This time the leap of her pulse, the sizzle felt right instead of scary. She enjoyed him holding her hand, enjoyed the little zip. "I'd like to go ice-skating."

"Ice-skating it is. You have your key?"

She patted her purse. "Let's go have fun."

Outside, they went to a waiting car. He opened the back door.

"We could have taken a taxi," Cicely said.

"It might be difficult to get one later. Besides, this is more comfortable."

And more intimate. "I'm sorry I kept you waiting," she said as the big black Lincoln pulled away from the curb.

He brought her hand to his lips, kissed it, then grazed his thumb across her knuckles. "Don't be. The skating rink closes at ten thirty, but we should have time to do a few turns."

She threw a frantic glance at her watch. "We don't have very much time."

"Then we'll just have to make the moments count."

Chapter 10

Cicely had looked forward to being with C. J. all day. However, her excitement dimmed when she saw the long line ahead of them waiting to be admitted to the skating rink. She glanced at her watch again.

"Do you think we'll make it?"

"Without a doubt." Her hand in his, he went to the head of the line. In less than a minute, they were on the ice.

"How did you manage that?" she asked, a death grip on his arm.

"Let's just say it's my secret."

She wanted to ask more questions, but he began to slowly move. Her concern became keeping upright.

"Just relax. I won't let you fall."

She tried to do as he said, her hold on him loosening as they circled the rink. Every time she lost her balance, he was there. If it hadn't been for his easy strength, her butt would have been on the ice after every cautious movement of her skates. He held her, encouraged her, always nearby in case she started to fall. By the time they turned in their skates, she could at least stand up on her own.

"That was fun," she said.

"It's not over." Taking her hand, he led her to the waiting car. "We're going to the observation deck of the Empire State Building. If you aren't too tired."

"Lead on."

The vast skyline of New York City spread out in front of C. J. and Cicely. "It's beautiful," she said from beside him as they stood on the seventieth floor.

"So are you." It seemed the most natural thing in the world to turn her to him, fit his mouth to her waiting lips, and take the kiss he'd been hungry for since she'd jumped out of the cab. The need had grown as he'd held her while she learned to skate.

He lifted his head, watched her face, wanting to see her eyes when they opened. When he did, he saw his desire reflected back at him. Kissing her again would test his tenuous hold, so he pulled her into his arms and held her until the need to take her slowly receded.

"Did you happen to eat anything substantial to-night?"

"A cube of cheese and two grapes."

He leaned her away from him, his gaze sweeping over her. "I figured. This time, I made reservations. Let's go."

They were seated almost immediately at the crowded restaurant. Cicely accepted her menu and smiled across the table at C. J. "You really have to tell me your secret."

"I know people." He lifted his menu in front of his face.

"It's a good thing I'm starved," she muttered, but she was smiling. And since she was, she ordered lamb, château potatoes with sautéed mushrooms, and iced tea. C. J. ordered the same.

When the waiter served them bread and their drinks, C. J. scooted the loaf of bread and butter closer to her. "Eat."

Shaking her head, she did just that.

The waiter quickly returned to served them their main course, asked if they needed anything else, and moved away when they said they didn't. The instant the waiter turned with the deck tray, C. J. tucked his head and said a blessing for their food. Finished, he reached for his knife and fork.

"What is your schedule like tomorrow?"

"Editorial staff meeting." Cutting into the bread loaf, she placed slices on each of their bread plates. "We're getting things in line for the next issue. It will showcase designers' collections from around the world, their spring/summer collections for next year. My team will—" Abruptly she stopped.

"What is it?" Alarmed, he reached out to cover her hand.

"They won't be my team if I get the job in Paris," she answered. "I guess it's sinking in more each day."

Squeezing her hand, he straightened. "Having regrets?"

"What? No." She shook her head at the absurdity of such a question. "I've worked for this."

"But you'll also be leaving friends and a place you've worked since you were a junior in college," he reasoned. "You must have a lot of attachments and memories tied to the magazine, not to mention your home."

Her hand closed around her glass of tea. "My first. My grandmother didn't like the idea of my living in an apartment, and left me enough in her will to make it possible for me to make a hefty down payment after I graduated from college. I haven't made any plans about what to do with it."

"Don't until you're ready. I'll look after it or you could hire someone." He motioned toward her plate. "Eat, and then we can decide on dessert. I don't want to keep you out too late."

She momentarily stared at his concerned face, then began to eat. "You're very good at this."

Lines radiated across his forehead. "At what?"

"Taking care of someone. I didn't think I would, but I kind of like it." She selected a mushroom. "My attitude and my schedule can't make it easy for you."

He looked uncomfortable again, and shrugged. "It's no problem."

She simply smiled and thought of the perfect way to say thank you when he took her home.

They reached for each other as soon as the door closed. C. J. didn't think he could have lasted another second. Cicely had been looking at him as if she'd like to crawl in his lap and take his mouth since they were at the restaurant.

His hand went under the oversized shirt, felt

warm, bare skin that heated more with his touch. Grabbing the material, he lifted it over her head. With a little tug, the sleeves slid over her wrists.

His breath stopped on seeing the white lace barely covering her full breasts. He wanted to taste, to touch. He did both, his mouth taking the turgid point into his mouth through the lace, suckling deeply.

Hearing her ragged moan, he teetered on the brink of pulling back or taking her standing up. She wasn't ready. He'd have this one night, but he intended to have more.

Pulling her to him, he held her tightly until the need tramping through him calmed. "You're a temptation I didn't count on."

"Same here."

Lifting his head, he kissed her on the temple, then headed for the door, not daring to look back. "Lock up. Call me tomorrow if you have time for a drink or coffee." Outside, he stood there until he saw her shadow. He was aware she could see him as well.

"Lock the door, Cicely," he said, as much to keep her safe as to keep him out.

He saw the doorknob begin to turn, felt his heart rate kick up. If she opened the door— The locks clicked.

Swallowing, he went down the steps and got into the waiting car. His hands shook. He wasn't used to wanting a woman and not having her. He wasn't sure what that said about him. He certainly wasn't as unthinking as Summer said. After one last look at the now dark house, he instructed the driver to take him home.

* * *

Friday evening, after leaving the software company, C. J. figured he might as well work at the bar while waiting for Cicely to call. Once there, he was glad to see business booming.

He easily fell into the routine of helping the waitresses, the bartenders. Whatever needed doing, he did, including bussing the tables, sweeping the floor. He had never figured he was better than his employees.

Callahan's Bar was located in an area with businesses, shops, apartments, and condos. His uncle probably had no idea when he opened the bar that the neighborhood would grow and change so much.

C. J. drew a customer a draft beer and moved to put the empty glasses in the dishwasher. The neighborhood might have changed, but Callahan's had remained the same. His customers appreciated that and he appreciated them.

He put another glass in the dishwasher, and wished the customers of Callahan Software were as easily pleased. Corporate always wanted more, better, faster. He'd been online today checking out the competition. Every day that went by and he sat on his tush and did nothing to affect the bottom line of Callahan, he felt more restless and, yes, worthless.

Not to mention a fraud. He wasn't sure he wanted to face his parents at his birthday party. Maybe there was a way for him not to go.

"Can I have some service?"

C. J. swung around to see Cicely standing between two men on bar stools, grinning at him. He rounded the bar, took her arm, and didn't stop until they were in his office.

Closing the door with one hand, he drew her into his arms with the other. The kiss was long and deep. His tongue thoroughly tasted hers, the inside of her mouth as she tasted and savored him.

"That enough service for you?"

Her heart galloping in her chest, her knees trembling, she murmured, "It will do for a start."

Laughing, C. J. hugged her again. "You'll never let me get a big head." He kissed her again. "This is a nice surprise."

Her fingers made little circles on his chest. "We finished thirty minutes ago. I called your place and when I didn't get an answer, I called here and Piper said you were working. I thought I'd stop by on my way home."

"I'll take you."

Shaking her head, she pushed out of his arms and adjusted her handbag on her shoulder. "I still have some work to do before I call it a night."

"It's past eleven."

"It still has to be done." She went to the door. "Good night."

"I'll see you to a cab, but I don't like it." He went with her to the street and hailed a passing cab that cut off two cars to pull to the curb. "Maybe you should get another one."

She chuckled and reached for the door. "You're doing it again. 'Night."

"How about tomorrow night?"

"I wish I could," she said, disappointment in her

face and voice. "There's a fashion event on Long Is-
land this weekend I have to attend. I'd invite you to
meet me there, but it will be hectic and nonstop. I'm
staying there and won't be back until late Sunday
night."

She worked hard while he worked at trying to
look busy. His hand covered hers. "How about
Monday?"

"I'd like that."

"I'll pick you up at seven thirty. We'll play it by
ear."

"If I'm late—"

"I'll wait." He kissed her. "Call me here when you
get home."

"Worrywart." She got into the cab and it drove
away, leaving C. J. on the sidewalk staring after her.

Cicely called Callahan's the moment she reached her
bedroom. C. J. answered on the second ring. "How
many lights on yellow did he run?"

Cicely stuck her tongue in her cheek. *Three.* "I'm
home safely with the door locked."

He grunted.

Smiling for the sheer pleasure of it, she kicked off
her heels and plopped on the bed. "How did your
day go?"

"The same. I better let you go so you can finish
and get to bed."

"All right." She wasn't sure if he wanted to get off
the phone for the reason he said or because he didn't
want to talk about the software company. "I might
not get a chance to call you while I'm there."

"I understand. Don't work too late, and I'll see you Monday night."

" 'Night, C. J."

" 'Night."

Cicely placed the phone in the holder and stood. If she stayed on the bed for too long, she'd fall asleep. She went to her closet to undress. She'd already packed for the weekend that, before meeting C. J., she'd looked forward to. Telling herself that she was getting in over her head didn't seem to do any good.

Still thinking about C. J., she pulled on a light robe and went to her office. From his abrupt answer, he was still having trouble settling in at the software company. If he discovered that his family's business was in trouble and no one had told him, there'd be hell to pay. And no matter what, she was a tiny bit afraid that she'd be included in the fallout.

After a hectic weekend, Monday wasn't any better. Cicely had a horrific day from hell. Nothing went right. The copy machine decided it had worked enough. The backup decided to join the strike. Two freelance writers were past due with their assignments. One of their biggest advertising accounts wanted a different placement in the magazine—one that was already secured by another account. To top it off, a false fire alarm had sounded and they'd had to walk down twenty-three flights of stairs.

She thought she was handling things relatively well and was back on track until Sami told her that the actress she was supposed to interview in a week needed to do the interview at 10:00 AM the next day at her Village apartment. No rescheduling was possible.

Cicely closed her eyes, counted to ten, and then counted again. The actress's current film had Oscar buzz and she was scheduled to be on the cover of *Fashion Insider*. Opening her eyes, Cicely said, "Please tell her I'll be there."

"You were planning on going to see her movie this weekend," Sami reminded her.

"I have it covered," Cicely said with assurance and waited until Sami left before snatching up the phone.

"Don't tell me you have to cancel," C. J. said moments later.

"Depends on you." She quickly explained. "If you think you can take a romantic comedy, I'll meet you at the theater."

Without hesitation he said, "Just tell me when and where."

Cicely gave him the information. "You're sure?"

"I'm sure. See you at seven."

C. J. didn't have any expectations of the movie, so he wasn't disappointed. He would have liked to have been nibbling on Cicely as a couple of guys were doing in front of him, but he contented himself with putting his arm around her shoulders. At least he wasn't the poor guy two rows down who snored at the exact moment the theater was quiet because the main characters were kissing. Laughter had erupted.

Moments later, he saw a woman storm out of the

theater. A man, probably the snorer, rushed after her, apologizing.

Cicely looked at him. He gave her a quick kiss on her lips. He figured he deserved it. "Wide awake."

Apparently satisfied, she went back to watching the movie.

C. J. could find something much better to look at. He let his mind wander where it shouldn't. The night he had gotten her emerald dress partially off, her barely there bra had been the exact same color. The night they went skating, she had on a lacy white bra beneath the long white blouse.

His curious gaze drifted over her slim body. She wore a bold floral multicolored dress. He wondered about the color of her lingerie and if he would have a chance tonight to find out. Sunny yellow maybe?

"Are you ready to leave?"

C. J. jerked his head upright and stared into Cicely's face.

"The credits are almost over."

He glanced around and saw people leaving. Standing, he reached for her arm. "Sure."

She stood as well. Her gaze almost level with his, she said, "I guess you really liked the movie."

He shrugged and they merged with those leaving the theater. He wasn't going to compound his bad manners with a lie. He hadn't done anything so juvenile since he was in high school.

"What would you say was the best part?" she asked when they were standing in front of the theater.

"I—er . . ." He searched his mind for a scene and couldn't come up with a one.

Her laughter lifted his head. Amusement twinkled in her eyes. "You were looking at something, but it wasn't the movie."

He hugged her. "I'd like to say I was sorry."

"It couldn't have been much fun for you."

His arm around her shoulders, they merged with the heavy pedestrian traffic that never seemed to end in New York. Horns blasted. Street vendors tried to sell their wares. "Anytime I get to hold you is fun."

"C. J., you could become a problem," she admitted as they walked down the busy street.

"Only if you let me." His lips brushed over her ear. She shivered. "Now, how about a pizza?"

She chuckled. "You know food is my weakness."

He turned her easily in his arms and moved out of the flow of foot traffic. "Is that your only weakness?"

Her body trembled as she felt the heated hardness of his body, looked into his passionate dark eyes, and barely kept from saying *you*. Her hands flattened on his chest. She leaned more heavily into him.

Abruptly he stepped back and took her hand. "If I kissed you the way your eyes say you want to be kissed, the way I want to kiss you, we wouldn't want to stop."

Cicely said nothing. He was right. She wanted him with a growing need and there was nothing she could do about it. The logical thing to do would be to escape while she could, but as they turned down a street she realized she wasn't going anyplace. If she did, she'd always have regrets—and she'd lived with enough of those to last three lifetimes.

Chapter 11

The next night they went to a Broadway play. Somehow C. J. didn't seem the theater type. She told him as much as they left the theater, merging with the heavy traffic on Broadway. People were taking pictures of the towering billboards, one another, laughing, energized.

For a moment, she didn't think he'd answer. "I read on your blog that you liked Broadway. Liked the costume designs as much as the play itself."

"You read my blog again?"

"I wanted to know what interests you," he said.

Her brows knitted. "That post was over a month ago."

"I had the time," he said, catching her hand and tugging her down the street. He hailed a cab and they got inside. He didn't say anything more about it and neither did she.

The cab parked behind his car, which he'd left there because it was easier to take a cab than to deal with parking. Paying the driver, he helped her out and they went up the steps together. Opening the door, she went inside and he followed.

"I didn't do it to invade your privacy."

Cicely tossed her clutch on the sofa—she was going to need both hands—and came back to him. He was still standing in the foyer, looking a bit unsure of himself. She couldn't imagine an unsure C. J., and it was because he was uncertain of her reaction.

Stopping in front of him, she curved her arms around his neck. "No one has ever given as much thought to pleasing me as you have. This is what I think." Her mouth settled on his, moving hungrily, this time the aggressor, giving without fear or caution.

She heard C. J. growl deeply in his throat. He pulled her flush against him. She felt his desire, felt her own. Her body went soft, yielding against him. His hands caressed her hips, pulled her closer. She idly wondered what it would be like if no clothes separated them.

He lifted his head, his breath as labored as hers, then dropped his forehead to hers. His hands trembled on her arms. "I better get out of here."

She opened her mouth to tell him to stay, then nodded instead. If they made love, she didn't want her decision to be based on her inability to control her body. "Why don't we have dinner here tomorrow night around eight?"

His gaze, still simmering with passion, stared down at her. "I'd like that. 'Night." Releasing her, he left.

Cicely took two steps toward the door to lock

it before she realized her wrap dress hung open. Beneath were her yellow bra and matching bikini panties. C. J. could undress her faster than she could herself.

Looking up, she saw his wide-shouldered shadow waiting for her to lock the door. He was a hard man to resist, and she wasn't sure she wanted to anymore. He didn't have to stop. Somehow he sensed her body might be more than ready, but not her mind. In his arms, need and hunger trumped common sense.

"Cicely, lock the door."

His voice sounded strained, hoarse. Once again, he'd put her needs ahead of his own. On trembling legs, she locked the door, then clicked off the night-light, wishing she could click off the desire rushing hot and fierce through her. The next time, she wasn't sure if either of them would be able to stop.

The next day C. J. had another forgettable day at work. Each day, he told himself the next day might be different, but it was always the same.

It was a quarter past six and all the employees had gone. He'd stayed. He wasn't sure why. Staring at the awards and accolades of those who had sat in the chair before him, though, he realized he did know why.

He wanted to do a good job. He wasn't, and that ate at him. He didn't mind hard work, but it seemed the employees weren't going to give him a chance. He admitted he hadn't minded at first; in fact, he was kind of glad they didn't bother him. He now realized that if things remained this way, it would eventually affect the bottom line.

His family was depending on him. He didn't plan to let them down. The ringing of his iPhone interrupted his unhappy thoughts. "Hello."

"C. J."

Cicely. Her voice sounded rushed, a bit breathless. Instantly alert, he rocked forward in his chair. "What is it? Are you all right?"

"Yes. Long story short, trouble at work, and I'm going to be working late. I have to cancel."

Disappointment and an unexpected feeling of loneliness hit him. He pushed it aside. "What about tomorrow night? I'll cook this time."

"I can't make any plans."

He heard voices in the background. Someone said Cicely's name.

"Sami, tell Lenora I'm on my way. Bye, C. J."

"Bye." he murmured, but she had already hung up. He replaced the phone. He'd really looked forward to tonight. He admitted he hoped it would be the night they'd finally make love, but he also wanted to see her. He liked being with her.

Standing, he rounded his desk. He was going to Callahan's. At least he didn't have any doubt he'd be welcomed. Alex would be home with Dianne, and Sin had left Dallas for his Chicago office. C. J. was on his own. He definitely deserved a beer.

Cicely couldn't make it the next night, either. Sitting alone in the back booth of Callahan's, C. J.

sympathized with his mother and sister-in-law for all the times his father and brother were no-shows. He'd never felt so restless. Sin was still out of town, but C. J. was sure if he called, he'd get him tickets to a sports event. But he didn't want to go to a game, he wanted to see Cicely.

He wasn't handling not seeing her very well. How was he going to take her moving to Paris? Oddly, he wanted her to get the job. She worked as hard as anyone he knew and deserved her success. Too hard at times, forgetting to eat and take care of herself. His mind lingered on the last thought.

Her building was only a short cab ride away. It would be a simple matter to pick up food and take it to her. The idea had no more than formed than he was scooting out of the booth and heading for the door. "I'll be back, Roy. I have to make a run."

"Sure thing, boss," Roy answered, but C. J. was already out the door.

Cicely's neck was sore from studying the layouts, the muscles in her back and legs in knots, but she kept working. They had to completely redo a fourth of the magazine and the cover story for the next issue. The tell-all interview of one of the leading fashion designers in the country had to be pulled. You don't take a chance when a high-powered attorney calls and uses the *sue* word.

"How is it going?" Lenora asked from behind her.

"We're almost there," Fred answered. "I could tap-dance on his cheating heart for doing this to us."

"Don't worry, his wife will do it for you," Cicely said.

"And enjoy every second," Lenora said. "I'll be in my office. Call when you have the final."

"Will do" came the chorus of agreements.

"Let's nail this sucker," Cicely said, and renewed her effort.

Thirty minutes later, they had the revised pages. Cicely massaged her lower back and studied the finished layout with a critical eye. "I'll go get Lenora."

"I'll do it." Eva rushed out of the room.

Cicely let her go. They'd all worked to pull this off and Lenora would know it. "What I wouldn't give for something to eat."

"How about a roast beef sandwich?"

Cicely swung around. "C. J."

Sami looked from C. J. to Cicely. "I met him trying to get into the building when I was going out."

"If you hadn't, I might have still been trying to explain to the security guard at the desk downstairs," he said easily.

"What are you doing here?" Cicely asked.

He lifted the large deli take-out bags. "I thought you might have been too busy to eat. I bought extra."

"I knew I liked him," Fred said, taking one of the bags and digging inside as others in the room crowded around him.

C. J. shoved the other bag toward Cicely. "I better go and let you get back to work."

He turned away. *That went well.*

He was almost at the elevator before he heard his

name and glanced over his shoulder. Cicely ran to him, her arms going around his waist.

"Thank you for thinking of me, of all of us. I'll probably fall asleep as soon as my head hits the pillow tonight, but tomorrow night, barring another disaster, I seem to remember you saying you'd cook steaks a long time ago. Say, around eight."

"Rare, right?"

"You got it." He wanted to kiss her, but he saw a couple of people in the hallway. He'd bet their appearance wasn't coincidental. At least it wasn't Lenora. "If you're late, don't worry. Just come."

"Count on it." Lifted on tiptoes, she gave him a quick kiss on the lips, then hurried back down the hallway.

Friday evening, Cicely rang C.J.'s doorbell at seven seventeen. Surprisingly, Sami and several people who had benefited from C. J.'s generosity had asked if she had a date that night. When Cicely said she did, everyone had seemed to be determined that she leave on time. She hadn't thought they cared enough to want to help her. She was pleasantly surprised to learn they did.

The door opened. Seeing C. J. made everything else fade. She just walked into his arms and put her mouth on his. Faintly, she heard the door slam, but she was too busy and too tangled up with C. J. to care. Her legs wrapped around his waist, the short emerald green jersey dress slid up her thighs.

"Hi."

His eyes shimmered with barely controlled desire. "Can you wait to eat?"

She knew what he was asking. With unsteady hands, she palmed his face, "Will you tire of me?"

"I . . . ," he began. His forehead touched hers before he let her slide to her feet. Tenderly cupping her face in his hands, he brushed his thumb over her trembling lower lip and stared deeply into her eyes. "I can't imagine that happening. I wake up thinking of you. I go to sleep thinking of you. I dream of you." He lifted his head. "I've never wanted anything as much as I want you. Things I want, I keep."

There were no guarantees in life. He'd given her an honest, thoughtful answer. No one had to tell her that C. J. wasn't the type of man to discuss his feelings. Neither was she.

"Is that enough?"

"Yes," she breathed, lifting her face to kiss him, giving to him without reservations or fear. This was what she wanted, not just her body, but her heart as well. The realization didn't scare her, it only made her want him more.

"Thank goodness."

Picking her up again, he quickly went to his bedroom, sitting her down by the king-sized bed. He'd left the bedside lamps on low. He wanted to see her when they made love. He'd never wanted so badly, but just as much, he wanted to savor the moment.

His hands trembled when he reached for the hem of her short dress and drew it over her body, his breath turning more labored, his heart beating crazily in his chest as inch by lovely inch of her incredible body was revealed.

Long, sleek legs, kissable knees, firm thighs, her woman's softness barely covered by a patch of emerald lace. He had to swallow before he could continue lifting the dress past her flat stomach, small waist, then over her breasts. His mouth dried as he saw the dusky nipple pushing against the lace.

He swallowed again and pulled the dress over her head, his gaze going to her. "You're incredible," he said, his voice shaky. No woman had ever reduced him to this need, this craving.

"I get to look, too." She reached for his polo shirt. Afraid she'd take too long, he whipped it over his head. He saw no reason for stopping there. He stepped out of his sandals, dragged off his jeans, taking his Jockeys with them.

Her eyes lowered, rounded as he jutted free.

He was thinking he should have waited, until he heard her say, "Oh, my."

He laughed, gathering her to him and falling into the king-sized bed. They landed facing each other. His laughter turned to a gasp as she cupped and then stroked him. He reveled in the pleasure before moving her hand. He was too near the edge.

He stared into her eyes, eyes that he'd never tire of looking into. "I've often thought of you here in my bed, and what we'd do to and with each other."

Cicely trembled. His words excited her as much as the lazy sweep of his hand down the slope of her back, over her hips. Skin that warmed and heated. She craved more. Staring into eyes that shone with desire for the first time in her life, she felt totally desirable. "No more than I've thought in my bed."

"Our wait is over." The last word was said against her lips, but his mouth didn't stay there. He moved to her breast. She was surprised when his mouth closed over the bare nipple, his tongue swirled, sucked. She realized he must have unfastened her bra when his hand was stroking her back—and she was infinitely glad he did.

She clutched his head to her. Nothing had ever felt so good, then he went to the other breast. She twisted beneath him as her blood heated, desire swamped her.

He continued downward, nibbling, kissing, and taking her panties with him. When he cupped her there, felt her wetness, she sucked in her breath, arched off the bed. His hands stroked her, petted her, and worshiped her until she twisted restlessly.

"Now, please."

Sheathing himself, he rose over her, lifting her hips. With their eyes locked, he joined them in one sure thrust. She moaned, arched, her eyes closing at the rightness of this.

He brought them together again and again, each stroke sending him closer to the edge, each stroke making him want more and more still. He felt her body tense, and quickened the pace. They went over together.

Breathing heavily, he rolled and pulled her to him. He didn't want to let her go. Another first. "Better than my imagination."

"Me, too."

He pulled her tighter, enjoying the softness of her against him. "You inspire me." He kissed her, felt his body stir again. "You eat today?"

She snuggled closer, kissed his chest. "Yes."

"When?"

Her head lifted. "A bagel around ten."

He came upright with her in his arms. "It won't take the steaks long to grill."

"You're taking care of me again."

"Yep. Because you're going to need your strength."

She'd worn his polo shirt while she helped him cook. They'd eaten on the terrace by candlelight. By her plate was a single hot pink rose—which she'd taken back to bed. He made her glad she had because he'd used the flower to stroke and tease her body before taking her again, this time achingly slow.

Afterward, Cicely felt more content than she had in her life. Caring for him didn't scare her. She'd waited too long for this. Thoughts of Paris tried to intrude on her, but she pushed them away. She'd think about that when and if she had to; now she was enjoying being held.

Holding her in his arms, C. J. realized that making love to Cicely, hearing her cries of pleasure, was much more pleasurable than he could have ever imagined. He stared down at her sleeping peacefully in his arms. Somehow she had come to mean a great deal to him. He wasn't sure how he felt about that, but he was sure he wasn't going anyplace. Kissing her on the forehead, he pulled the covers over them and drifted off to sleep.

* * *

Saturday morning, C. J. was awakened by the annoying ring of the phone on his bedside table. He felt Cicely's warmth, the slight weight of one leg across his, her arm thrown across his chest. He reached for the phone, intending to get rid of whoever it was as quickly as possible.

"Make it fast."

There was a slight pause. "C. J.?"

He recognized Sin's voice. "Let me call you back."

"You okay?"

"Yes, Sin, I really can't talk." Cicely stirred against him and so did his body.

There was another pause. "Would it be a fair assumption to say you're not coming to brunch and then going to the baseball game, and that you're tied up with other things."

"Yes." And enjoying every moment.

"Sorry to disturb you. Give Cicely my best."

The line went dead before he could reply. Carefully, he replaced the receiver. The game had been on the schedule for weeks. He'd looked forward to it, but once Cicely had walked though his door, he had completely forgotten about it.

Her head lifted. "Did I hear you on the phone?"

"Yes." He drew her more fully over him.

"Was it important?"

"Not as important as this." He rolled over and joined them in one sure thrust.

Saturday afternoon, Cicely had to cover a fashion show at Bloomingdale's. C. J. took her home to change, then to the event. After dropping her off, he headed to the bar to wait for her to finish. The usual crowd was there, yelling at the umpire, the Red Sox. The bar was as busy as he'd ever seen it, yet the moment she called he signaled Roy that he was leaving. He didn't look back. He made one stop on the way to her house, to pick up food.

He'd just parked in front of her brownstone when her taxi pulled up. Grabbing the handled bag, he got out of his car. She met him on the sidewalk with a smile and a kiss.

"Hi."

"Hi," he returned and watched her run up the steps in a gauzy dress with swirls of color. It amazed him that she could run and be so graceful in heels that had to be five inches.

"You coming?" she asked, going inside.

Quickly following her, he closed the door and held up the take-out bags. "Eat now or later?"

"Later." She began to unbuckle his belt. "Much later."

Hearing the take-out containers hit the floor she laughed, then moaned as C. J. cupped her breast. Yes, much later, she thought when his mouth covered hers.

Waking up with C. J. on Sunday morning definitely had its perks, but there was also something to be said for the benefits of showering with him, making love with him. The man had magic hands, a wicked mouth, and knew how to use both.

"You look awfully happy this morning," he said.

"You look smug." Lying naked on top of him, she

ran her finger across his mouth, which earlier had done incredible things to her body.

"Your fault entirely." He brushed her hair away from her face, lifted enough to kiss her lips. "Like I said, you inspire me."

The thought tried to intrude of how many women he had said those same words to. She refused to think about it. She had no right to be jealous or territorial. Except she was.

"What is it?" he asked.

Shaking her head, she lay down on his chest. "Nothing."

His hand stroked her back. "When I finally figured out the reason I tried so hard to dislike you, I quickly learned that you spoke what was on your mind the same way I do. I liked that about you."

So he wasn't easily fooled. So he expected honesty. Her head lifted. "For a moment, just a moment, I wondered how many women you'd said those same words to."

"You don't trust easily, do you?"

There was only one answer. "No." She half expected him to lift her off his body, roll out of bed, and leave. C. J. put a lot of stock, as well he should, in trust.

His hands tenderly cupped her face. She trembled with relief. "You're the first. The first woman who spent the night at my place, the first woman I've spent the night with. I wake up in my own bed alone. Fewer complications that way. Any more thoughts you'd like to share?"

"One."

"Go for it."

"How about chicken and waffles for breakfast?"

"You cooking?"

She chuckled at his doubtful expression. "Restaurant down the street."

He gave her a quick kiss. "Sounds like a plan."

Chapter 12

Monday morning, Cicely arrived thirty minutes early and in a fabulous mood. C. J. had dropped her on his way to his apartment to change and get dressed before he went to work as well. On the elevator ride up to her floor, her good mood slowly vanished. In her office, she placed her attaché case on her desk, took a seat, and picked up the phone. She couldn't put off the call any longer.

"Hello."

"Ariel?"

"Yes. Is this Cicely?"

"Yes." Too nervous to sit, Cicely came to her feet. She might be sticking her nose in where it didn't belong, but if she was right, C. J.'s family was doing him a disservice. "I've been thinking about what you said about C. J. and the family company."

"You didn't tell him I came to see him, did you?" Ariel asked, her voice panicky.

"No, but I think *you* should." Cicely paced the length of her office. "I'm not much for beating around the bush so I'll come out and ask, is Callahan Software in trouble?"

"No."

The answer came too quickly and held a hint of fear. "Ariel, if there is a concern at Callahan, C. J. has a right to know. You and your family can count on him. He might not like running the company, but he is proud of what his family has accomplished, and if it's not his dream, he is aware it's yours. He loves his family."

"It sounds as if you two have come to a decision about your relationship," Ariel evaded.

And in a very satisfactory way, Cicely thought, her body heating. "Yes. We did."

"I'm glad what I said didn't make you walk away, and I apologize," Ariel told her. "I guess I forgot what a great guy he is. Thanks for reminding me."

"You still haven't answered my original question about Callahan," Cicely reminded her.

"The Callahan women aren't kept abreast of business," Ariel said crisply.

"But you'd like to be," Cicely said.

"A lot of good it will do me," she said in frustration. "My parents, especially my mother, feel a demanding job at Callahan wouldn't allow me to have a family."

Cicely frowned. "I thought your mother was very liberal when it came to women working."

"She is, just as long as it isn't her only daughter," Ariel said. "I've developed a program that will help grocery stores keep better track of their inventory. I know companies would want it, but I won't be allowed the opportunity."

Ariel rounded her desk and sat down. "Have you spoken to C. J?"

"I was going to the other night."

"He's at his office. Give him a call," Cicely suggested.

"I think I'll wait until he comes up for his birthday party here this Sunday."

"He has a birthday coming up?" she asked, feeling a bit disappointed he hadn't told her about the party. It was probably a family affair.

"Yes." Ariel laughed. "He'll be the big thirty-five. It's supposed to be a surprise, but he knows. He has a lot of friends and business associates so the place will be packed, but you'll see for yourself."

"He hasn't invited me," Cicely said, trying not to sound hurt.

There was a slight pause. "It probably just slipped his mind."

Nothing got past C. J. "I suppose." She wasn't going to read anything into it.

"I hear Mother calling me."

Cicely wouldn't read anything into Ariel's being conveniently called away, either. "Well, good-bye, and remember what I said."

"I will. Good-bye."

During the next two days, C. J. and Cicely spent as much time together as possible. He found being with Cicely put him in a good mood, so much so that in fact he decided to show up for his surprise birthday party on Sunday. He hadn't mentioned it to Cicely because he wasn't sure he was going. Now that he was sure, he couldn't imagine her not being with him.

Grinning, he picked up the phone on his desk at work and dialed. It would save Sin and Alex the trouble of trying to come up with a way to get him there.

"Hello."

"Hi, Mom, how are you doing?"

"Hello, C. J.," she said. "You sound happy."

His grin widened. "I just thought I'd let you know I'm coming up Sunday, so you can stop bugging Alex and Sin."

"I wasn't worrying them," his mother defended. "I'm glad this year they didn't have to practically kidnap you."

Last year, Sin had told him they were going to Dallas on his private jet to watch a Texas Rangers baseball game. Instead, the limousine that was supposed to take them to the airport delivered them to his parents' house, where fifty or so of his friends were waiting. "I'm bringing a guest."

"Oh." Her voice perked up. "Anyone we know?"

"Cicely St. John," he said, hearing pride in his voice.

"Cicely St. John! Oh, Clarence, that's wonderful! She's a lovely young woman," her mother said. "It's about time you thought about settling down."

"What?" He rocked forward in his seat. He was so distressed that he forgot to correct her about calling him by his given name. He liked Cicely, but he wasn't ready for marriage. His mother was worse than Alex and Sin. "We're just dating. Don't embarrass either of us by acting as if there's more to it."

"You know I wouldn't do that," she said, sounding a bit hurt.

"Sorry, Mother," he placated, instantly contrite. "It's just that we're still getting to know each other."

"Of course."

She didn't sound convinced. "Take care, Mother. I'll see you Sunday."

"Please give Cicely my best. We'll expect you around eleven. Good-bye."

"Good-bye." C. J. hung up, wondering if he should have told his mother he was bringing Cicely. She'd sounded much too pleased with the idea.

"Why the frown?" Cicely asked as she opened the take-out container of baked beans. It was past nine, but she hadn't eaten and C. J. had picked up the food on the way to her place. It never ceased to amaze her how he seemed to effortlessly think of her.

"I called my mother today." He picked up a similar container of potato salad. However, he made no move to open it.

Cicely paused in removing the turkey and ham sandwiches from the bag. Unlike her, C. J. was close to his family. "Is she all right?"

His gaze glanced up toward her, but the frown didn't clear. "She's fine."

Deciding the direct approach was necessary, she removed the container from his hands, placed it on the table, then caught his arms, turning him toward her. "Then what's bothering you?"

Instead of answering, he asked a question of his

own. "Are you free Sunday around eleven and beyond?"

The birthday party. Her hands lowered. She was scheduled to attend a fashion brunch, then fly to Paris later that same afternoon. Cicely did some quick thinking. She'd assign Sami to cover the brunch. She deserved the opportunity. As for Paris, Cicely could catch a ride with a designer friend on her private jet Monday morning. Her schedule that day was fluid. "Yes. Why?"

He heaved out a sigh and looked uncomfortable. "My parents are giving me a birthday party Sunday and I wanted you to go with me."

"And?" she questioned, positive there was more. "What aren't you telling me?"

"When I told my mother I was bringing you, she might have gotten the wrong impression about us."

"And what impression would that be?"

"You know," he evaded.

"If I did, I wouldn't have asked."

"Like we're serious."

Cicely pushed aside the quick stab of hurt. "I hope you told her we're just dating."

Anger flashed in his eyes. "We're doing more than just dating."

Some of the ache eased. "But we're not ready to send out wedding invitations."

His head snapped back, his eyes widened. He looked shell-shocked.

She smiled. "I wish you could see your face, but

that proves my point. Now, let's finish getting this food on the table so we can eat."

He caught her arm when she started to move away. "Maybe not, but I care about you," he said, staring into her eyes.

"I care about you, too."

He nipped her ear. "How hungry are you?"

She hooked her leg around his. "Depends on the kind of hunger you're talking about."

"I can't get enough of you." He gave her a boldly erotic kiss. Lifting his head, he caught her hand and headed for the bedroom. He was grateful the covers were thrown back. Bending, he caught the hem of her clinging short black dress and pulled it over her head, tossing it toward a chair. "I've wanted to do that since I walked in the door."

She laughed and ran her tongue across the seam of his mouth. "That was the idea."

Chuckling, he caught her to him and tumbled them both into bed, then rolled to come up straddling her. "You're beautiful."

Her hand trembled as it cupped his cheek. It still threw her when he said things like that.

"You don't believe me?"

Sensing it was important to him, she grinned. "That's what my assistant thinks about you. She keeps hoping that you'll visit again."

"I'm not letting you change the subject."

"Wanna bet?" She pressed her lips to his, kissing him deeply, while her hand sought him. Raking her nails lightly over him, she felt his shudder.

Muttering, he grabbed her hand and stared into her eyes. "I have a better idea. Let me see if I can let you see what I see." His lips went to her nose, her lips, the curve of her shoulder with a gentleness that had her shivering. "Your skin is the softest I've ever touched, yet there is strength there as well." His lips moved over the swell of her breast, licked the nipple. Blew.

Air hissed though her teeth, her nails dug into his arms. He didn't seem to notice.

"Beautiful, lush, and proud. You know what it does to me to see you respond with just a touch?"

Unable to speak, she shook her head.

"You might hit me later, but I feel cocky and proud because I know it's just for me." His mouth took the turgid point of her nipple and the farthest thing from her mind was hitting him . . . until he left her breast and started kissing his way down her stomach, her legs.

"You're delicately made."

Lifting her hips, he joined them together. She met him stroke for stoke. Each time they made love was better than the last. There was tenderness, passion that strained to be free. There was fierceness this time that she reveled in. Sensation splintered through her as she felt her release, felt him reach his own satisfaction.

Rolling, he tucked her back against him as his hand continued to stroke her body, not in passion, but with tenderness.

She twisted her head until she faced him. "I'm slow. Perhaps after we eat you could show me again."

"Why can't it be now?"

"I thought you might be tired or something."

He pulled her closer to his erection. "You were saying."

"Pleasure now, eat later."

Thursday morning, C. J. arrived at work whistling. Cicely put a smile on his face. He'd never come close to enjoying a woman as much. He enjoyed her more each time he was with her.

He looked forward to her waking slowly, rubbing her sleek, elegant body against his. It aroused him so much that by the time she was fully awake he was sliding into her satin heat, stoking her, filling her, taking them on a slow easy ride of passion. He couldn't imagine waking up a better way.

Going behind his desk, he checked his schedule. There was only a meeting with marketing at two. There had to be more going on with running the company, but everyone was still avoiding him. That stopped today. He wasn't a man to sit around doing nothing.

His brother and father had entrusted him to run the company, and he'd done very little of that. He thought the employees would eventually come around and learn to look to him for leadership, advice.

His father and his brother hadn't gotten their health problems by sitting behind a desk being bored for eight hours. The software business was highly competitive. Just as his bar had to have something to draw the patrons into Callahan's instead of the hundreds of other bars in the city, Callahan Software had to offer that something.

As the CEO, he had to be on top of things, and he hadn't been. There was no way he was going to let the company take a nosedive because his employees feared involving him in their projects or concerns in case he didn't want to deal with them and bailed.

He punched in the intercom button. "Alice."

"Yes, Mr. Callahan."

"I'd like to see the quarterly reports for the past year, and please have all the department heads call me, starting in fifteen minutes at ten-minute intervals. Start with program development and end with marketing," he told her.

There was a slight pause, then "Yes, sir. I'll call them right away." The line went dead.

C. J. rocked forward in his chair. He understood his secretary's hesitation. Another person who thought he wouldn't stick it out. Heaven only knew what she thought of his sudden interest in the company.

There came a brief knock on his door. "Mr. Callahan?"

"Come in, Alice."

Her back arrow-straight as usual, his secretary crossed the room and placed the thick file on his desk. "If you have any concerns, I'm sure the department heads would be happy to discuss them with you when they call."

He didn't take offense at her suggestion. He'd showed no interest in running Callahan before now. "Thank you, but I'd rather read it for myself." He pulled the thick bound report toward him. "That will be all. Please notify the departments and put them through as soon as they call."

"Yes, sir." Turning, she left the room, closing the door softly behind her.

C. J. opened the report, wondering why his brother's old secretary—whom Paul had called unflappable—seemed worried. But he dismissed it as he began to read.

He stopped to take the first phone call, and the ones afterward. He asked each department head to have a full report ready to give him on Monday. By then he would have finished the quarterly reports. He'd expected the excuses and flatly told each his request wasn't negotiable. He'd finished the calls and went back to reading the report.

He might not want to be there, but he certainly planned to leave the company in as good a financial position as when he arrived—or better. For some odd reason, he thought about the future of his niece and nephew. Perhaps that's what his brother's worry was all about, his family's security.

He told Cicely as much late that night on the phone. She'd had to attend a private opening of a boutique. He'd considered dropping by, but hadn't wanted to disturb her at work. And he didn't want Lenora to give her any grief. Like a teenager, he'd dived for the phone the second it rang on the table, then hearing her voice he'd muted the sound on the television, and settled in to talk until he heard her yawn a couple of times.

She'd been as reluctant as he was to hang up. She, indeed, worked hard. It made him feel like a slacker, knowing all he had planned for that week was to check over the new program designed for a school district's health service that would allow them to track students' clinic visits and their health screenings more efficiently. He'd had to practically insist on the information. His father and brother had gotten stress and he was getting a sore butt.

In his office the next morning, he opened the report for the second to last quarter. Callahan's future was in his hands and he intended it to be solvent for his niece and nephew and beyond. He wasn't sure why he was thinking more about the future—perhaps because it was getting closer to the day when the new editor-in-chief would be named for the Paris office.

He flipped another page of the report. He'd continue to take one day at a time with Cicely and enjoy each moment. Her busy schedule just made the time they did see each other that much better.

He was halfway down the page when he saw figures that didn't add up. He flipped back a page, then read the next page. The figures stayed the same. Quickly, he turned to the end of the report, then pulled the final quarterly report in front of him and went to the last page.

He didn't want to believe it, but there it was in black and white. Profits at Callahan had been down the last two quarters. "How can this be?" he murmured. Surely his father and brother would have told him if the company was in financial trouble. He'd soon find out.

He jabbed the intercom. "I want to see the head of each department in my office now. No excuses."

In less than two minutes, the men were there. To a man their gaze went to the report on his desk. C. J. could see the fear in their eyes. They'd known.

"James, you're head of marketing and were in charge after Paul became ill." C. J. rounded the desk and picked up the report. "What happened?"

"That's not my fault," the man blurted, his eyes flickering to the report, then back to C. J. "You can see sales were down even before Paul left. These are tough times."

"When I asked for a report from each department, why wasn't I told about this?"

"I was instructed not to by your father. You'll have to ask him," James replied.

That hurt. His family didn't trust him, either. "That will be all."

C. J. had the phone in his hand, dialing his father's number before the last man hurriedly left, closing the door behind them.

"Hello."

His grip on the phone tightened on hearing his mother's voice. He wondered if she had known. His father usually discussed everything with her. "Is Dad there?"

"Yes, he's down at the boat with Paul. Is anything wrong?" she asked.

"I just need to discuss something." If she was as

in the dark as he was, there was no sense worrying her. "Can you tell them I'm on my way."

"Today? Now. You sure nothing is wrong?"

"Positive. I just need their thoughts on something. Bye." Hanging up the phone, he started for the door. His father and brother had a great deal of explaining to do.

Chapter 13

During the drive, C. J.'s hurt feelings evolved into anger that they hadn't confided in him. By the time he pulled up in the circular driveway in front of the house, his brother and father were on the porch. Neither was smiling as they had been the last time he'd seen them.

Getting out of his car, he slammed the door. "I always thought that despite everything, we would be up front and honest with each other."

His father visibly winced. "We'll talk in the study." Without waiting for C. J. to comply, his father entered the house. C. J. was right behind him. His silent brother brought up the rear.

The study door had barely closed before C. J. spoke again. "Why didn't you tell me the company was in trouble?"

"I take full responsibility," Paul said, his expression somber. "Dad wanted to tell you. But I convinced him not to."

C. J. whirled on his brother. "Just tell me why."

Paul glanced at his father. "We all knew that you didn't want the job. If we'd told you that the company was going through a tough time, we weren't sure you'd take it."

Hurt and disbelief splintered through him. "How could you think that? How could you think I wouldn't do everything in my power to help my family? I love you. Apparently you don't love or trust me." Whirling, he headed for the door, brushing past his brother, who looked stunned and remorseful.

"Don't you take another step," his father roared.

Long years of obedience stopped C. J. in his tracks.

"That's a lie I won't listen to. I loved you from the moment I knew of your existence, and that love has only become stronger as I watched you grow up to be a man I've always been proud to call my son. Now be the man I know you to be, and face me. I let you have your say, now it's my turn."

Love and respect had C. J. turning, but the ache in his chest grew more painful with each breath.

His father crossed to C. J. and clutched his forearm, his gaze direct. "Blame us for being scared, but not for not loving you. Once you have your own family, perhaps you'll understand that with love comes responsibility." His father swallowed. "It wasn't just ourselves we were thinking about, it was your mother, Ariel, Paul's family."

"Then, too," Paul said, stepping closer. "It wasn't your problem."

His father nodded. "Neither one of us wanted to ask you to clean up a mess we'd made. A bit of pride, perhaps, but it didn't sit well with either of us. We kept waiting for you to find out, dreading the day.

It's a relief to get it out in the open. I know it's a shock, but please try to understand. It's hard when you've given your best and it's still not enough."

There was a brief knock on the door before it opened. C. J. wasn't surprised to see his mother. Neither his sister nor the servants would have dared come in without permission. Lines of strain bracketed her mouth. She must have heard everything. He'd certainly been shouting loudly enough.

"Callahan Software can fail, but it will not tear this family apart," she said firmly, catching her husband's and C. J.'s hands. "I won't have it."

Ariel came in behind her mother and closed the door. "I think I've found a way to help the company."

"No." Releasing their hands, her mother moved to curve her arm around Ariel's shoulder. "I'd hoped to keep this from you, but you must realize how much time and dedication it takes to run a company."

C. J. winced this time. He should have become involved from day one. He'd wasted valuable time whining when he should have been working hard to get the company back on its feet.

"You'll have no chance of a family. Some women are meant to be homemakers. Now, let's leave your father and brothers to figure out what to do next," her mother said.

"I want to stay, Mother," Ariel protested, but it did little good. Still holding her daughter's arm, her mother kept walking.

"Things have changed, Mother. Women can have a career and a marriage," Ariel tried one last time.

"But one will suffer." With those last words, her mother opened the door and left, taking Ariel with her.

For just a moment, C. J. thought of Cicely. They weren't in this for forever, but so far they hadn't let her hectic schedule come between them.

"Thanks for staying, C. J. I hope this means you're willing to listen," his father said.

"We need you," Paul said. "I'd go back but my doctor won't release me, and if I do anyway, I stand to lose my insurance. When Sharon heard me talking to Dad about going in, she wasn't too happy with me."

"Are you crazy?" C. J. turned on his brother.

"The company's profits started declining under my leadership." Paul glanced away, then met C. J.'s gaze. "It's my responsibility to fix things."

"Not at the risk of your health," C. J. told him. "If you come to the office, I'm calling Sharon."

The look of fear on his brother's face almost made C. J. laugh. Sharon was easygoing until it came to her family; then she was in the league with his mother. Mess with those she loved, and suffer the consequences.

"Does . . . does that mean you're willing to stay for a bit?" his father carefully asked.

C. J. glanced first at the hopeful expression of his father. His brother wore the same expression. He felt trapped.

"It's all right, son," his father said. "We'll think of something."

"Sure we will," Paul added, trying to sound cheerful and failing miserably.

How? What? The words swirled around in C. J.'s head. He was it and they all knew it.

He'd always known and accepted that he thought differently than his father and brother. His work habit was to roll with the punches, one reason he didn't want the nine-to-five job of being regimented—deep down he didn't want people depending on him.

"I need to think." He walked to the windows with the floor-to-ceiling swag draperies his mother had insisted on, and stared out at the boats on the calm water. Callahan wasn't just a company, it was tradition built with pride and a strong work ethic. Failure would be a blow that he wasn't sure his father or brother would recover from.

What would he have done if Callahan's Bar had faltered instead of thrived? What if he'd had to turn it over to someone who openly didn't want to be there? He easily recalled the strain and sacrifice on his father and grandfather's faces after a long day, even that of his brother. They'd do whatever it took to keep Callahan Software solvent. Would he have done any less for Callahan's Bar?

His mind made up, he crossed to them. "I'll do everything in my power to bring profits up." He extended his hand to his brother and father. "Now, let's get to work, and try to figure out what's causing the drag and how to fix it."

"Take a seat behind my desk," his father offered.

The gesture was more than symbolic and caused

C. J. to feel pride he didn't recall feeling before. "All right. And, Paul?"

"Yes?"

"I meant it when I said I'd call Sharon."

"Now that you know the score and are ready to work, you won't have to."

Two hours later, C. J. walked out of his parents' house. His father's attaché case in his hand was filled with notes. It wouldn't be easy, but he was turning the company around.

He smiled on seeing Ariel waving to him from the end of the drive. Tossing the attaché case in the backseat, he pulled the car up to where she had been waiting, obviously trying to evade being seen by their mother.

Rounding the car, she got in. "You have Dad's case. Does that mean what I think it does?"

"I'm going to do everything in my power to turn the company around," he said. Callahan wouldn't go under on his watch.

"I'm glad." She folded her hands primly in her lap. "Dad and Paul didn't tell you because they didn't want to do anything to make you leave again. We love you."

But they didn't trust him to stick. That still bothered him, but perhaps he hadn't given them a reason to think anything else. He planned to change that. "I'm staying."

She moistened her lips and turned to him. "I've been working on a program that will impact grocery stores. I also have some marketing ideas," she said. "I could help. I want to help."

He didn't have to think about his answer. "Be in my office at nine Monday morning. This is a family business. You should be a part of it. I'll help you work on Mother."

Screaming, she hugged him. "Cicely was right about you."

"What?" He frowned. "When did you talk with Cicely?"

"Over two weeks ago," she told him. "I'd come to the bar to talk with you, but you were in your office. I'd heard Dad and Paul talking and realized the company was in trouble. I was afraid you would walk away and go back to the bar. That you wouldn't stick. She made me see things differently."

Cicely had known and hadn't told him. He'd deal with that later. "Differently how?"

"You always treated me as if I could do anything. I doubted myself and made you the cause." She shook her head of long black hair. "It makes me a bit ashamed that Cicely had more faith in you than I did. I let my fear rule me. Cicely never did. I'm glad you're seeing each other." Leaning over, she kissed him on the cheek. "Bye. I'll see you Sunday. I can't wait to give Cicely a hug and thank her for helping me to remember what a great big brother I have."

Ariel ran back around the side of the house. She might have run faster if she had seen the angry expression on her brother's face.

* * *

Growing angrier by the minute, C. J. drove back to New York. He easily recalled Cicely asking him the first night they made love if he would tire of her. Like his family, she didn't think he would stay around. Apparently she was really just killing time until her Paris appointment came through. He'd thought they meant something to each other, thought they were honest with each other.

Leaving his car at his apartment, he took a cab to her office. She had fooled him completely.

It was an effort to contain his anger on the elevator ride to her floor. Exiting, he stopped at the receptionist. "Cicely St. John's office please."

"Is she expecting you?"

"No, but I'm a close friend," he said, smiling. He'd use charm if he had to.

The woman studied him instead of smiling. "You're the one. The one who brought the staff food. The one she rushes home to meet."

He wouldn't find comfort in that. She was just killing time. "Yes."

The smile finally came. Standing, she peered over the top of the wooden counter before retaking her seat. "I just wondered if you'd brought anything today."

"Just me."

"I'd say that was enough." She pointed down the hall to the right. "Next to the last door on the right. Her assistant just went to lunch."

"Thanks." He went down the hall and opened the door to the assistant's office. He didn't bother to knock, just opened Cicely's door, closing it softly when he really wanted to slam it shut.

Cicely's head came up. Surprise, then pleasure widened her eyes. Smiling, she started around the desk. "What a—" Her words abruptly stopped and so did she. "C. J., what's the matter?"

"Why didn't you tell me about Ariel's visit to the bar? About the company being in financial trouble?"

She slipped her hands into the pockets of her black slacks. "It wasn't my place."

"Not even when we started sleeping together?" he yelled, no longer able to contain his anger.

Her chin came up. "I can understand anger, but you want blood."

"I expected you to be honest with me. You're not the woman I thought you were. Good-bye." Turning, he opened the door and barely caught himself before slamming it. Going through the outer office into the hallway, he started down the hallway. Yet no matter how fast he walked he couldn't get the picture of hurt and disbelief on Cicely's face out of his mind.

Cicely refused to cry. She had foolishly thrown caution to the wind and followed her heart. She could regret it and be miserable or believe that once C. J. calmed down he'd figure out that it had taken a large leap of faith to offer him her body and give him her heart.

If he didn't . . .

Cicely went back to her desk and continued making appointments for her trip to Paris on Monday for four days for Paris Fashion Week. She'd planned to tell C. J. about the trip after his birthday party. That wasn't about to happen now.

C. J. took a cab to work. He stopped at his secretary's desk. "From now on, you owe your loyalty to me. I need someone I can trust. If you can't be that person . . ."

She swallowed. "What is it that you need, Mr. Callahan?"

"Call me C. J. I need all the department heads in the conference room in five minutes. I want you there as well to take notes. Route the phone until we get back. I'll wait in the conference room."

By the time he opened his door, his secretary was already speaking, "Elton, meet Mr. Callahan in the conference room in four minutes,"

C. J., standing at the head of the conference table with his shirtsleeves rolled up, pointedly looked at his wristwatch when Thomas Dean, the head of public relations, sauntered into the room two minutes late with a cell phone to his ear. C. J. waited the thirty seconds it took for him to finish his conversation.

"Was that a business call?" C. J. asked. Thomas paused with his hand on the back of the seat. "Before you answer, think carefully. I might have left things in the hands of the department heads because I thought they were going well. I learned today they're not." He looked at the head of his HR department. "Ms. Parsons isn't here just to occupy a space. Your job might be on the line."

Thomas tugged at his tie. "My girlfriend. Sometimes it's difficult to get her off the phone."

C. J. might have had sympathy if he'd given any other excuse. "I suggest you find a way and don't be late to my meeting again. Is that understood?"

"Yes."

C. J. straightened. "Please take a seat. I called this meeting to see where we are on delivering contracted programs, and determine how close we are to acquiring new contracts." He looked at Thomas. "You first."

C. J. took his seat and listened to Thomas tell him about the tough economic times, and how people weren't buying as much as they were. The reports from project development and marketing weren't much better. They were good people; his father and brother wouldn't have kept them otherwise.

"This company can't survive on excuses, so leave them at the door. We make the impossible possible. Thomas, I suggest you tell your girlfriend she might not be seeing you as frequently. If there's a problem with the program integrating with the other systems, find out what it is and fix it. I'll look it over personally."

They looked at each other.

"Have you forgotten I developed computer games? I know how to write programs. Come to work Monday ready to put in the hours it's going to take to make things happen. They won't happen by themselves. In the meantime, Thomas, you and I are going to contact all the firms we've sold to within the past year. Customer service always has been and always will be key. How many clients are you calling weekly to see how things are going, if you can be of any assistance?"

Thomas bristled. "Of course I contact them after the sale, but I don't check back after a couple of weeks. That would take too much time."

"Make the time," C. J. said. "If you don't have time for them, they'll feel the same way about you. Callahan has to be not just about selling the program, but being there for the customer for the long run. New program needs occur all the time. How likely do you think the client will be to purchase again if he only hears from you when you're trying to sell something?"

"Not very," Thomas admitted slowly.

"Exactly." C. J. glanced down at the files on the table. "I want the name of the contact person and their phone number of every sale within the last quarter on my desk within the hour. I'm going to call them. You take the two quarters before."

He looked at the head of marketing. "Marketing has to up their game. We have to think of innovative ways to get Callahan out there."

"Advertising is expensive," Elton said.

"Then find unconventional ways," he told him. "This is a company founded on ideas. We need something that will get a company's attention and let them know that if they have program needs, Callahan can develop them." He turned to the head of program development. "You're up next, Perry."

Perry Wallace, balding and in his midfifties, glanced around the table before speaking. "The bank-

ing program we're working on will take at least another couple of months to complete," he said.

"Make it five weeks. I'll look at it myself Monday." C. J. stared at everyone in the room. "I don't
have to tell you that we're in a fight I plan to win. If
you can't give your all, see HR, but before you do,
please know that I value each and every one of you.
You helped build Callahan."

"I'll get you the phone numbers," the PR head
quickly said.

"I'll get to work on shaving the time," Perry told
him

"I'll come up with some ideas to get us out there,"
Elton said.

"Thank you." C. J. came to his feet. This was the
cooperation he'd hoped for. "This meeting is ad-
journed."

The department heads piled out of the conference
room. C. J. picked up his stack of notes.

"You remind me of your brother," his secretary
said.

"I just hope I can be as good as he was."

"You're off to a fine start." She held the pad to her
chest. "I'll get these notes typed up and on your
desk."

"Thanks." C. J. followed her out the door. Working together, they could turn the company around.

"No one is going to leave. They believe in you,"
she said.

He thought of Ariel saying Cicely believed in him
and pushed it away. "Let's get to work."

* * *

With the list of their most recent accounts in front of him, C. J. began making phone calls. With some, he had to leave a message; others, he was able to speak directly with the department head where the program was being used. After introducing himself, he always gave the same positive spiel.

"Thank you again for relying on Callahan to make your business run more smoothly. As the new CEO, I just wanted to touch base with you and remind you that, if you have any questions, feel free to call me or the account manager."

Thankfully, no one had any problems. A couple of the account reps had minor questions about connection issues that he easily answered or solved.

He ended each conversation by saying that the calls would be monthly from the person assigned to handle their account so they would always have the same person, but if they had a problem not to hesitate to get in touch.

The people he spoke with seemed genuinely pleased and impressed that the CEO of Callahan had called. "When you're a client of Callahan, you have the entire staff at your disposal."

"That's good to know."

"Good-bye, Mrs. Williams." As soon as he heard the director of nursing at a large midwestern hospital hang up, he disconnected the call and dialed the next company, Eagle Automotive in Los Angeles, the third largest supplier of automobile parts in the country.

Because of the time difference, C. J. was able to talk to the vice president of operations, and he made two calls after that. By the time 8:00 PM rolled around, he had made twenty-nine phone calls. He'd make more Monday.

Leaning back in his chair, C. J. stretched his arms over his head, rolled his neck and shoulders. His muscles were tight. He'd been hunched over his desk for almost five hours. He refused to entertain that some of the tension was due to his breakup with Cicely.

He reached for the notes he'd made when speaking with his father and Paul. Profits had started to decline when Paul had to cut back the time he spent with follow-up calls or visits to prospective clients. He had also made the mistake of letting program development work on programs they "thought" companies would need instead of developing programs contracted for by companies. That was changing.

He'd look at Ariel's program. But they wouldn't take one minute on development unless they had a company interested. They couldn't afford the manpower hours and expense of developing another program they couldn't sell. He hoped marketing could find an interested company and then, once they saw what Callahan could do, get the sale.

Paul had been a top salesperson. He had a winning way with people, and could explain the products in simple terms, making the person believe that those on his staff who were over thirty years of age wouldn't mutiny when they had to learn a new way of doing their jobs. The big boss might want a change, but those who would actually be doing the work, especially older employees, usually weren't so receptive.

Now that job of selling would fall to C. J. He

could charm most people, especially women, or at least he once could. Pushing up from his desk, he shoved the papers into the attaché case. There was nothing more he could do until Monday. He'd give everyone time to regroup and recommit.

Whatever happened, he planned to be ready to lead. Callahan was coming back strong. Picking up the case, he left the office.

Chapter 14

Cicely made herself get ready for the baby shower of co-worker Ginger Adams. She'd told the expectant mother the other day that she wouldn't be able to make it. Ginger, being sweet and in love, with a twinkle in her eyes and having heard about C. J., said she understood.

She wasn't sure what excuse she'd give for showing up, but she wasn't staying at home no matter how much she wanted to in case C. J. came to his senses and came over to beg her for forgiveness.

Since she loved him, she would.

Cicely stopped brushing on her lipstick and stared at her reflection in the mirror. Her eyes looked too big for her face. At least they weren't red and puffy.

She could take pride that she hadn't cried, had been able to tell the receptionist who asked about C. J.'s abrupt leaving that he was just late for a meeting. She'd said it with a smile when her heart had been breaking.

Putting the brush away, she closed the compact and dropped it into her nearby handbag. This wasn't supposed to be happening to her. Her life was planned, but as Dianne had said, she wouldn't trade not finding love for the heartache.

Turning the light off, she went to the front room and picked up the gigantic pink gift bag full of fashionable accessories well-dressed babies were supposed to have, including monogrammed cloth diapers, blankets, and bibs.

Ginger was ecstatic about being a mother for the first time, and so was her husband of two years. She hadn't seemed to mind that she had been passed over for the promotion to art director.

Lenora, in her straightforward way, had told her that the magazine needed someone who could work the long hours demanded and also travel. Ginger had placed her hand on her bulging stomach and said her baby came first, and that she was content being an assistant.

Cicely would never be content settling. She wanted to reach the top, but reaching the top sometimes meant reaching it alone.

Loud music from the jukebox greeted C. J. as he entered his office from the back door. The Yankees were playing tomorrow and their loyal fans were getting ready. He'd planned to take Cicely. He scowled, tossed his keys on his desk, and went into the bar.

Greeting a few regulars, he started cleaning up tables, taking orders, trying to smile when teased by some of the patrons that he wasn't as pretty as their waitress, Piper. He took the teasing in stride, and replied that they weren't, either, so they were even.

"Hey, boss," Piper greeted, picking up a stack of dirty dishes from a table. "Cicely have to work tonight?"

He couldn't keep the anger from rushing across his face.

The waitress's eyes widened. She held up one hand. "Forget I asked. I like my head where it is."

He caught up with her as she was going through the swinging door into the kitchen. "Sorry."

She smiled. "Forget it. I've been there. It sucks."

"You'll find someone else," he said. Piper was a good woman.

"But I wanted him." She bit her lower lip, shook her head, then held up the dishes. "I better get to work before the boss fires me."

C. J. caught the door as it swung toward him. *But I wanted him.* For Piper, there was no substitute.

"Hey, C. J., can you help at the bar for a bit while I restock?" Frank, one of his bartenders, asked.

"Sure." C. J. moved behind the bar. Just because Piper couldn't forget some guy who'd probably cheated on her was no reason to think he would be the same way. Women had always come easy to him. Confident he was right, he asked the first man he saw without a drink in front of him, "What will you have?"

Two hours later, when the bar was under control, C. J. left. For once Callahan's hadn't helped smooth out the rough edges. He was restless and he knew exactly the annoying reason. He couldn't stop thinking about Cicely.

Starting the car, he backed out and went home. In

the elevator, he punched Alex's floor instead of his. He wasn't ready to listen to his own thoughts. Ringing the doorbell, he shoved his hands into the pockets of his slacks.

He waited, then lifted his hand to ring the doorbell again before it hit him that they were probably doing what he'd intended to be doing with Cicely. Head lowered, he started back down the hall.

"C. J."

He turned to see Alex and Dianne, grinning, their arms around each other, her hair disheveled, her blouse out of her skirt, and his unbuttoned shirt out of his slacks.

"I'll catch you later."

Frowning, Alex released Dianne and went to C. J, buttoning his shirt on the way. "You all right?"

He rammed his hands into the pockets of his slacks and stared down at the floor. "Yeah." He felt like hell. His insides were in knots.

Concern on her face, Dianne joined them, placing a hand on C. J.'s tense shoulder. "Did you and Cicely have a fight?"

He hunched his shoulders. "Sort of."

"Bring him inside, Alex," Dianne said. "I'll get you two a couple of beers."

The crazy thought ran through C. J.'s head that Cicely hated beer. "None for me." Inside the apartment, C. J. took the same seat he and Cicely had shared the night of Dianne and Alex's first dinner party.

"You want to talk about it?" Alex asked.

"I have some work to do in the office." Kissing

Alex, she left. A few seconds later he heard the sound of the door closing.

"I think I might have misjudged Cicely," C. J. said, misery in every word. While he was still smarting a bit from his family not leveling with him, learning Cicely had known had been like a punch in the gut. He'd taken his anger and hurt feelings out on her.

"You let your temper get the best of you," Alex said. "You must really care about her. No other woman ever got to you the way she does."

He was too unhappy to deny it. Worse, he now realized this was his fault. Cicely was honest. She wasn't into subterfuge. It had taken more courage for her to make love with him than to walk away, especially considering she hadn't let many people into her life.

"Well, are you going to sit here miserable, keeping me from my woman or go find yours and beg her to forgive you?"

"She's not my woman," C. J. said.

"But you want her to be. You're just too stubborn to admit it."

"Things are different between us," C. J. said, but from the look on Alex's face, he wasn't buying it. "I mean it. You've always been the serious one. You got lucky with Dianne."

"Luck had nothing to do with it." Alex leaned forward in his chair, his expression serious. "I saw my chance to make her mine and I took it. Sometimes we only get one opportunity."

C. J. frowned, his worry about his earlier behavior increasing. "Cicely impresses me as a woman who can keep a grudge and make you regret pissing her off."

"Then you'll just have to change her mind." Alex stood and took C. J. by the arm. "Get out of here, and put both of you out of your misery."

C. J. grinned. "You just want me gone so you can get your hands on Dianne."

"True, but I also want you to be happy." Alex stopped in front of the door. "I also happen to like Cicely."

"She's wonderful. She gives her all. I've never met a woman like her," C. J. said.

"Shouldn't you be telling *her*?"

C. J. slapped Alex on the shoulder. "I will, among other things. Thanks. Kiss Dianne for me, and tell her thanks for letting me barge in on you two."

"Thank us both by making up with Cicely."

"It's as good as done." Grinning, C. J. pulled his iPhone from his pocket, dialing her cell phone as he continued down the hall to the elevator.

"Cicely St. John, fashion director of *Fashion Insider*. Leave a message or call back later."

"Cicely, it's C. J. Call me when you get this."

Slightly annoyed that she didn't pick up, but admitting that it was no more than he probably deserved for what he'd put her though, he called her home and got her answering machine. "Cicely, it's C. J. Call me."

Stepping into the elevator, he punched G for the garage. She should be at home. They were supposed to spend the evening at her place. She didn't have anything on her schedule.

In his car, he headed for Harlem. She was just probably being stubborn. In less than thirty minutes he was on her doorstep, ringing her doorbell. There was the usual light she kept on upstairs, the glow from the lamp in the living room.

She could be in her office in the back of the house. He called her on her cell and house phones again, and listened to the messages on her answering machines.

He didn't know whether to be annoyed or concerned for her safety. He made another call. It was answered abruptly on the fifth ring.

"C. J., you're really pushing our friendship."

Well aware that Alex was annoyed rather than really angry, C. J. dismissed the snarl in his voice and rushed on to tell him, "Cicely won't answer her cell, her house phone, or her door. She was supposed to be with me, so she should be at home. I don't know if she's pissed at me or if I should be worried. I know she can take care of herself, but . . ." His voice trailed off. He swallowed and shoved his hand over his head.

"Pissed would be my guess. Hold on while Dianne calls her on her cell."

"Thanks." C. J. stared at her house. "She should be at home."

"Women, I've learned, never do what you expect them to. It's one of their many appeals."

"I just want to know she's safe." C. J. paced in front of the steps.

"She's safe. Dianne has her on the phone, but Dianne left the bedroom to talk to her."

There was a hint of worry in Alex's voice. "What?

Why did Dianne do that? Did she tell Cicely I want to talk to her?"

"I'm not sure, and since I have no intention of spending the night on the sofa, we'll just have to wait until one or both of them are ready to let us know what's going on."

C. J. stared at the phone before raising it to his ear. Alex wasn't afraid of anything. In the courtroom he went for the jugular, especially if you were trying to screw over his client. "You serious?"

"As a heart attack, as they say. You can't push a woman. She'll push back and she'll do it meaner," Alex said with complete conviction.

Shaking his head, C. J. leaned against his car and crossed one leg over the other. He had that right. Cicely didn't push worth a damn. "You can't have learned that in the short time you've been married."

"Life lessons from my mother and baby sister. Now go sit in your car, put on Maya's new CD, and I'll call you as soon as I know anything."

"Can you at least peep and try to gauge from Dianne's expression how much trouble I'm in?"

"Nope, because I don't want to be in the same trouble. Chill, and hang tight."

C. J. disconnected the call, but he was too nervous to sit down. What if she didn't want to forgive him? The little voice that said *It's your own fault* wasn't comforting.

"All right, Dianne. I can talk now," Cicely said, stepping outside the apartment building. She'd ignored C. J.'s name on her caller ID because she'd wanted him to stew in his own juices for a bit longer. She'd accepted Dianne's call because she'd needed to talk to a friend. The moment Dianne mentioned that C. J. was worried about her and looking for her, Cicely had asked her to hold, bid the baby shower hostess and Ginger good night, and left.

"C. J. came by here tonight, looking worse than the night you didn't show up for the pool game. I went to my office while he and Alex had their man-to-man and then he left. He called back later, worried when he couldn't contact you."

"I ignored his calls," she said with satisfaction.

Dianne chuckled. "C. J. has met his match."

Cicely's lips curved into a smile. The evening was definitely looking up. "Where is he?"

"At your place," Dianne told her. "I think he's in a groveling mood. If you're interested, you might want to hurry home."

She'd already started walking. She'd taken a cab over because of the gift bag. "I'm interested."

"Thought so. I'll call him, and tell him you're on your way. It's better if they grovel in person."

"Alex?"

"No. Me. It was a night we'll both remember." Dianne's laugh was pure wickedness.

Cicely's laughter joined hers. "Good-bye, and thanks."

"We're glad to help. 'Night."

C. J. had his iPhone in his hand when it rang. "Where is she? Is she all right? When is she coming home? Does she know I want to talk to her?"

"She's on her way home," Dianne calmly told him. "I told her you were in a groveling mood. Make it good. 'Night."

C. J. might have taken exception to Dianne's phrasing if he weren't so relieved that Cicely was all right and coming home. He could finally relax. He took a seat on the steps to wait. If Cicely forgave him that was all that mattered. If it took groveling, it would be a small price.

C. J. saw Cicely when she was half a block away. He wanted to run to her, hold her. He made himself stay where he was. He didn't want her to brush him off before he got a chance to ask her to forgive him.

She stopped a few feet away. "C. J."

Her voice was clipped. She was rightly pissed. He had to talk fast. "You're honest and up front. I was wrong. I shouldn't have taken my anger and frustrations out on you."

Lifting a brow, she folded her arms. "Are you finished?"

"No, not by a long shot, but what I have to say is rather personal and I'd rather not say it out here."

Unfolding her arms, she brushed by him, went up the steps, and opened her door. C. J. was right behind her when she stepped inside. "You were saying."

"I get that it took more courage to make love with me. I also get that Paris means a lot to you. I'm firmly in your corner on that. I'm not sure how I'll handle it when you leave, but I'll be happy for you. You need to be focused, just as I need to be focused for the coming weeks to turn my family's business around. One thing I don't want is for either of us to be worried about our relationship."

"Relationship?"

"Yes, relationship," he said firmly. "I don't know where this is going, but I know being with you is where I want to be, and I'm hoping you feel the same way."

"Finished?"

He wasn't sure. "For the moment."

Her mouth twitched and he breathed a little easier. "I'm glad Ariel decided to go after what she wants, and you had a talk with your family about the business."

"Why didn't you tell me about your conversation with her?"

"As I said, it wasn't my place," she said. "In my office, were you angry with me or yourself?"

"Myself. I should have discovered the problem weeks ago. I was a jerk."

"Self-discovery is good," she said with absolute conviction.

Laughing, he kissed her, or at least tried to. Their lips had barely met before she pushed out of his arms. "You can make me angrier than anyone I know and that's saying a lot considering some of the people I work with. I finally realized it's because I care about you," she admitted.

"You were blindsided about the company and might not have been thinking too clearly. I'll give you that one, but you had better be on your best behavior from now on. Just because your eyes draw me as much as your voice, which caresses and soothes me even when I try to fight it, they won't give you another pass."

Moved, C. J. kissed her again. This time she was with him all the way. The heat and the need quickly built.

Cicely felt herself being caught up in a whirlwind of passion, and all she could do was hold on to C. J. She was fire burning in his arms. It felt so incredibly right. Their lovemaking had never been so intense. She went to sleep with a smile on her face.

Cicely awakened the next morning with C. J. beside her, his hand propped under his chin as he stared down at her. Smiling, she cupped his face. "Good morning."

"Good morning. Can you spend part of the day with me? I want to take you to a Yankees game."

C. J. took his baseball seriously. "I have to finish a layout. What time does the game start?"

"One thirty."

She pushed at his shoulder and got out of bed. "Then we better shower and eat breakfast so I can finish."

Grinning, enjoying the sight of her naked, elegant body, he debated whether he should follow her into the bathroom. If he did, he'd make love to her. He wasn't sure how much time she needed to finish. Shaking his head, he pulled on his Jockey shorts and pants, and went to the kitchen to start breakfast.

C. J. looked at his watch. Eleven thirteen. Cicely had been at it for over two hours. Since there was a Yankees game, the bar was opening earlier. He could go by to check on things, but he decided to stick around until she finished.

He wandered into the dining room with its silk-covered walls, polished-antique Chippendale table, and padded chairs with a color scheme of yellows, beiges, and creams. Across the hall in the living room was a formal sofa with a built-in case for books. On the shelves were awards, and framed and signed *Fashion Insider* magazine covers. He was pleased to see that one of the covers was of his mother and sister.

His pleasure dimmed when he didn't see any personal photos of her and her family. She deserved so much, and accepted that she wasn't going to get it. The thought made him want to shake her and then her uncaring parents. Didn't they realize what an amazing woman she had grown into?

His troubled gaze went back to her office down the hall. He'd peeked in earlier to check on her. She was hunched over her writing desk, her eyes narrowed in concentration on her computer screen, her hand on her mouse.

She'd looked up and smiled. Just her smile had made him feel . . . happy. He shook his head. He didn't think he'd ever been on such a roller-coaster ride of emotions as he was with Cicely. From the way he caught her looking at him at times, they were in the same boat.

He needed to walk. He wandered outside to the backyard. The grass was surprisingly green and manicured, but unlike his mother's yard there were no flowers. Lines radiated across his forehead. Cicely liked flowers. There were flowers—daisies and carnations—on her nightstand and long stems of gladiolas in a crystal vase on the polished dining table.

He paid attention—albeit occasionally for ungentlemanly reasons—to what she wore, so he easily recalled that she wore floral prints and had floral influences in her home. He didn't have to think long to figure out why her yard was bare of flowers.

Her hectic schedule didn't allow her time to care for them. And although she obviously had someone cut the yard, it was so small, they wouldn't come often enough to care for flowers.

Stepping farther into the yard, he saw a two-tiered stone fountain—only there was no water. He started toward it. She might not have any flowers, but there was no reason she should do without her fountain.

Cicely saved the file, shut down the computer, and went in search of C. J. She hadn't heard the television, or perhaps she had just tuned it out the way she did everything when she was working . . . or at least used to.

The man she was looking for had changed that, and that was never more evident than in the disappointment she felt when she didn't see him in the living room or kitchen. He wouldn't leave without saying good-bye. Seeing his car proved her point. He wouldn't have gone upstairs. The front door was still locked from the inside so he hadn't taken a walk.

Turning, she retraced her steps to the kitchen and went out the back door. He stood at the far corner of the yard with his hands on his hips staring down. "It doesn't work," she said.

His head lifted. Turning, a wide grin on his face, he stepped aside. "It does now."

She squealed like a teenager meeting her favorite rock star, and rushed across the yard. Reaching out her hand, she let the running water trickle through her fingers. "I paid a fortune to have an electric socket put out here only to have the yard guy not be able to fix it. It belonged to my grandmother."

"The wires were messed up."

She glanced down at the tools she kept in the closet in her utility room and never used. The only reason she had them was that the last homeowner had left them.

"Thank you." Kissing him on the cheek, her arm went around his waist. She stared back at the fountain. "I wanted to landscape the backyard around the fountain. Perhaps a tiny pond, rosebushes on a trellis, a small seating arrangement around a fire pit. Since I couldn't get the fountain going, I wasn't too optimistic about the other things."

His arm tightened. "We could start working on it today if you want."

She turned in his arms. "That was then. Now I might be leaving for Paris."

His gaze darkened. "I could have done without the reminder."

"Maybe this will help." She kissed him, molding her body to his hard length.

Lifting his head, he drew her into his arms. "You finish what you were working on?"

So he didn't want to talk about it. Neither did she. "Yes. There's a software program, as you well know, to help me design the layout, see if the article and pictures will fit in the allotted space, what it will look like. It's like putting the pieces of a puzzle together. It's tedious and the least favorite part of my job."

"Yet you do it and give it your all."

Leaning her head back, she stared up at him. She knew he was thinking about the software company. "Now that you know the situation, you're going to kick butt."

His eyes narrowed with determination. "I'm going to give it my best shot. We have a lot to make up for in a short time."

"Whatever it takes, you'll do it," she said with absolute conviction.

He stared at her strangely. "You have that much faith in me?"

She rolled her eyes. "You're relentless when you want something. I should know. You'll find a way to fix whatever problem the company is having. You won't settle for anything less."

"I should have discovered there was a problem earlier," he said slowly. "I was too busy feeling put-upon and annoyed."

She palmed his cheek. "You can kick yourself or kick butt. I'd rather go with the latter."

"I bet." He finally smiled. "I told Alex how intelligent and wonderful you were and he said I should tell you. You're intelligent and wonderful."

She continued to smile up at him, but it occurred to her that *wonderful* and *intelligent* were nice but rather tepid.

"What?"

She shook her head. He read her too easily. She could evade. "Intelligent and wonderful sounds rather ordinary."

He gathered her closer, brushed his lips against hers. "How about passionate?" The curve of her neck. "Elegant?"

She sank more fully against him. "My neighbors can see into my backyard."

Catching her hand, he sprinted toward the back door, their laughter trailing behind them. In the house he strode toward her bedroom.

"Won't we be late?"

"It will be worth it."

Chapter 15

All smiles, C. J. and Cicely, hand in hand, entered the suite at Yankee Stadium at one twenty-three. They saw Sin almost immediately. He looked at them, his gaze going to their joined hands.

Cicely was unaware of her hand tightening in C. J.'s. Baseball was sacred to some men; perhaps she shouldn't have come.

"Cicely."

Cicely turned to see Dianne and Alex. She accepted the hug from Dianne; in fact, needed it. Sin, who was usually so happy, hadn't said one word. "Hi, Dianne, Alex."

"It's good to see you," Alex said.

Cicely glanced over her shoulder at the still-silent Sin. "Yes."

"Hey, Sin." Dianne looped her arm with Cicely's. "Summer is supposed to be catering again. Let's go say hi."

Realizing that something was going on, she allowed Dianne to lead her away.

"It's like that?" Sin asked C. J., when the women were out of hearing range.

"Yes," C. J. admitted. "I messed up once with her. I don't plan on doing so again."

"So you brought her here."

C. J. twisted his head to one side. "If it's a problem, we can leave."

"All right, you two." Alex stepped between them. "Cool it."

"He started it," Sin said. "You know I don't mind her being here."

C. J. briefly tucked his head. "Sorry. I just don't want her hurt."

Sin's eyes narrowed dangerously. "You think I'd do that?"

"You already did."

"Hell." Sin shoved his hand over his head. "I better go correct that and give her my sympathies since she has to put up with you."

"You don't know the half of it," Alex said. "Last night—"

"Is better left forgotten," C. J. quickly interjected.

"He was a mess," Alex said with a laugh. He clapped C. J. on the shoulder. "Welcome to the club."

"What club?" C. J. asked.

"The one where a woman teaches a man that she's not to be messed with," Alex told him.

"Glad I'm not a member and never will be." Sin looked over the crowd of people filling the suite, which looked out onto the infield. "I better find Cicely and apologize."

"Thanks, man. Sorry about earlier." C. J. searched the crowd as well. "I better make sure she's okay."

Sin waited until C. J. was out of hearing distance.

"Do you think we could have stopped this from happening?"

"No," Alex answered. "It started the moment he first saw her at his bar. Being C. J., he was too stubborn to admit it then or admit now that he's in love with her."

Sin turned to Alex. "I'm happy for him, but it's never going to happen to me."

"Just like C. J., you can't control your heart," Alex told him.

"We'll just see about that." With determined steps, Sin moved through the crowd toward the buffet table.

"The suite used to be sacred to them. No women were allowed until I came along. C. J. almost had a coronary when Alex brought me. Now he brings you." Dianne laughed softly. "His change of heart probably just shocked Sin."

"But you said Summer often caters on Sundays," Cicely reminded her.

Summer waved her slender hand. "I don't count. I'm C. J.'s cousin, and one of the boys."

Cicely raised an eyebrow, her gaze running over Summer in a coral sundress that complemented her complexion, the chandelier earrings, and the statement necklace. Chic and elegant. "Hardly. You're beautiful with a figure to die for. Women would kill for the natural curls in your long black hair, not to mention your fashion sense. You always look great."

"Well." Obviously pleased, Summer unfolded her

arms. "If I ever need a pick-me-up, I know who to call."

"Hi, Summer." C. J. joined them, throwing a playful arm around Cicely's shoulder. "I thought you'd have a plate by now."

Cicely lightly elbowed him. Laughing, he caught her hand and brushed his lips across the top.

Sin saw the exchange and pulled up short, his eyes narrowed speculatively, then he was moving again. "Cicely."

"Yes." Since C. J. hadn't tensed, perhaps things would be all right. She hoped so for C. J.'s sake.

"If you're going to hang out with us, you should look the part." He handed her a Yankees T-shirt and cap, then turned to Dianne and Summer with the same items. "Dianne, yours are long overdue. Summer, I'm not sure how you'll work them into your catering wardrobe, but I didn't want to leave you out. Welcome, ladies, to our little part of the world."

Dianne and Cicely hugged him. His questioning gaze went to Summer, who hadn't moved. "No hug?"

"You have too many women hugging you now." She went behind the table laden with food and picked up a plate. "Preparing you a plate will have to do."

Releasing the women, he stepped forward and smiled. "I'll take it."

The next day C. J. drove Cicely to his parents' house in East Hampton for his birthday party. When they arrived, cars were lined up on the street and the driveway. Giving one of the waiting valets his car keys, he took Cicely's hand and went inside. His mother would most likely be in the kitchen to make sure everything was going smoothly.

"Your parents' home is beautiful," Cicely said in the grand entrance, a sequence of three rooms, each with a different shape: a square foyer, a larger elliptical hall, and finally a long stair hall. They passed the living room with its yellow Venetian plaster wall that Cicely could only describe as regal, the dining room as sumptuous.

"Thanks. I grew up here," he said as they went by the octagonal sitting room.

"You probably have a lot of great memories."

"I have better ones now." Pausing, he briefly kissed her on the lips.

She sighed, placing her hands on his chest. "You can say the nicest things."

He brushed a finger down her nose. "You sound surprised."

"I am."

"Well, wait until I get you alone. I'm just getting started." His heated gaze ran over her bare shoulders. Today she wore a strapless multicolored sundress in strong hues that stopped three inches above her gorgeous knees, a twisted crystal necklace, and strappy coral—last year's "in" color, she'd told him—wedge sandals that had to be four inches high. "Did I tell you how much I like the dress you're wearing?"

"Every time you look at me."

His hands circled her waist. "I'm going to enjoy taking it off more."

Her breath hitched. "And I get to return the favor."

His hands tightened. He stepped back and caught her hand. "Come on before you make me forget where I am." He pushed open the kitchen door to find a beehive of activity. The two islands could barely be seen because so many people were there.

Since his mother loved to cook almost as much as she loved gardening, the cabinetry was intricately carved, the stove the best money could buy, the countertops Italian marble. "Mom, are you in here?"

Wearing a pretty pink-and-white sleeveless sheath, she appeared from behind three men in white shirts holding sterling-silver serving trays. She smiled and rushed to him, barely able to keep her gaze from Cicely. "C. J., Cicely. It's nice to see you again. I'm so glad you could come."

"Thank you, Mrs. Callahan. I'm glad to be here."

Mrs. Callahan beamed at C. J. "So am I."

C. J. had seen the look on his mother's face before. It was the same, only brighter, on the day she'd introduced him to Ariel's friend. "Is Evan here?"

"No." Her smile faded. "He called, but Ariel hasn't gone out with him again."

Smart girl. "Where is she and the rest of the family?"

His mother looked around the kitchen. "She and Sharon were here a moment ago, helping out. They must be seeing to your guests. Your father and brother were making sure the games were all in place."

C. J. rubbed his hands together. "I plan to take on all comers."

"I'm not sure that's wise," Cicely murmured.

"Why?" he asked, frowning down at her.

She folded her arms and stared up at him. "Because you're such a poor loser."

"I am not."

"Yes, you are, son," his father said. He was dressed casually in linen pants and a white shirt. Paul, who was with him, was dressed in toffee-colored slacks and a knit shirt. His wife, Sharon, wore a white sundress with wide straps, while Ariel had on a peasant blouse and pink slacks. "It's good seeing you again. Cicely. I think you met everyone."

"Yes, sir." Greetings were exchanged.

"I am not a sore loser," C. J. insisted as if he couldn't let it go.

Cicely patted her small bag. "I have a camera in here, so be warned if you happen to lose."

His family laughed. "She knows you," Paul said. "He hasn't changed since we were kids."

"Gotten worse, if you ask me," his father put in.

"I believe it," Cicely said, looking askew at C. J. "You should have seen his face when I beat him at craps."

Five stunned faces stared first at her, then at C. J.

"That's one of his favorites," Ariel finally explained.

"So I gathered by his reaction when he lost." Cicely grinned.

C. J. tried to remain stern, but seeing Cicely having such a good time he couldn't. He hadn't felt the trepidation he'd thought on introducing her to his family; instead he was proud. "You're never going to let me forget that, are you?"

"In a word, no."

Chuckling, he threw his arms around her shoulder. "Come on, let's get out of here. Thanks, Mom and Dad."

"You're welcome," they said in unison, both looking at them a bit wistfully.

Passing a tray of croissant roast beef sandwiches, C. J. gave one to Cicely and took one for himself. Outside, they took the stone path to the backyard. Several people were already playing badminton, horseshoes, and volleyball.

On the side terrace were teak cushioned-seating arrangements, interspersed with topiary in teak box planters. Waiters with drinks and food moved through the crowd, as did C. J. and Cicely. He was pleased that several of the women knew of her, read her magazine, and were on her blog.

He saw Alex, Dianne, and Summer watching the sailboats and joined them. "Hi," C. J. and Cicely greeted.

"Hi, Cicely. C. J." Dianne leaned over and whispered to C. J., "I see groveling worked."

Releasing Cicely, he hugged Dianne. "Thanks."

"C. J., take your hands off my wife," Alex said, reaching for Dianne.

He released her, then pulled Cicely to him. "I have my own woman."

"Don't brag." Sin joined them, then threw his arm around Summer. "Let's me and you hook up."

"I'd have to fight too many women." Summer playfully patted his cheek.

Sin glanced around. "I don't see any other women."

"We both know how quickly that can change when they find out you're here," Summer said.

All playfulness left Sin's face. "If—"

Summer lightly touched her fingertips to his mouth. "I didn't mean anything. Let's hook up, as you said, and take on all comers at horseshoes."

The smile transformed Sin's bearded face, making him look even more gorgeous. He threw his arm around Summer's slim shoulders. "From this day forward, we'll be known as the annihilators."

"You hate to lose." C. J. curved his arms around Cicely.

"Never said I didn't," Sin said. "You're the same way. You get in the game to win."

"I couldn't agree more." C. J. kissed Cicely on the lips.

Cicely pushed against his chest and glanced around. "Your parents?"

"Couldn't be happier you're here," he said. "Here's Ariel, she'll tell you."

"He's right." Ariel offered the tray of drinks. "You're the first woman he's brought home since he was a college freshman."

Cicely accepted the mimosa, pleased and oddly annoyed about some woman he'd probably forgotten. Over the rim of the glass, she asked, "Whatever happened to her?"

Alex cleared his throat. Sin coughed.

Cicely didn't bother looking at them; her entire attention was centered on C. J. "Should I be concerned?"

"No. I saw her a couple of years ago on a trip," he said. "Let's go play horseshoes."

"Where did you see her?" Cicely asked, not sounding at all casual.

"I'll go get us next in line," Alex said, leading Dianne away.

"We'll help." Sin caught Summer's hand and followed.

"I better check on our other guests." Ariel left with the hasty group.

"On second thought, I don't want or need to know," she said. "It's none of my business. I'm sorry."

"Really?" he asked a bit cautiously.

Cicely screwed up her face. "No, but I'll get there."

He chuckled, then palmed her face, enjoying the brief spark of jealousy. He'd never cared for how possessive and territorial some of the women he dated became. With Cicely, he wanted to preen. "I saw her when Sin, Alex, and I went to Vegas. She tried to interest me in cheating with her on her second husband."

Cicely relaxed against him. "She didn't know you very well."

"No." His thumb grazed her lower lip, his eyes narrowed.

"What?" she asked.

It still amazed him that she could read him so easily. "Remind me never to play cards with you."

"I'll add it to craps. Now talk. They're waiting on us to play."

He grabbed her hand and went to his mother's greenhouse. The earthy scent of soil and the fifty-odd specimens of roses surrounded them. Closing the door, he took her hands. "Just thinking about next week. I have to find the answer to jump-start the company and that means I'm going to be putting in a lot of long hours."

"And I'm flying to Paris in the morning."

"What!" His hands flexed on her arm. "For how long?"

"I'm coming back on Friday. It's Haute Couture Paris Fashion Week," she told him. "I should be on the last flight out this afternoon, but I convinced Lenora I wanted to cover an event that I sent Sami to."

His frown didn't clear. "What's going to happen when she learns you sent your assistant?"

"Hopefully Sami will do a fantastic job."

"You evaded my question, and that's not like you." His hands moved to rest on her bare shoulders. "You don't look happy about leaving."

She cut him a look. "Crazy, isn't it. I love Paris, but even more during Fashion Week. All the great designers and the new ones looking to make their names known will be there. It's a multicultural event. I have a hectic, impossible schedule from the moment I get up until the wee hours. It's the epicenter of the fashion world. Four weeks ago I would have been on the plane Friday."

"Four weeks ago, I might have helped you pack. Now." His hands curved around her small waist, bringing her to him, nibbling on her ear. "I don't suppose you could 'lose' your passport."

"Lenora would have my head."

"And mine." He lifted his. "We'll leave early, so you can rest and get to bed early."

"We will not. You have an incredible family, amazing friends. They're warm, affectionate, and funny. Sharing them with you is wonderful." Grabbing his hand, she headed for the door. "I'm not going to let either of us miss that. Let's go play horseshoes."

Since Cicely had never played horseshoes, she and C. J. came in dead last. He didn't appear the least worried about the loss when Dianne declared Alex was on a roll or when Sin mumbled that this time he was having a wine pairing with each course to soothe his loss. Summer had simply looked at him.

C. J. refused to get another partner. Taking off her wedge heels hadn't helped as Cicely had hoped. Win or lose, they stuck. He'd said the words with such conviction that Cicely's crazy heart thumped. At least she loved someone who cared about her. Her record wasn't the best.

"Time to open the gifts," his mother said, rushing everyone to the terrace.

C. J. groaned as Sin and Alex took his arm to lead him to the waiting chair. "I thought I told you guys, no presents."

"A man of your advanced years needs to mark his special day." Sin pressed his hand on C. J.'s shoulder.

Alex pressed on the other. "Sit down, old man."

Since he *was* older, if only by months, and his mother was hovering, C. J. took the seat. Ariel gave a pad and pen to Cicely. "You can keep track. Perhaps this time you can help C. J. remember to send out thank-you cards."

"I thanked them then." He looked dubiously at the box wrapped in black paper. "At least those that deserved thanks." He tore into the paper and pulled out a retractable walking cane. Everyone laughed. "Ha. Ha."

The next present was a tube of dental cream, and so the gifts went. Cicely didn't join the laughter. She hadn't known they were giving gag gifts. She'd smuggled hers into the backseat of his car under a blanket. Dianne had gotten it out of the car for her. She felt better when C. J. opened a lovely wrapped box and pulled out season tickets to the New York Yankees, until he said, "They're for last year, Sin."

"Oh, my mistake." He grinned.

"All right, Alex." C. J. picked up the next to last box, shook it, and listened.

"Dianne picked it out," he said. Obviously trying not to laugh.

"Really." C. J. perked up, tearing open the paper to reveal a rectangular-shaped foam garden knee pad.

"I thought that might come in handy," she said, her tongue in her cheek.

C. J. grinned. "Hopefully, I learned my lesson." He picked up the last present, read the neat script, and turned to Cicely. "A ruler to rap my knuckles if I get out of line?"

She shook her head, tried to smile. "No."

His own smile faltered. He turned to his guests. "I think I'll open this later." He came to his feet, drawing Cicely with him. "Thank you for coming." He waved his mother over and hugged her with one arm, keeping the other around Cicely. "Thank you and Dad."

"Our pleasure. Lunch is being served in the main dining room, and then C. J. will cut the cake." She beamed up at her son, then at Cicely. "C. J. and his special guest, Cicely, will lead the way."

Chapter 16

"How did you do it?" Cicely asked C. J. as she stood beside him on the driveway of his parents' home watching Sin, Summer, Alex, and Dianne leave in a limousine. Unlike C. J., both men preferred a car service to dealing with a car.

"I might give you an answer if I knew what you were talking about."

"It's barely five. Ariel said your last birthday party lasted until almost ten," she explained.

He kissed her furrowed brow. "A man of my age needs his rest." He kissed her again when her brow lifted. "I had Sin and Alex spread the word that you were leaving for Paris in the morning and I'd rather be with you than them."

Her eyes widened in horror. "You didn't!"

"Alex probably put it more politely, but you can never tell about Sin," he explained. "But all they had to do was look at me looking at you and they got the message." His forehead touched hers. "I'm going to miss you."

"I'll miss you, too," she said. "With a six-hour time difference, it might be difficult to talk."

"We'll make time." He caught her face in his hands. "All right?"

"All right."

He gave her a quick kiss. "Let's go say good-bye to my family and we can go."

"I'm glad things worked out with them," she said. "Family is important."

He heard the wistfulness in her voice and pulled her closer. "Love and respect got us through," he said, opening the front door so they could go inside.

"That's the way a family is supposed to be."

He stopped. She was thinking about her parents. "Maybe they'll come around."

"I've almost given up."

He hugged her and cursed her parents. It wasn't in her to give up. She'd just keep getting hurt. He'd just have to be there for her.

"C. J., what is this Ariel tells me about her going to work for you on Monday?" His mother met him in the living room, her face wreathed in annoyance.

"I'm sorry, C. J." Ariel's gaze bounced between her upset mother and her brother. "I was just so excited, it slipped out."

"It's all right, Ariel." He went to his mother. "Callahan is family-owned. She has every right to work in the family business."

"I won't have it." Mrs. Callahan looked over her shoulder to see her husband, her son, and his wife approaching. "You tell him, Frederick. Ariel is not going to work for Callahan. Monday is our day to volunteer at the shelter. Your shelter, C. J."

"You have a shelter?" Cicely asked.

"I try to help when I can," he said mildly.

"He's the main benefactor of Home Place, a homeless shelter," Ariel explained. "For the past seven years he's asked his friends to contribute to the shelter instead of buying him a birthday present."

"And you'll be with me when we go to help serve lunch," her mother said adamantly.

"Mother, give her a chance." C. J. stepped in front of his mother. "Being a woman doesn't make her less of an asset." He looked at his father. "Dad's a strong man, but it probably helps that you were in his corner."

"No probably to it." His father curved his arm around his wife's tense shoulders. "There's nothing like having someone there who's always in your corner, who understands you, who'll tell you if you're wrong even when you don't want to hear it."

"Mother, Ariel is smart, intuitive. If she's right about the program she's developed, it could bring in much-needed contracts," C. J. told her.

"I won't let her jeopardize her chance for a family." Her mother's chin lifted. "You'll find a way without her."

C. J. decided to try tact. "Women can do both. Just look at Cicely. She's at the top in her field, respected so much that she's one of three candidates for the editor-in-chief position of *Fashion Insider* in Paris."

He caught Cicely's hand. "She might not have picked the best guy to date, but I'm glad it's me. We both have busy careers that are about to get busier. The main thing is to believe in yourself, then do the work. Cicely could give all of us lessons on determination and perseverance. Let Ariel have her chance."

His mother heaved out a defeated sigh. "We'll take it a week at a time."

Ariel gave an unladylike scream and hugged her mother. "Thank you, Mother. Although I'm not ready to get married, I hope to one day. Like C. J. said, women can handle a busy career and a family."

"We'll see." Mrs. Callahan spoke to Cicely. "I fixed you and C. J. a bite to eat later. It's in the kitchen."

"Thank you," Cicely said, but she was sure his mother had more on her mind than food.

"I hope there's a big slice of my lemon birthday cake," C. J. said.

"Of course." His mother continued from the room. In the stainless-steel kitchen, she handed Cicely a picnic hamper. "Can a woman have it all?"

"Some women can," Cicely answered, her hand closing on the hamper. "Dianne is ecstatic."

"She and Alex share a business, but soon she'll have to travel to promote their line and Alex won't be able to go," Mrs. Callahan pointed out.

"They'll make it," Cicely said with absolute conviction. "Both of them waited a long time for each other. From what I've heard, Alex loved Dianne long before they started dating, yet he supported her in her career. Their marriage will stand the test of separation."

"What about you and C. J.?"

She was glad the basket was still on the counter. "W-what?"

"If you go to Paris, what happens between the two of you?" Mrs. Callahan asked bluntly, then went on to say, "I'm not being nosy, or perhaps I am, but C. J. seems as taken with you as you are with him. I like you and want the both of you to be happy."

"I like you, too, I like your whole family, but what's between C. J. and me is between us," Cicely said.

"He wouldn't be this interested in a weak woman, and I suppose I wouldn't want one for him who couldn't hold her own," his mother said.

His mother's words sounded suspiciously like she thought she and C. J. were serious. "We're just dating."

"So he said." Going to the refrigerator, she removed a plastic container and placed it inside the wicker hamper. "Shrimp salad. One of C. J.'s favorites. I didn't want to leave it out."

"Thank you." Cicely lifted the hamper and was surprised by the weight. "You've made C. J. a happy man."

"No, Cicely," his mother said, looking directly at her. "You did that."

Cicely didn't know what to say, so she said nothing.

"I don't want you to think badly of me, but I'm torn between wanting you to get the Paris assignment and staying in New York."

For the first time, Cicely found that she was torn as well.

Cicely was quiet during the drive to her brownstone, a marked contrast to the drive up to his parents' house. C. J. thought the reason was a combination of her present, which he had yet to open, and her trip to Paris. He'd seen the worried expression on her face, her lower lip tucked between her teeth, and known. She could read him better than anyone, but he could read her just as well.

Parking in front of her house, he grabbed his present wrapped in light blue paper with plastic dice hanging from the center of the blue satin bow, then the picnic hamper. He had a feeling if he didn't, he might not see the present again. "I can't wait to see what you got me."

She glanced at him over her shoulder, then opened her front door. "I've been thinking, perhaps you shouldn't open it. I can give a check to your shelter."

He'd seen her nervous, but never unsure of herself. "Not a chance." He went to the kitchen and placed the hamper on the kitchen table. "I'll send the shelter a little extra for expenses this month." He took his seat, shredded paper, and opened the box. Inside were ten metal hooks with CALLAHAN engraved on the round head.

"It's a purse hanger." She moistened her lips. "I know you have mostly male clients, but women come there as well."

"Thank you. Believe it or not, a few men have messenger bags and purses."

She picked up one of the brass holders, then replaced it in the box. "It's hard to shop for a man who has everything."

He put the gift on the table and pulled her onto his lap. "I don't have everything. I thought I did until you walked through Callahan's door." His mouth took hers in a boldly erotic kiss. At least in this, neither one of them was unsure.

She was trembling by the time he lifted his head. "You say the dandiest, sweetest things."

"I just say what I feel," he said simply.

For how long, she thought, and knew she couldn't be as direct or honest. He wasn't ready for anything more, and she wasn't sure she was, either. Paris sat squarely between them, and no matter how they danced around it, if she got the assignment, things would change. But she wouldn't let it intrude on them tonight.

She bit his ear. "From where I'm sitting, I'd say you're feeling pretty good."

"It's going to get a lot better." He came to his feet with her in his arms.

They were almost to the kitchen door before she remembered. "Your shrimp salad."

"It'll keep."

"Not if I plan to do the things to you I've been thinking about all day," she whispered in his ear.

C. J. stopped in his tracks, passion burning in his eyes. Turning smartly, he went back to the kitchen and stopped in front of the hamper.

Laughing, Cicely reached inside. As soon as the salad cleared the top of the hamper, C. J. started for the refrigerator. Once there he placed her on her feet, then picked her back up once the refrigerator door began to close.

"Anxious, are we?" she teased. There could never be any doubt that he wanted her. The thought always sent shivers through her and increased her own desire.

"Yes, because before you have your way with me, I get to do all the things I've been fantasizing about doing to you." He put her down by the side of the bed, then reached for the hem of her sundress, bringing it over her head. He sucked in his breath. "I wondered what you had on under here. I'm a lucky man,"

Cicely trembled with desire just from the way his hungry gaze roamed over her naked breasts, the string bikini panties. She'd purposely chosen the strapless sundress with a built-in bra. She hadn't thought they'd spend much time undressing. C. J. seemed to be savoring each moment.

He reached out with one finger and touched her nipple. It hardened immediately, the ache transferring to her lower body. She sucked in her breath.

He kicked off his sandals. She stepped out of hers. He jerked his polo shirt over his head, shucked his knee-length shorts, taking his underwear with them. Together they fell into the bed.

"Cancel the car and I can take you to the airport."

He'd repeated the same thing several times that morning before, during, and after making love. She'd almost given in. She'd finally had someone in her life who would miss her, whom she'd miss.

"No, because a car is scheduled to pick me up any minute. We have to swing by and get Ming," she said, then glanced at her watch. "It should be here in less than five minutes."

"Is that my cue to leave?"

Her arms went around his waist. "Since I can't be one of those women being kissed breathlessly in the airport, I can have the next best thing." In her five-inch heels—which she planned to remove once she was on board the private jet—she only had to lift a couple of inches on her tiptoes before meeting his mouth. He took over, his tongue thrusting with hers.

The doorbell rang.

Lifting her head, she stared into his eyes. He'd picked her up again.

"Buy something that will make me drool." Placing her on her feet, he fiddled with her hair, straightened her top.

The doorbell sounded again.

"It won't go in the issue. It will be just for you." She reached for her handbag on the little chair she'd placed there for just that purpose.

"Ready?" C. J. asked, her two pieces of Henk Travelfriend luggage in his hands.

"No, but I'm going anyway."

"I'd kiss you again if it wouldn't throw you off schedule."

"And I'd let you. Kick butt today at work." Stepping in front of him, she opened the door, kissed him, and quickly went to the waiting limo.

He didn't have any recourse except to give the waiting driver her suitcases. Her suitcases might be among the most exclusive in the world, but Cicely was infinitely more valuable. "Drive carefully."

"Yes, sir." Putting the suitcases in the trunk, the driver got inside the black stretch limo and drove away.

* * *

C. J. went home to shower and dress. It was barely six, but he didn't bother trying to go back to sleep. He could dwell on missing Cicely or figure out how to stop the red at Callahan. He sat down at the computer.

Hours later, he still didn't have the answer. Frustration weighing heavily on his shoulders, he grabbed his keys and went to the elevator. It opened moments later. Dianne and Alex were already on board.

"'Morning, you two." He stepped on and pushed G for garage.

"Good morning, C. J."

"'Morning," Dianne said. "Did Cicely get off all right?"

C. J. slid his hands in the pockets of his slacks. "Yes. A car picked her up."

Dianne touched his arm in sympathy. "Like I told Cicely the night Alex won the pool game, Paris might be beautiful, but it doesn't compare to being with the one you love."

"We're just dating," he said. Why did everyone insist there was more?

Dianne lifted a brow. "Fashion Week started this morning. She might be on a private jet, but the flight is still almost eight hours. She'll only have time to go to her hotel before she hits it all-out for a full day. She probably won't get back until around midnight. Knowing that, she still stayed for your birthday party."

His hands came out of his pockets. He frowned. He should have known.

"I didn't tell you for you to worry," Dianne

quickly said. "I've flown over and gone straight to work. Cicely probably has, too. She wanted to spend your birthday with you."

"She should have told me," C. J. said.

"It would have changed nothing." Alex smiled at Dianne. "Women generally do what they want."

His best friend was right. Cicely had already taught him that lesson. He'd make it up to her when she returned. "What's that you're holding, Alex?"

"Dianne's new sketches. She and Greg Dickerson, our other designer, are going to go over them today." He leaned over to kiss Dianne on the cheek as the elevator doors opened and closed without anyone boarding. "I already told her they were brilliant."

"You say that about everything I design," she said, an indulgent smile on her face. "Luckily we have a designer who is a bit more objective to evaluate my designs before we go to the trouble and expense of making a pattern and buying the material to make the design. We'd waste an unbelievable amount of time and money otherwise."

C. J. thought of Cicely. "Cicely likes seeing how things will fit for her magazine as well. She called it her least favorite thing to do, but it's extremely important."

"She's right." Dianne nodded. "It has to catch the viewer's attention. After so long, you develop an eye for what works and you know immediately." She wrinkled her nose. "I'm still working on the last part, but I'm getting there."

It hit C. J. at once. He straightened and grabbed her arms, grinning for all he was worth. "It makes perfect sense. I could kiss you. You've helped me more than you can imagine."

"It had better not be on the mouth," Alex grumbled.

Laughing, C. J. kissed her on the cheek as the elevator doors opened on the first floor. "You and Cicely might have solved a problem I've been wrestling with all weekend. Alex, you have a smart wife."

"If I didn't know how sane you were, I might worry." Alex took Dianne's arm and stepped off the elevator.

"I'll explain later. Thanks." The door closed. He pulled out his iPhone on the elevator's continued ride down to the garage. "Cicely, thanks to you and Dianne I might have an answer to our problems. Call me when you land. Lo—" He caught himself in time. He'd almost said *love*. He shoved his hand over his head. He was so psyched. He'd almost made a terrible blunder. "Talk to you later," he finally finished.

Replacing the iPhone, he stepped off the elevator and headed for his car. He had work to do.

Ariel by his side, C. J. was still fired up when he stepped into the board meeting an hour later. She was just as enthusiastic. He'd discussed the idea with her and together they had come up with an outline that would explain the new direction he intended to take Callahan. When the clock struck nine, all the department heads were in their seats.

"Good morning, thank you for being on time." There were nods and murmurs from those seated. "I'm sure all of you know my sister, Ariel." More nods and unsmiling faces. Unlike a week ago, C. J. wasn't discouraged.

"Among the problems Callahan Software has encountered has been the expense of developing software for what we felt companies wanted. That stops today. Unless we have a signed contract, we're not going to do any speculative development of software."

There was a loud murmur this time—with disapproval. "Perry, the bank project you mentioned is speculative, so it will be stopped."

"But we've already spent a lot of money and time on the program," the man said.

"And we'll lose more if we continue." C. J. planted both hands on the conference table. "It stops today. Is that understood?"

"Understood." He glanced around and then asked, "What will I be working on?"

"A new program that will allow Callahan's representative to make a prototype of what the client wants," C. J. answered. "This way clients will be able to see exactly the functions they want and we can evaluate those in the developmental process and stop problems before they occur."

"Developing that program is going to take time," Elton James, the head of the marketing department, said.

"But once it's done it will save considerable time and make the client a real stakeholder." C. J. glanced down at his sister. "Ariel is going to work with me, and since you'll have some time, Perry, I'd like you on my team as well."

Perry pushed up his eyeglasses with one finger. "Yes, sir."

"Marketing, I want you to find out who wants what in new software and get back to me." C. J. looked around the table once again. "Innovation and customization, along with customer satisfaction, are going to be the keys that will put us ahead of the competition." He briefly paused.

"We'll get the software to our clients faster and cut down on cost for them and us," C. J. told the department heads. "On your computer screens, you should have a working representation of what I'm proposing. I'm open to suggestions and ideas on how to incorporate aspects of client needs."

People traded glances, but no one said a word. This wasn't what C. J. had hoped for.

Ariel scooted forward in her chair. "The product we produce will be an exact replica of what the client wants so the company can see how it works for them. Interaction should be the first step, don't you think, Perry?"

Perry pulled his laptop closer. "Yes. People dislike change. If the prototype mimics the planned system, they would see the effectiveness of the program ahead of time, make suggestions, which would make them feel as if they were stakeholders as C. J. said." His dark lead lifted. "I like the idea. We've worked on projects in the past, and gotten down to the last synchronization and it didn't work. This should cut that out."

Elton in marketing spoke up. "If I can take this to clients where they can actually see how the product will work early, they'll sweat less during development and, frankly, so will I."

Laughter joined his. C. J. sent Ariel an appreciative glance. She had gotten things started. They had a long way to go, but he felt they were on the right road, thanks to three women—Cicely, Dianne, and Ariel. And he couldn't wait to tell them, and his mother.

The first things C. J. saw when he entered his office three hours later were the dozen or so boot-shaped balloons on his ceiling. *Cicely.* He chuckled.

"I don't get it," Ariel said with a frown.

Staring up at the dancing balloons, he explained. "Cicely told me to kick butt. This is her way of reminding me," he explained. The smile faded. He whirled on his sister. "She forgot to tell me the name of her hotel. She likes flowers. I'd like to send her some."

"Then it's a good thing you persuaded Mom to let me come in today. During the interview for the article Mom and I were in, she mentioned the name of the hotel where she always stays."

"Tell me you remember the hotel's name."

She folded her arms. "The Ritz Paris."

"Thanks, Ariel." He rounded his desk and picked up the phone. "As soon as I order her roses, we'll meet with Perry in the lab."

"Thank you for letting me be a part of this." Ariel unfolded her arms. "Mom and Dad were up when I went down for breakfast. Ten minutes later, Paul walked in. All three of them kept cautioning me on driving in. I think Mom is hoping that the drive will discourage me. It won't."

C. J. hung up the phone. "You don't have to be here for us to work together. I'll drive you back and you can pick up some things and stay with me the rest of the week. After that, you can work from home."

Ariel's lips twitched. "And isn't it a coincidence that Cicely comes back Friday afternoon?"

He grinned. "Isn't it?"

Chapter 17

It was close to midnight when Cicely arrived back at the Ritz Paris hotel. She went straight to her room. She didn't remember ever feeling this tired, but helping C. J. celebrate his birthday had been worth it, she thought, as she let herself into the Coco Chanel Suite. The famed designer had stayed at the Ritz from 1927 to 1971. Cicely always tried to stay in this suite because it reinforced her dream to keep reaching for the top.

Cicely had only gone a few steps inside before she saw, then smelled, the large bouquet of pink roses on the glass-topped coffee table. Rushing over, she tossed her satchel on the sofa with one hand and plucked the card from the bouquet with the other.

The tiredness she'd felt immediately disappeared.

Missing you. C. J.

Pressing the card to her chest, she leaned over and inhaled the scent. She missed him, too. She hadn't realized how much until now. He was probably working. But she wanted to talk to him, see how his day went. If he laughed when he saw the balloons as she'd intended.

Her iPhone rang. Wishing, hoping, she rushed around the sofa, pulled it from her purse, and felt tears crest in her eyes even as she was grinning

"They're beautiful. Thank you."

"I got a kick out of the balloons. No pun intended."

Slipping off her shoes, she sat on the sofa and drew her feet under her. "How did it go today?"

"Because of you, Dianne, and Ariel, better than I expected. We're developing a new interactive way for clients to integrate a program to see if it works first. Kind of the same way you do with your layout and Dianne does with her sketches."

"I knew you'd do it! Congratulations."

"You never doubted me, did you?"

"No." She leaned back in the sofa. "You're too stubborn to let anything get the best of you."

"I thought so once."

She caught the change in his voice. "What happened? What is it?"

"You. I miss you. You're probably bone-tired because you stayed to go to my party and, knowing this, I'm still keeping you on the phone because I wanted to hear your voice and pretend you're here instead of there."

She slid her feet from under her. "This was important. I have to travel."

"And soon you might be in Paris permanently."

"Yes." The silence seemed to go forever. "C. J.?"

"I was just wondering if I could be as good a man as you are a woman."

"What?"

"You never complain. Never. You just do your job and care for me like I never thought a woman could."

Tears clogged her throat. "Oh, C. J."

"Don't you dare cry when I'm not there to kiss the tears away. Stop it now."

She nodded. "Stopping it now."

"I better let you go so you can get some sleep."

"Thanks for calling."

"Thank me by not forgetting to go shopping for that outfit."

"It's on the top of my list."

"'Night, honey."

Honey. "Good night." Still a bit stunned, Cicely hung up. She had to come thousands of miles to hear C. J. call her honey. She wished she could have seen his face when he said it. Picking up her bag, she headed to the bedroom. She wouldn't try to read anything into it. He was just feeling a bit lonely, the same as she was.

C. J. hung up the phone and stared at it. *Honey* had just slipped out. He hadn't missed the slight pause before she said good night. He ran his hand over his head and blew out a breath. He wasn't the sentimental type. He didn't call women honey, baby, and sweetheart. He also didn't use the L word. He liked Cicely. He didn't love her. He was just missing her.

Sure he had explanations for his lapses today, he

gave his attention to the computer screen. He had work to do.

In the coming days, C. J. worked tirelessly to complete the new program to turn the company around. They worked ten to twelve hours a day. He'd had to postpone the monthly pool game with Sin and Alex. Ariel and Perry worked well together. He quickly found she had a knack for analyzing data the same way he did.

He also consulted with his brother and father. Both were invaluable. He admired them even more. Their love of Callahan Software was obvious.

Marketing kicked it up a notch and, by Thursday, Elton had a lead on a prospective client who agreed to meet the next day. There was just one problem: The district manager of the grocery store couldn't meet until 3:00, and the last flight out of Memphis that could get them back to New York left at 4:00 PM. He'd have to spend Friday night there and fly back Saturday.

"Make flight and hotel reservations for three. Ariel and I are going with you," C. J. said.

Relief swept across Elton's face. "I was hoping you would. You know the new program better than anyone. I'll get right on it."

"And Ariel has researched the grocery store chains enough to be able to help with the presentation."

"I'm on it."

C. J. waited until his office door closed then picked up the phone and dialed.

"Hi, stranger," Cicely greeted cheerfully.

The corners of his mouth curved upward. They'd managed to talk twice yesterday in between her schedule and his. He hadn't minded the early-morning call one bit. Thankfully he hadn't had any more slips with words. "Hi, yourself. Still busy?"

"No, we're taking a breather to grab a bite at a beautiful sidewalk café."

The day before she'd told him she had rushed from place to place and hadn't had time to eat. "Change of plans. I have a three o'clock meeting in Memphis on Friday and won't be back until sometime Saturday. I need to be there to explain the new program." He wanted her to know that he didn't have a choice.

"Of course you do. Kick butt, and we'll celebrate with your present when you get back."

Was there ever a woman like Cicely? "I'll call as soon as I get back."

"Just come over. I'm going to the office that morning to work, then home by one. I'll cook."

"I won't be hungry for food."

"Neither will I."

"See you Saturday. 'Bye."

"'Bye. Safe travel." Cicely hung up, a wicked smile on her face. His present was going to make him beg.

"Don't you look happy?" Eva almost cooed as she pulled out a chair at the table and took a seat. "Guess I don't have to ask who you were talking to. Why you were late getting to Paris."

Cicely dropped her phone in the pocket of her satchel. "No, you don't, but I'm sure you'll keep bringing it up. Where's Lenora?"

"She's coming." Eva steepled her fingers and propped her elbows on the table. "Everyone knows you've lost focus. Why don't you just take your name off the list?"

Cicely's smile was as cold as ice. "Because I'm going to win no matter what rumors you try to spread or how you try to influence Lenora. The work is what counts."

"And yours is slipping." The other woman tsked. "Letting Sami do the fashion tea for a start."

Cicely opened her mouth to tell Eva off, then saw Lenora approaching and waved. "Glad you made it."

"I am, too." The older woman took her seat. "You two seemed to be having a serious conversation. We're a team. I don't have to tell you that *Fashion Insider* always comes first."

"Not me, but I think Cicely must have lost the memo," Eva commented nastily.

"I haven't," Cicely said, trying to rein in her temper.

"I've begun to wonder about that myself," Lenora said, signaling a waiter. "Three white wines, please."

Cicely straightened. Her stomach knotted. "How can you say that?"

Lenora faced her. "Before you let Sami cover the fashion brunch you said you were going to cover it. So where were you?"

"Your wine, madame."

Cicely wanted to snatch up the wine to ease her dry throat, to stall. "At C. J.'s birthday party."

"I see." The disappointment was clearly written on Lenora's strong face. "You can have a man, or you can have a career. I thought we'd already had this conversation. I don't like repeating myself." Lenora picked up her menu. "I suggest you decide what you want."

Cicely no longer felt like eating. She had to choose, and heaven help her when she did.

They'd done it! They'd sold the new C-It software program to the largest grocery store chain in the South. C. J. couldn't have been prouder of Ariel, who had helped them nail the account. Anxious to hear all the details, his father and brother had met them at La Guardia Saturday afternoon.

"Ariel can tell you as well as me," C.J. said, slapping his father on the back as he glanced at his watch. It was 1:13 PM. "I have a date with a beautiful woman."

Frederick told him to say hello to Cicely as they headed for the parking garage. C. J. grabbed a cab. He felt like pumping his fist, shouting at the top of his lungs.

He grinned. He'd named the program after Cicely. After all, she'd gotten him to thinking, had faith in him when his family and employees at Callahan had doubted. Granted, it was a play on words, but it clearly said what the program brought to the table.

He couldn't wait to share the news with Cicely. He'd called a couple of times last night and once this morning before boarding the plane in Memphis for New York. He'd gotten her voice mail on her cell and home phones. He'd figured she was probably busy.

Of course, traffic was a mess. Horns were honking, drivers were taking unbelievable risks. He shook his head. There was no place like New York.

A couple of blocks from Cicely's place, he scooted to the edge of his seat. He couldn't wait to see her, hold her. He'd told Sin and Alex he'd be busy and would catch up with them Monday.

The taxi stopped in front of Cicely's house. C. J. already had the fare and a generous tip in his hand. "Thanks." Grabbing his overnight bag, he got out of the taxi, hurried up the steps, and rang the doorbell.

The door opened. Grinning, he dropped the suitcase and he hugged her. It took him a few seconds to realize that she wasn't hugging him back. A strange foreboding came over him. Slowly, he released her and stepped back

There was no light dancing in her eyes, no smile on her beautiful face. "What is it?"

"Please come in."

The words carried none of the warmth he'd come to associate with her. Picking up his bag, he stepped over the threshold, heard her close the door behind him. For a moment, he didn't want to turn, didn't want to see her face, hear what he knew was coming.

"There's no easy way to say this, and I owe it to you to say it to your face."

He turned and knew it was over between them. "Paris won."

She slid her fingers into the slanted pockets of her dark chocolate skirt, which stopped five inches above her knees. She'd paired it with an orange silk blouse. The collar draped to a V and tied in a large bow just below her breasts. The voluminous sleeves stopped above her elbow. On her feet were lace-up, ankle-wrap wedges with lace detail on the wood heels. Orange crystal earrings dangled from her ears. She was absolutely stunning; so near yet ever so far away.

"I told you from the beginning about the possible assignment to Paris."

"Possible? You don't have the job yet?" Hope flared within him.

"No, and I won't if I keep seeing you." She pulled her hands from her pockets and shoved one through her hair. "You're a distraction I can't afford. Lenora wants someone whose entire focus is on *Fashion Insider.* She realized that I can't be focused if I'm going out with you."

"That's a bunch of crap and you know it. My birthday party is the only time you've let our relationship get in the way of your job," he told her.

"I gave an assignment to my assistant that I should have covered so I could go to the party." She shook her head. "The magazine has to come first."

He felt her withdrawing, felt a mild sense of panic. "I understand that. I might want you with me, but I understand when you have to work, just like you understand when I have to work. I'll be busy myself in the coming weeks."

"But my focus might be splintered between you and the job. I'm sorry, C. J., but I've worked too hard and too long to mess up now over an affair that's leading nowhere."

"We had more than an affair," he snapped. *Affair* was too casual a word for what she meant to him.

"We're still not ready to send out wedding invitations. And I'm not looking to do so. My life is the fashion industry. I shouldn't have forgotten."

Anger at the situation hit him. "Your parents won't change their minds no matter what you achieve."

She flinched. "You don't know my parents. You don't know me." She went to the door and opened it. "Good-bye, C. J. I don't want to argue and end up saying ugly things we'll both regret later."

He wanted to, he realized. He wanted to rant and rage at her. She'd blindsided him. For what? For parents who ignored her? A boss who wanted her to sacrifice her life for a magazine? "Give us a chance, Cicely. We can work this out."

"I can't. The price is too high."

He'd argue if he thought he had a chance. He didn't. There was too much to overcome. C. J. picked up his overnight case and walked out the door, heard it close quietly after him. He felt like howling.

Cicely leaned her forehead against the door. She'd made the only logical choice. What C. J. felt for her was white-hot lust. And, like heat, it would eventually cool down, but by that time she would have lost the Paris assignment. She had done the right thing, even if it felt as if her heart was breaking, her soul shattering into a thousand pieces. And she didn't even have the luxury of tears.

Pushing away from the door, she went to pick up her tote that matched her shoes. She wanted to visit some of the couture stores to see what they thought of the designs she'd seen in Paris. She'd blog the results that night.

She'd show Lenora that she was still in it to win it. She just had to remember that C. J. was in her past. Paris was her future.

C. J. walked several blocks before he had the presence of mind to flag down a taxi. This time when he got in he wasn't happy. You couldn't be happy with as much pain as he felt. He rubbed his chest with the heel of his hand. What got to him most was that she refused to fight for them.

Cicely was a fighter. She hadn't cared enough. The realization hurt. But he'd get over it. He just wished he knew how long it would take.

To say that he had a hellish weekend would be putting it mildly. Arriving at work Monday morning shortly after eight and being greeted with words of praise for a job well done instead of polite nods only marginally helped. Walking into his office and seeing the balloons at eye level was a kick in the gut.

Spinning on his heels, he went to his secretary's desk. Seeing a pair of scissors sticking out of a holder with pens and a letter opener, he picked them up. He took savage pleasure in bursting all of the balloons. When he finished, the tattered remains were scattered on the floor. Picking them up, he started from the room, only to stop short on seeing his secretary.

"The noise—" Alice began. "Is everything all right?"

"Yes." He handed her the balloon shreds. "Get rid of these, please."

"Yes, sir." Gathering the balloon pieces to her, she took the scissors he held out.

"That will be all." He went behind his desk. She hadn't moved. "Was there something else?"

"I just wanted to congratulate you on getting the account. Your C-It program is brilliant." The corners of her thin mouth lifted. "You came up with the perfect name."

His mouth tightened. "Thank you. That will be all."

Nodding, his secretary went to the door. Pausing, she looked over her shoulder at him, then left.

He was in an ugly mood, but that was no reason to take it out on his poor secretary. It was his fault that he'd believed Cicely cared. But he'd forget her, as he had all the women before her.

Cicely wore a Chanel black microdot-printed three-button suit and black Valentino ankle-wrap sling backs with golden metal stud and chain detail to work on Monday. If ever there was a time she needed to show she was on her game, it was today. She was too close to her goal to mess up. If she only felt half alive, no one would know it but her.

She stepped off the elevator and headed to her office, head high, back straight as if the world was hers for the taking.

"Wow." The receptionist whistled and came to her feet to give Cicely a once-over. "You look sensational,

Cicely. Makes me want to lose these last stubborn thirty pounds. You're seeing him later on?"

Just like that, despair hit her. She knew her face reflected the misery she'd tried so hard to hide, but it was also a way to get the word out. Rea gossiped more than Eva. "I'm solo again. As for the clothes . . ." She laughed and hoped it didn't sound as brittle as she felt. "After seeing all the fabulous fall fashions, I felt like dressing up a bit. Paris is wonderful this time of year. See you later."

Keep walking. Just keep walking. You can do this. She opened the door to Sami's office and saw the young woman on the computer. She glanced up. Her usual smile was gone.

"What's the matter?" Cicely asked because she cared and because she wanted to stop thinking about C. J.

"I heard Lenora wasn't pleased that you let me take the assignment." She bit her lip. "I know I asked to do it, but I didn't want to get you or me in trouble."

"You're good or I wouldn't have sent you," Cicely said, aware it was the truth. She might have wanted to be with C. J., but she had confidence in Sami. "Shoot it to me in an e-mail and I'll take a look at it."

The young woman's face brightened. "Thank you." She turned to the computer, then swung back around. "By the way, you look sensational. You meeting him?"

"I won't be seeing him anymore." Cicely kept walking. Inside her office, she wanted to put her head on her desk and bawl. And when she finished, it would change nothing.

Taking her seat, she placed her attaché case on the desk, took out her laptop, iPhone, and tape recorder. She didn't have time to mourn the loss of C. J. She had a magazine to help run.

Chapter 18

The call C. J. expected and dreaded came shortly after ten. His father wanted to congratulate him again, his mother wanted to know how Cicely had enjoyed Paris. Because he still felt raw, and he knew this wouldn't be the last time he had to say she dumped him, he took a few moments to answer.

"Cla— C. J, is everything all right between you two?" his mother asked.

With a mother's uncanny perception she'd picked up on his hesitation. His hand clenched and unclenched. "You were right. Cicely wants to concentrate on her job."

"C. J."

He heard the disappointment, the sympathy He didn't want either. "I'm fine with it. Tell Ariel we'll sync up in about an hour. I wish you could have seen her, Mom, she was brilliant. With her program for monitoring stock and expiration dates, it will save grocery stores a mint. We're going to make it."

"Are you?"

He hadn't thrown his mother off. He hadn't thought he would. Family meant everything to her. "Mom, she's not the first woman I've dated or broken up with." But he'd never felt as if his insides were tied in knots, his temper boiling just beneath the surface.

"She wasn't just any woman," Mrs. Callahan said quietly.

C.J. swept his hand over his head. *No, she wasn't.* "Mom, I have to go."

"I love you, son. We're proud of you. 'Bye."

"Love you, too. 'Bye." C.J. hung up. Why wasn't he enough? If he had been, she wouldn't have walked away so easily. Cicely had accomplished so much because she was determined to succeed, determined to show her parents she could make a name for herself. She wasn't a quitter. If she cared, she would have stayed. Together they would have worked something out.

The ringing of his phone interrupted his thoughts and sent hope shooting through him that Cicely was on the line. He pushed the speaker. "Yes."

"Perry just called. Elton and he are waiting for you to begin working on the software program whenever you're ready."

"Please tell them I'm on my way." Rounding his desk, he headed for the door. He wouldn't keep doing this to himself. It was over between them. He'd move on just as he always had.

Monday afternoon Cicely received a call from Lenora asking her and Sami to come to her office. Since Lenora had never asked to see them together, Cicely knew it was about Sami's article that she'd sent to Lenora earlier in the day.

"I don't think I've ever been this nervous," Sami said as they walked the short distance to Lenora's office at the end of the hall.

"You wrote a great article." Cicely tried to reassure her assistant, but the younger woman was trembling so badly it was a wonder her teeth weren't chattering.

"I love this job. I love it here." Sami blinked back tears.

"Then you better grow a backbone," Cicely snapped, causing her assistant's eyes to widen, her shoulders to snap back. "You'll be eaten alive and spit out if you don't. Have confidence in yourself, even if no one else does. Fight for what you want."

Sami bit her lower lip. "I'm not sure I can be as strong as you."

Had she been strong or weak to give up C. J.? Either way, the decision was made and there was no going back. "Then you won't make it." Cicely knocked on the door. She'd come too far, given up too much to fail.

"Come in," Lenora called.

Cicely couldn't tell from her voice if she was going to flay them alive. Lenora could cut you to shreds with a smile on her face, her voice sugary sweet. Opening the door, Cicely entered Lenora's plush office furnished with eighteenth-century antiques.

On a side table was a bouquet of calla lilies in a slim crystal vase. Lenora, her head bowed, sat behind her writing desk, flipping through white sheets of paper, probably Sami's article. She still preferred reading hard copies of material.

"You wanted to see us," Cicely said when seconds ticked by and Lenora had yet to acknowledge them. It was a trick she often used to make people nervous.

Lenora's head came up, her assessing gaze moving from Sami to Cicely. "I wanted to talk to you both about this." She waved her long-fingered hand toward the sheets of paper in front of her. The glitter of the diamonds matched the glint in her eyes.

"Yes, what about it?" Cicely asked.

"You tell me." Lenora leaned back casually.

"Sami did a good job." Cicely would not be intimidated. She glanced at Sami out of the corner of her eye and hoped the trembling woman didn't pass out. "I wouldn't have given her the assignment if she hadn't been up to the job."

"What if I say differently?"

"Oh, my goodness," Sami moaned in distress, grabbing Cicely's arm.

Cicely didn't hesitate to speak. "We've disagreed before, Lenora, but frankly I'd be very surprised if this is one of those times. You trained me."

Long seconds ticked by before Lenora leaned forward and placed both arms on the desk. "It seems . . . I did a damn good job, and so did you, Sami. It goes in the issue as planned, with your name on it."

Sami gasped, squealed, and squeezed Cicely. "Thank you. Thank you."

"Thank me by being less exuberant."

Sami instantly loosened her stranglehold and stepped back. "Sorry. Thank you, Lenora."

"It was no more than you deserve." Lenora stood. "I need to talk to Cicely alone."

"Certainly." Sami closed the door behind her.

Lenora rounded the desk, folded her arms, and leaned back against it. "I read your blog Saturday and Sunday night. Good solid pieces. You got a lot of hits. Circulation tells me there was also a bump in subscriptions that can be directly attributed to the blog."

"It's part of my job."

"You broke up with him," Lenora said, watching Cicely's face closely.

"Yes."

"How do you feel about it?"

She wouldn't lie. "Like hell."

"Yet you did it. You put the magazine first."

"I want that Paris assignment."

Lenora rounded her desk and retook her seat. "You'll get over him. You have your whole life ahead of you to find another man. That will be all."

Cicely left. Lenora might know fashion, but she didn't know men. Some were irreplaceable, and C. J. was at the top of that list.

C. J. was working in his home office Monday night when the doorbell rang. His hands paused over the computer keys. He couldn't keep on thinking it was Cicely every time the phone or doorbell rang. She had her life. He had his.

The landline phone on his desk rang. He glanced at the readout. ALEX STEWART. For a split second, he considered not answering. It was past ten. There was only one reason he'd call this late.

He punched the speaker. "Hi."

"Hi, yourself," Alex greeted. "You have company, so open the door." The line went dead.

C. J. pushed up from his desk and started for the door. He'd never avoided problems or run from them. She wouldn't make him start. But, man, he didn't want to see the pity in their faces.

Opening the door he stared into the concerned faces of Alex, Dianne, Sin, and Summer. Ariel must have told Summer, and she'd told the rest. Being his friends, they were here to comfort him.

"I'm all right," he said. "So you can all go home and Summer can get back to Radcliffe's."

"We won't stay but a moment." Summer brushed by him and so did the others.

C. J. blew out a breath and closed the door. He hadn't thought it would be that easy.

"We're with you, man." Alex laid a comforting hand on his shoulder.

Sin briefly placed his hand on the other shoulder. "Always will be, no matter what."

"She chose her career and Paris." Saying the words brought back the anger, the feelings of inadequacy. "It was her decision to make. I knew going in. I've moved on."

"You're sure?" Sin questioned.

"She made it clear that I'm not what she wants," he told them, the words tasting bitter in his mouth.

Dianne frowned. "From the way she looked at you, I'd say she wants you."

"Dianne's right," Alex told him.

C. J. shrugged. "Looks can be deceiving, as they say." He tried to say the words flippantly, but they came out hoarse.

Summer gave him a hug. "If you want her, fight for her."

Dianne nodded. "She cares about you. Sometimes women make emotional decisions out of fear." She reached for Alex's hand. "Giving your heart, laying your feelings on the line can be scary."

Alex nodded. "She's right. I was afraid to tell Dianne I loved her in case I scared her away."

"Whoa. I don't love her," C. J. protested. "I just . . ." He searched for the right word. "She was fun to be with."

"Stubborn and scared." Sin shook his dark head. "She's not just another woman to you. Negotiate. Put everything on the table."

C. J. stared at his friends. They meant well. "I'm not running after any woman. She chose her job."

"What if she doesn't get the Paris assignment?" Summer asked. "What will you do?"

Somehow he knew she'd get the assignment. "She made her decision. It's over."

"There you go, being stubborn again, C. J.," Alex said. "You care about her. Learn to bend a little."

"You've never given up without a fight," Sin added.

C. J. turned on him, some of his anger boiling to the surface. "I thought you'd be happy we broke up."

Sin's midnight-black eyes narrowed dangerously. "If I didn't see how much this is eating at you, I'd punch you. You're one of my best friends. I want you to be happy. If Cicely makes you happy, that's what I want for you."

"Damn." C. J. shoved his hand over his head. "Man. I'm sorry. I know that. It's just . . ."

Sin clamped his hand on C. J.'s shoulder again. "I've never loved a woman so I don't know what you're going through, but I do know that, when you put your mind to something, nothing can stand in your way."

"Cicely said the same thing about me," he murmured.

"Maybe she thinks you don't care enough to fight for her." Summer said.

"I'd be fighting a losing battle," C. J. told her. "I appreciate more than you know you coming here tonight, but it's over. The sooner I accept that and move on, the better. So please drop it."

His friends stared at each other, then C. J. "Do you want to come back to the restaurant with us?" Summer asked.

"No, I need to work." *And brood.*

"Ariel mentioned the new contract. Congratulations," Summer said.

The others congratulated him as well.

"Thanks," he told them.

Sin took Summer's arm. "We'll get out of your way. If you change your mind, you know where to find us."

C. J. shook his head. "I won't. Thanks for coming by."

"Friends help each other," Alex said. "'Night. We'll see you Wednesday night for our pool game."

He didn't want to go. "Sure."

After exchanging good nights, the small group left the apartment. C. J. headed for his office. He had good friends, a successful business, the respect and love of his family, but it wasn't enough. There was a gaping hole in his life he was beginning to fear could be filled by only one person.

Cicely had her head bent over the proposed layout of the next issue of *Fashion Insider* when her phone rang. Since she had specifically asked Sami to hold all calls, she hit the speaker. "Yes."

"Summer Radcliffe and Dianne Harrington-Stewart are here to see you," Sami said, awe and admiration clear in her voice.

Cicely straightened. Her heart thudded in her chest. She was out of her chair in seconds and striding across her office to open the door. "Is he all right?"

"Yes." Dianne took Cicely's arm.

"Let's talk in your office." Summer took her other arm, closing Cicely's door behind them.

"But he'd do better with you." Dianne said as soon as they were alone.

Cicely briefly closed her eyes and tried to get her emotions under control. "It was just the suddenness of our breaking up. He'll be fine by the end of the week."

"If you can make yourself believe that lie, you're not the woman I've come to know and admire," Summer said.

Cicely winced and accepted the reprimand. "I

didn't have a choice. My boss is aware that I put C. J. ahead of the magazine when I attended the birthday party. I'm on notice. Mess up again, and I won't be considered for the Paris position."

"Then tell her to stuff it." Summer didn't even try to hide her irritation. "She can't dictate to you about your personal life."

Cicely shoved her hand through her short curls. "I'm afraid she can." She spoke to Dianne. "You must remember when you were The Face of Harrington, and your life wasn't your own. You did what you were told for the good of the company."

Dianne's face harshened for a moment. "And look where it got me. Fired because I didn't fit the image the new CEO wanted. C. J. cares about you. Don't throw it away."

"Caring is not enough. This assignment isn't just a whim, it's what I've worked for since I was a little girl. It will finally show my parents that I made the right choice instead of going into academia as they wanted." She swallowed. "Both of you understand the need to make your parents proud of you. Would you do any less?"

Dianne and Summer looked at each other. "No," they both said in unison.

Cicely swallowed again. "I have to give this my all. I can't do that with C. J."

"What if you don't get the assignment in Paris?" Summer asked.

"I refuse to think I won't be chosen." Cicely's face hardened into determination. "I've sacrificed too much not to."

"At the risk of sounding disloyal to C. J., I hope you get it," Summer said.

"Me, too," Dianne told her.

"Thank you, that means a lot."

"No matter what. We stay friends," Dianne said, giving Cicely a hug.

"I'd like that." Cicely turned to Summer. "Take care of C. J. for me."

"You got it." Summer hugged Cicely, then stepped back. "I wish things could work out for you two."

"We both knew going in it wasn't forever," Cicely told them, but it still hurt.

"I thought the same thing when Alex and I got together." Dianne said thoughtfully. "Life has a way of throwing you a curve and I couldn't be happier."

"Alex loves you," Cicely said. "C. J.'s feelings for me don't go that deep."

Summer shook her head of dark hair. "I'm not sure even he knows what he's feeling, but I can say it's stronger, deeper than anything he's felt for any woman before you."

"I'm uncertain if that makes me feel better or worse," Cicely said. "I don't want him hurt."

"How do you feel about him?" Dianne asked, watching her closely.

Cicely's heart thudded. "Naturally, I care about him."

Summer and Dianne traded looks again. "Both of you are too scared to look deeply at your feelings," Dianne said. "One of you had better before it's too late. Real love only comes to some once."

"We're not in love," Cicely insisted. She was, but he wasn't, so technically they weren't "in love."

"You and C. J. are both stubborn, but don't let it take away a love that will last a lifetime." Dianne headed for the door. "Come on, Summer."

Summer touched Cicely's shoulder again. "I've never even been close to falling in love, but I'd like to think if I were, I'd fight tooth and nail to save it. Good-bye. Remember, no matter what, we remain friends." She joined Dianne at the door.

"Thank you for coming."

"When will you know who gets the position?" Dianne asked.

"Sometime this week."

"Please call us when you know." Summer reached for the doorknob.

"I will, and thanks again."

" 'Bye," Summer and Dianne said and then they were gone.

Cicely returned to her desk. She wanted to put her head down and howl. She went back to the layout. She'd come too far to fail. She had work to do no matter how badly she hurt and wanted C. J. in her life.

Cicely went to work Wednesday morning, trying not to remember that tonight C. J. and the rest would be playing pool at Callahan's, or that afterward he would have taken her home and to bed.

She'd barely taken a seat at her desk when her phone rang. Absently she picked up the receiver, mentally berating herself for not being able to move on. "Yes, Sami."

"Lenora wants to see you. She also asked to see Fred and Eva."

The other two candidates for the editor-in-chief position. Her heart raced for a wild moment. This was it.

"Cicely?"

"Please tell her I'm on my way." Hanging up, she checked her appearance in the floor mirror in the corner. Today she'd worn a black Chanel suit with her grandmother's pearls. She'd needed to feel as if someone cared, and to remember her dream.

She stared into the eyes of the woman staring back at her. There should be excitement. There wasn't. She should be smiling. She wasn't.

Her phone rang. She didn't bother answering it. It was probably Sami again, reminding her to get moving—or worse, Lenora. Leaving her office, she went directly to Lenora's office, passing several co-workers. Obviously, the word was out that Lenora was naming the editor in chief that morning.

Taking a deep breath, she knocked on the door.

"Come in."

Opening the door, Cicely wasn't surprised to see Fred and Eva already there. Greeting them, she took the one remaining chair arranged in front of Lenora's desk. The polished surface was bare except for three folders on top. It didn't take much thought to surmise it was their files.

"Now that Cicely is here, we can start."

Lenora's reprimand didn't bother Cicely. Lenora didn't make snap decisions. She would have thought long and hard before calling the candidates to her office. Cicely's being late wouldn't cause Lenora to change her mind . . . if she were the one chosen.

"I value all three of you, and appreciate the contributions each of you have made to *Fashion Insider* magazine," Lenora said, her poker face firmly in place.

"Thank you," was echoed by all three.

"But there can only be one new editor-in-chief of the Paris office." Lenora placed her clasped hands on top of the middle folder, the large diamond on her finger glittering. "We need someone who has shown themselves capable of leadership, but who can also listen. A person who is focused, has an uncanny sense of fashion's fickle direction, and knows the ins and out of *Fashion Insider.*"

Murmurs of understanding came from Fred and Eva. Cicely just stared at Lenora. This was the moment she had waited for. She'd worked her butt off to be noticed, then worked even harder to do better than anyone else. The editor-in-chief position would finally validate her to her family. They'd have to finally admit that she was somebody, admit she hadn't made a mistake by choosing a career in fashion.

Her thoughts jumped to C. J. She'd given up a lot to be here. Her sacrifice couldn't be for nothing.

"I want to personally thank the two candidates who will not be chosen, to know that this is no reflection on your work, but in all things there is someone who is better." Rising, Lenora rounded her desk to stand in front of them. They all stood as well.

Chapter 19

"The new editor in chief of the Paris branch of *Fashion Insider* magazine is Cicely St. John."

Stunned, Cicely blinked and accepted Lenora's hug.

"Congratulations, Cicely." Lenora stepped back and studied Cicely's shocked face. "Don't you have anything to say?" Lenora asked, her blue eyes as sharp and discerning as ever.

"Thank you," she managed, then laughed and palmed her face. "I can't believe it."

"Neither can I," Eva murmured.

Cicely laughed and accepted the brief hug from Eva. Cicely didn't hold any animosity toward Eva for trying to place her in a bad light with Lenora. She would have been a bit miffed as well if she hadn't won.

"You have two weeks to clear everything and help me select your replacement before you report to the Paris office," Lenora said.

"Two weeks," Cicely repeated.

"Will that be a problem?" Lenora asked, her perfect eyebrow arched.

"No," Cicely told her. There was nothing to keep her. "I'll be ready to go."

"Good. Now, let's go make the announcement to the staff."

Thirty minutes later, Cicely was finally able to get back to her desk. There was a lot of work she'd have to do before leaving. But first she had a call to make.

Picking up the phone, she dialed her parents' house. Her father had an early class on Wednesday, but her mother's first class wasn't until eleven.

"Hello, Cicely, I'm in a bit of a hurry. Let me call you later," her mother said on answering the phone.

On occasion, Cicely wished they could go back to the days before caller ID. "Mother, I got the position. I'm the new editor-in-chief of the branch office in Paris."

"I don't suppose you'll be home for Thanksgiving or Christmas this year, either," her mother said, a hint of disapproval in her voice. "I don't like making excuses for you."

Cicely closed her eyes. How did every conversation with her parents somehow always come down to chastisement or disappointment in her? "No, Mother, probably not. This is an important position. They looked both in-house and out to name the editor. I'll have the task of keeping with the style and elegance and fun of the magazine, while putting my own stamp on things."

"And what good will it eventually do?" her mother asked. "You have an IQ of a hundred eighty-eight.

You could have done some good in the world instead of wasting it on something as frivolous and fleeting as fashion."

"Can't you be happy for me?" Cicely sank heavily into the chair behind her desk.

"Happy that you've wasted your life? Hardly," her mother said. "Do you know why I was in such a hurry?"

"No." Cicely massaged her forehead.

"Your sister is being honored at a luncheon by her sorority. She's just been accepted at the university to teach medieval history. She'll have an impact on people that will prepare them for a future."

And I'm next to worthless. "I better let you go."

"You should call and congratulate Estelle. Perhaps send flowers. She's worked hard to get her doctorate and she did it with honors. Your father and I planned to take the entire family out this weekend and celebrate."

And, of course, the entire family didn't include her. "Please tell Estelle congratulations for me."

"I will, but don't forget to call. Good-bye."

"Good-bye." Cicely hung up and finally accepted the truth. She'd never be a part of her family. They didn't accept her, or want her. Love was out of the question.

She was twenty-eight years old and was almost alone in the world. She'd worked hard to impress her family, who didn't care. Now all she had was the job, and when she went to Paris she'd be alone again.

* * *

C. J. had never felt less like playing pool, but he wouldn't let Cicely take anything else from him. She'd already taken his peace of mind, his joy of living. He didn't want to talk, so he'd racked up the balls and grabbed his cue stick, ready to play when Alex and Sin finally arrived.

He was more than a little surprised to see Sin and Alex walk in together. Dianne couldn't possibly have taken Sin banning her seriously. "Hi. Where's Dianne?"

"Cicely's place." Alex picked up his cue stick. "Who plays first tonight?"

C. J. didn't even try to mask his surprise or concern. Where Alex went, so did Dianne. It had to be important for her not to be with him.

"I feel lucky tonight." Sin picked up his cue. "I'll take C. J. on. Glad to see you're ready."

C. J. waited for Alex to say more, but when he didn't, he heard himself say, "Is something wrong?"

"Depends on how you look at it." Alex propped his hands on the cue stick.

"You want to go first?" Sin asked.

The farthest thing from his mind was playing pool. C. J. got in Alex's face. "Will you stop being so cryptic. Is Cicely all right?" The last words were almost yelled.

"He wasn't being cryptic this time," Sin said.

"Will you two please just spit it out," he asked through clenched teeth.

"Cicely got the Paris job," Sin explained.

C. J. didn't expect the deep sense of loss to hit him so hard. His hand clenched on the cue stick.

"Cicely and Summer went over to help her celebrate since her mother was more interested in what her sister was doing than Cicely's accomplishment," Alex told him, anger creeping into his voice. "No one in her family even called her back to congratulate her."

C. J. muttered an expletive. "She wanted them to be proud of her. How could they treat her like that?"

"Not our problem or yours." Sin picked up the eight ball and tossed it lightly in his hand. "You don't love her. It's not like you're going to marry her or anything. What's it to you?"

C. J. whirled on Sin with a snarl. "She deserved better." Tossing his cue stick on the table, he stormed out of the bar.

"I'd say that went well." Sin let the ball fall on the table.

"You do like to live dangerously," Alex said.

Sin's eyes darkened. "Just because I won't have love is no reason I don't want you and C. J. to have it."

"Sin—"

"I'm happy for the both of you." Sin cut Alex off. "Let's grab a taxi and go pick up Summer and Dianne. I think C. J. is finally ready to admit that he can't live without Cicely."

Cicely never felt less like celebrating. What should have been the best day of her life left her feeling lonely and out of sorts. She could barely keep the smile on her face as she talked to Summer and Dianne. They'd arrived thirty minutes earlier with a bottle of aged Madeira and a box of imported Swiss truffles.

After her mother's uncaring response, she'd needed to share her success with someone and had called them on a three-way. Before she knew it, she'd told them about her mother. Summer had immediately said they'd be over that night to celebrate.

"I'm sorry, I'm not very good company tonight," she said.

"You've been through a lot emotionally in the past few days." Summer picked up the bottle. "Let's open this. Dianne, tear open the chocolates. People think champagne is better with chocolate, but they're wrong."

Cicely uncurled her legs from beneath her. "I'll grab some wineglasses." By the time she returned, the wine and chocolates were open.

Summer took the glasses and expertly poured the wine, then placed the bottle on the table. "A toast. To Cicely finding happiness and success beyond her wildest expectations."

Cicely barely sipped her wine. There had been few times in her life that she was completely happy. Most of those moments had been with C. J. or the women with her now. And in two weeks she'd leave it all behind her.

The doorbell rang, impatiently rang again.

Cicely placed her glass on a coaster. "Please excuse me." Going to the door, she opened it and got the surprise of her life. C. J. stood there. Strong, powerfully built, his eyes flashing, his mouth tight. He was still angry with her, and she wanted nothing more than to fling herself into his arms.

"Your parents don't know squat. It took grit and determination to make it to where you are. Don't let them make you feel less."

"Excuse us. 'Night, C. J. Cicely." Summer and Dianne scooted around the pair, closing the door after them.

Cicely didn't know why her throat felt tight, why she had to fight back tears.

"Ah, honey." He pulled her into his arms. "Don't cry." He swept his large hand over her head, down her back, then up again. "You're going to make a great editor-in-chief. I'm proud of you."

The first tear fell. A bit panicky, he talked past the lump in his throat, the knot in his stomach. "Maybe, just maybe you'll let me come and visit you." She stiffened against him.

"I won't pressure you, but I don't want to let you go. You should know by now that I fight for what I want."

Her head lifted, and she stared up at him. It made the knot in his stomach worsen to see the sadness shining though the tears in her eyes. He swallowed his own sense of loss. "I am so darn proud of you. You'll be the best."

"My mother didn't think so," she murmured. "She called me this afternoon, berating me for not calling to congratulate my older sister for being hired to teach at the university where my parents and brother already teach. She called me selfish and uncaring."

"Bull!" C. J. tilted her face up to his. "You care. Too much. That's why they can hurt you."

"You've always had wonderful parents." She glanced away. "You don't understand how much it hurts when your parents don't love you."

"Their loss."

"No, mine," she whispered softly. "Deep down, I've always wanted their love, for someone to appreciate what I've accomplished. Is that asking too much?"

"No," C. J. answered. "Deep down I've always wanted a woman who looked beyond my face, my temper and stubbornness, and my money to the man beneath. A woman who makes my heart beat faster with just a smile. Do you think I'm asking too much?"

He looked at her with such love that she had to swallow a couple of times before she could answer, "No."

"Good, because I never knew what I wanted until our first tempting kiss, then you spitting at me like a cornered cat. Once I held you in my arms, made love to you, everything seemed to click into place. It happened so quickly I had no time to prepare, to defend myself. Looking back I wouldn't change a thing. You're the one. You make every one of my hormones stand to attention and pant, but it is *you* that I treasure most and refuse to do without."

He reached into his pocket and pulled out a little replica of the Empire State Building on a gold charm bracelet. "I picked this up a couple of weeks ago. It's so you won't forget me. I was going to give it to you the night before you left."

She looked from the bracelet to him. "You had that much faith in me?"

He almost smiled. "You had that much faith in me." His face grew serious. His hold tightened. "I want you in my life. I refuse to believe that we can't work through your Paris assignment. That is, if you're willing to fight for us."

She saw the fear, the vulnerability in his eyes. There was no way he'd ask her to give up what she'd worked for and stay in New York. "Are you asking me to continue the affair?"

"No. I'm tired of fighting it." He gathered her closer to him. "I love you. I'm asking you to marry me."

Her eyes rounded. "W-what?"

He grinned sheepishly. "It sort of snuck up on me. I didn't accept it until Sin said I didn't love you or want to marry you and I wanted to take him on. I know now he was just goading me. I might be able to join you in six or seven months, depending on how the company goes. I can fly back and forth every couple of weeks or so until then."

She couldn't take it all in. "What about the bar? You love that bar."

"I love you more. Marry me?"

Tears streamed down her cheeks. He panicked. "You love me. I know you do. Don't throw away what we have."

"I thought you said I was smart. I won't need the bracelet," she said. "I love you more than the job in Paris."

"You're not leaving me?"

"How could I leave my heart?" She palmed his face. "I wanted something to make my parents proud of me. I finally realize I was trying to live my life to please them." She shook her head. "From now on, I'm living my life to please me, and that means a life with you."

"Honey." His forehead briefly touched hers. "I don't want to live without you in my life."

"I feel the same way. I'm not scared of my feelings anymore." She smiled up at him. "I want to share so many things with you. I want you because I love you, and I refuse to live without you. I'll tell Lenora in the morning."

"She's not going to be happy."

"But I will be." Her arms went around his neck. "I love you. You sort of snuck up on me, too. I was miserable without you."

"I was the same way, and determined to get over you."

She playfully punched him on the arm. Laughing, he gathered her closer. "In case you haven't figured it out, forgetting you is impossible. You're the woman I love, the woman I adore, the woman I want to grow old with. I'm proud of you, proud of my woman."

"And for the first time in my life, that's enough."

"I don't guess you bought that outfit to make me drool."

Her finger traced his lower lip. "I did, but I'm saving it for our honeymoon."

His hands tightened around her. "Thank you for trusting me, trusting our love. You'll never be sorry."

"I know."

He picked her up. "Let's go to bed."

"Yes." Passing the lamp in the living room, she snapped out the light.

Outside the dark brownstone, Alex stood with his arm around his wife's waist. Sin had his arm across Summer's shoulders. "They're going to be all right," Summer said.

"He stopped being stubborn," Sin said. "He loves her."

"Something you know nothing about," Summer teased.

"Nope. Now let's go play some pool." Sin turned toward the waiting taxi.

Only Alex saw past the easy smile to the pain beneath. Sin was doomed to live without love and there wasn't a thing under heaven either of them could do to change things.

Epilogue

The next morning Lenora took Cicely's decision to remain in New York surprisingly well. She admitted that she hadn't wanted to lose her and be bothered with finding a replacement. Some people were irreplaceable. Cicely told her that was what C. J. was to her, irreplaceable. Lenora harrumphed and dismissed her, but not before warning her that her quality of work better not suffer.

"It won't," Cicely said with confidence as she left Lenora's office. She'd only gone a few steps before she saw C. J. with his parents, coming down the hallway. Grinning, she went to meet them.

She and C. J. had called them this morning to tell them they were engaged. They'd been ecstatic. Her own parents were less enthused. With C. J. by her side, it hadn't mattered.

Mrs. Callahan enveloped Cicely in a hug, then it was her husband's turn. "We have another daughter" Mr. Callahan said once they were in her office.

She couldn't have been more pleased. She finally had a family who loved her. "Thank you."

"The engagement party will be at our home," Mrs. Callahan said.

"We were thinking of having it at the bar." C. J. grinned down at Cicely, who smiled up at him. "It's where we first started falling in love."

"Only we didn't know it then." Cicely leaned against him.

"Let them do what they want, Hillary," Mr. Callahan said. "You know how stubborn he is when he wants something."

"I hope you'll let me help plan the wedding," Mrs. Callahan said, a bit anxious.

Cicely went to her. "I was hoping you'd ask. I planned to ask Summer and Dianne, but I want your help as well. I know, with your keen insight and impeccable taste, it will be a day that all of us will remember and cherish."

His mother sniffed, dabbed her eyes, and took Cicely's hands. "C. J. couldn't have chosen better." She reached for her husband's hand. "Good-bye, Cicely. We expect you both for Sunday brunch to celebrate."

"We'll be there." C. J. hugged his mother, shook hands with his father. "Thanks for driving down. We'll see you on Sunday."

"Happy?" C. J. asked when his parents had gone.

"Ecstatic. I love you so much."

His eyes darkened. "I'll never get tired of hearing you saying that." Reaching into his pocket, he drew out a six-karat diamond ring circled with emeralds. Taking her trembling left hand, he slid the ring on her third finger, then kissed it. "Each day I fall more in love with you. Thank you for loving me, for looking past my faults, for teaching me what real love is."

Tears streamed down her cheeks. He kissed them away. "Thank you for loving me, for looking past my faults, for teaching me what real love is," Cicely repeated.

"Always." He kissed her, thinking of the days to come when she would be in his life. He'd found something to make his life complete. Cicely St. John, an incredible woman whom he'd love a lifetime and beyond.

As soon as C.J. left, Cicely went to her computer and pulled up her blog.

I have some incredible news. I'm engaged!! Yes, you read that right. He's the most caring, stubborn, not to mention mouth-watering gorgeous man I've ever met. Since I'm a bit stubborn, we'll butt heads a time or two, but love will always see us through.

I met him on assignment. I wore Prada. He couldn't have cared less. His preference of dress is laid-back casual. Just as I want my readers to do, he dresses to please himself, and not to please others. With his muscular build, six-four height, and self-assurance, he nails it every time. Women take a second and third look when we go out. Since he's looking at me, I don't mind.

I'm giddy with excitement. My life is about to become richer and fuller because of him. When he proposed last night, I was wearing Chanel and my grandmother's pearls. He just left my office after slipping an incredible diamond ring on my finger. I'm typing despite the lump in my throat, the sheen of tears in my eyes. Being in love is the greatest natural high. It trumps finding that special dress, incredible shoes, and knock-out accessories at a deep discount the first time you go shopping. Some of you might agree, while others are shaking your heads. For the disbelievers, I hope one day you'll find that special someone and discover for yourself what unconditional love feels like.

How could I have known that with just one kiss my life would irrevocably change? My toes curling in my favorite Jimmy Choos should have been my first clue. LOL. Whatever I wear now, he compliments me, but he doesn't have to say a word—his incredible midnight-black eyes speak volumes!!! I'm the luckiest woman in the world.

Until next time—remember—make your fashion your own, don't let fashion own you.

Diva

William H. Ray

Francis Ray (1944–2013) is the *New York Times* bestselling author of the Grayson novels, the Falcon books, the Taggart Brothers, and *Twice the Temptation,* among many other books. Her novel *Incognito* was made into a movie that aired on BET. A native Texan, she was a graduate of Texas Woman's University and had a degree in nursing. Besides being a writer, she was a school nurse practitioner with the Dallas Independent School District. She lived in Dallas.

"Francis Ray is, without a doubt, one of the Queens of Romance."

—*A Romance Review*

DON'T MISS THESE OTHER NOVELS
BY BESTSELLING AUTHOR

FRANCIS RAY

THE GRAYSONS OF NEW MEXICO SERIES

Only You

Irresistible You

Dreaming of You

You and No Other

Until There Was You

THE GRAYSON FRIENDS SERIES

All of My Love (e-original)

All That I Desire

All That I Need

All I Ever Wanted

A Dangerous Kiss

With Just One Kiss

A Seductive Kiss

It Had to Be You

One Night With You

Nobody But You

The Way You Love Me

AGAINST THE ODDS SERIES

Trouble Don't Last Always

Somebody's Knocking at My Door

THE FALCON SERIES

Break Every Rule

Heart of the Falcon

A FAMILY AFFAIR SERIES

After the Dawn

When Morning Comes

I Know Who Holds Tomorrow

THE TAGGART BROTHERS SERIES

Only Hers

Forever Yours

INVINCIBLE WOMEN SERIES

If You Were My Man

And Mistress Makes Three

Not Even If You Begged

In Another Man's Bed

Any Rich Man Will Do

Like the First Time

STANDALONES

Someone to Love Me

The Turning Point

ANTHOLOGIES

Twice the Temptation

Let's Get It On

Going to the Chapel

Welcome to Leo's

Della's House of Style

AVAILABLE WHEREVER BOOKS ARE SOLD

 ST. MARTIN'S GRIFFIN